THE BRIGHT DA

She had climbed a grassy bank and was well into the hedge, her hair falling down but her arms full of the coveted blossoms, when she heard someone approaching. She turned, blushing, and looked down on a young man, striding along slashing moodily at the tall meadowsweet with a stick he had cut from the hedge. Just as she was thinking, 'if I keep still he may not notice me,' the young man glanced up to the top of the bank and saw her.

His initial amusement slowly turned to appreciation as his eyes took in the tumbled fair hair, the shapely figure and the flushed face of the girl poised on the bank above him. For her part, Amy saw a tall young man with bright dark eyes which were fixed on her face. His black hair curled thickly on his head but he was beardless, and his skin was tanned a golden brown by the sun.

'Let me help you down, mistress,' he said in a deep young voice which held a hint of laughter.

Amy, accepting his proffered hand, laughed outright and he joined her, so that they stood smiling into each other's eyes like old friends instead of strangers.

The Bright Day is Done

The story of Amy Robsart

Judith Saxton

CORONET BOOKS
Hodder and Stoughton

For my parents, Dorothy and Ivor Saxton

Copyright © 1974 Judith Saxton

First published in Great Britain 1974
by Constable and Company Limited

Coronet edition 1976

Printed and bound in Great Britain for
Coronet Books, Hodder and Stoughton, London
By Richard Clay (The Chaucer Press) Ltd.,
Bungay, Suffolk

ISBN 0 340 20650 0

Contents

Acknowledgements

I should like to express my thanks to F. D. Sayer, the Colman & Rye Local History Librarian, Norwich, and his staff, for their help in my research work; to Mervyn Payne of the Eastern Daily Press, for advice on sources, all of which I used; to Dr Jean Infield, whose medical advice was invaluable; to the Rev. Albert W. Hollands, Rector of Syderstone for an interesting morning in his parish examining the sites of Syderstone Manor, Cockisford Priory, etc., and to the staff of Wymondham Branch Library.

Counsel for the defence

My Lord, Members of the Jury. The apparently unexplained death of a young woman is always a cause for concern. When the young woman is the wife of the Queen's favourite, the concern becomes intense public interest. It is not surprising, therefore, that this case has twice been heard by a jury: nor perhaps is it surprising that the verdicts, in both cases, were death by misadventure, which has never really satisfied the majority of the people.

However, in the past it has always been the death of Amy Dudley, and that alone, which has exercised the minds of those investigating the tragedy. Never before has a jury looked into the *life* of Amy Dudley, born Amy Robsart in the year of our Lord 1532.

Now, over four hundred years later, we realise how much more significant, in attempting to resolve such a vexed question, it is to examine the life which formed the character of the dead woman.

It was not a long life, Members of the Jury. Nor, towards its close, could it have been a happy one. But we must not presuppose that because she died unhappy, her life was one of continual gloom. When you see the evidence which I shall present to you, I hope you will have a much clearer picture than those presented to earlier enquirers.

In the past, Amy Robsart has been dismissed as a mere nonentity. Some said Robert Dudley fell violently in love with her fresh country beauty—and as speedily tired of her. Others put forward the theory that Amy was a rich Norfolk heiress and the Duke of Northumberland arranged an advantageous marriage for his son. She has been accused of being a neurotic, staying away from court from choice; or a hypochondriac, enjoying imagined illnesses.

Yet even at the time, to people who disliked Robert Dudley heartily, the facts did not support such accusations. William Cecil, Queen Elizabeth I's trusted minister, and a very real enemy to Robert, wrote that the marriage had 'begun in passion and ended in tragedy': scarcely likely if Robert had been smitten by a transient lust for Amy—even less likely when one considers that a year elapsed between their first meeting and the marriage. The marriage settlements (which, Members of the Jury, are still in existence today) show that far from giving her lands and wealth, Sir John Robsart dowered his daughter with only twenty pounds a year—hardly the sort of sum with which to buy an eligible son-in-law!

Why then, did Amy and Robert marry? Is love so improbable? She certainly had beauty, to attract such an extraordinarily handsome young man. During the time of his greatest need she comforted him by her presence, and Robert showed his total trust in her capability by leaving to her the work of superintending the sale and management of their lands.

If Amy had been the spineless neurotic alleged, why was Robert faithful to her for the first eight years of their marriage? His worst enemies never accused him of infidelity during that time. If her love for him had died, why did she not rebel and proclaim herself hard-done-by when her adversities were greatest?

My Lord, Members of the Jury, I shall now call my evidence—the life of Amy Robsart.

The evidence

'Finish, good lady; the bright day is done, and we are for the dark.'

from *Antony and Cleopatra*,
by William Shakespeare

I

The beloved

A pale shaft of early morning sunlight stole through a gap in the curtains, striking the silver candlestick so that it glistened, and making the candle flame look foolish. The watchers who had sat all night waiting patiently for the woman on the bed to begin to give birth to the child within her, smiled at their mistress and drew back the heavy curtains further, so that she could see for herself the bright new day.

The woman in labour hardly noticed the dousing of the candle flame and the tentative fingers of sunlight shining into the room. Her only concern lay with her task of bringing new life into the world; life that already fought to be free of the quiet security of her womb.

Outside the room, the normal life of the house went on, though the father of the child about to be born paced the floor, afraid for his wife and impatient for the sight of his son and heir.

'He's like a young bridegroom,' giggled a nursemaid to the midwife, who said impatiently, 'Any man worries over his first child, however old he may be. Though Sir John is no longer young, the only child he has is his bastard son. *This* one, born in wedlock, means a great deal to him. It's his heir.'

The woman on the bed felt the surging pain suddenly change as the urge to push came over her. She was no inexperienced young bride for she had been married before, and had given birth to other children. She reached up to grasp the knotted sheet tied to the fourposter and even as she did so, the sun reached the foot of the bed and shone gaily on her new London gown with its square neckline and hanging sleeves.

11

It was like an omen, she thought. She had come to Syderstone already ungainly with the child so she had not worn the dress. But seeing it was a reminder that when she had recovered from the birth, she would be able to wear the new fashion that Anne Boleyn had brought to England from the Paris court.

Steadily, the sunshine filled the room like golden wine in the cup, and by the time it had reached her sweat-bright face, Lady Elizabeth's job was almost over.

'One more push, my lady,' encouraged the midwife. 'I can see the head already. One more push will see him into the world.'

Outside the door Sir John stopped his pacing as the small thin wail rent the air. He entered the room shyly, almost sheepishly, to find his wife saying in a disappointed voice, 'Oh, it's a girl. I know my husband . . .'

'Wanted a girl above all things, for he has a son already,' interrupted Sir John, smiling at his wife's weary face.

He eyed the small pink body as it was vigorously washed by the nurse, and gently touched the child's quiff of damp blonde hair. 'She will be beautiful and beloved,' he told his wife firmly. 'What shall we call our daughter, my dearest?'

'I'd like to name her Amy. That's French for beloved.'

Sir John smiled fondly. 'Aye, a pretty name. Amy Robsart. It sounds well. We are a family that likes an unusual name once in a while. Now I'd better go and tell the girls they have a sister—or rather a half-sister. They are eager for news, naturally.'

The girls were at their tasks in the kitchen when their stepfather brought his message that they might see their mother and the new baby. Giggling with excitement and relief from tension they tidied themselves and took off the big aprons that had been protecting their gowns.

Frances and Anne were the children of Sir Roger Appleyard, Lady Elizabeth's first husband. So was little John, who came running from the nursery to see the new baby. Arthur Robsart was Sir John's only other child, a bastard son already in his teens.

12

The girls entered the room on tiptoe, but both boys were told firmly by the midwife that their mother's lying-in chamber was no place for them that day, and they should see their new sister in the morning.

'Come on then, Johnny, I'll show you my new falcon,' Arthur said good-naturedly. He felt rather glad the child was a girl; relieved almost. After all, a son was a father's natural heir even though he'd been born on the wrong side of the blanket. Sir John could still give him lands and property. Had the mewling brat been a boy, of course, things might have been different. Arthur grinned to himself and helped John to swing open the heavy side door which led to the stables.

Elizabeth eyed her tall, pretty daughters with affection. It wouldn't be long now before they found themselves husbands, yet they behaved with the baby like little girls with a new doll.

'Isn't she sweet? How small and fair she is,' said Anne. 'What are you going to call her, Mother?'

'We thought—Amy. It's an uncommon name. Do you like it?'

'Oh yes, it's very pretty. Amy Robsart. Why didn't you call *me* Amy, Mother, instead of Anne? Every dairymaid is called Anne.'

'What about me, then?' demanded Frances. 'When we lived in Wymondham I must have known half-a-dozen girls named Frances at least!'

'Frances-at-least! What an odd name,' mused Anne, and the two girls left the room laughing and pushing each other as sisters will.

Without their presence, the room grew quiet once more. The midwife, tired after a wakeful night, dozed before the log fire. In her carved oaken cradle, the baby Amy Robsart slept. Unaware of anything except the comfort of soft blankets and the warmth of sun and fire after her long struggle for birth, she knew calm at last. Lady Robsart too, allowed sleep to overcome her, welcoming forgetfulness of her ordeal.

Peace reigned over Syderstone Hall.

*

13

And during the years of Amy's early childhood, Syderstone was a peaceful place. She saw her half-sisters rarely, for they had returned to their mother's dower house, Stanfield Hall, in Wymondham, where life was so much more exciting. John Appleyard was sent away to an uncle to get an education as a gentleman's son, and Arthur was placed in a noble household for the same purpose. Only Amy and her parents remained.

She was a real country child, enjoying country pastimes and rather frightened by what she saw of town life. She was spoilt of course, the pretty darling of elderly parents. Very much Sir John's favourite, she soon became quite a tomboy, riding, hunting, and following her father round their estates.

When he had business in the nearby port of Wells, Sir John would take his daughter with him down to the docks. There she would watch the tall ships sail in, though she shrank shyly from the sailors who came strolling by and smiled at the rosy-cheeked child.

To Amy, it seemed that Wells was the hub of the world. Flanders merchants came to bargain over the good Norfolk wool which was shipped away, sometimes in its raw state, sometimes already woven into fine cloth. Even the sailors, with their mahogany skins and tarred pigtails, their foreign languages and their quick, expressive hand movements, had an air of romance and delight.

Amy would stand for an hour at a time, finger in mouth, gazing at the scene whilst Sir John talked interminably of wool. Her round blue eyes saw the paily painted ships unloading onto the quay their fascinating cargoes of wines from Gascony, whispering silks and spices from the Mediterranean, and oil, leather and iron from Spain. The spicy scents intoxicated her, and so did the bright colours of the materials and the voices of the sailors, slurred and guttural, quick and lilting.

If the delights of the dockside palled, there were the pleasures of the market to enjoy. Highly-coloured sweetmeats jostled with strange foreign toys and baubles; and these in turn rubbed shoulders with the honest farm produce which the sailors came to buy. Amy watched fascinated as some bold,

14

black-eyed lad with gold rings in his ears strolled amongst the stalls, eating a handful of ripe berries or sweet apples, whilst he eyed the pretty wenches appreciatively.

'You make the most of Wells whilst you may, my girl,' Sir John would tell his daughter. 'Folk hereabout say that the channel is silting up so that the sea flowing into the harbour grows shallow. Maybe one day the sand will come right up here, to the quay, and Wells won't be a busy port any longer.'

'What about the floods, Father?' questioned Amy. 'Tell me about the flood when you were a lad, and came down with *your* father to help rescue the sheep.'

Nothing loth, Sir John told how the sea had come roaring in, right up and over the good salt marshes where the sheep grazed. He and his father had indeed come into Wells, for they owned some of the sheep, and had even managed to rescue a few of their flock by going out in a little cockleshell of a boat and heaving the half-drowned animals to safety.

'Well, the floods will wash away the silt,' Amy remarked comfortably as she always did. 'Aren't folk foolish, Father, to say Wells might lose its harbour and become an ordinary town?'

Father and daughter laughed together at the absurd idea.

Back at home in Syderstone, life continued its simple, uncomplicated course. The Robsarts went to church three times each Sunday, as their ancestors had doubtless done before them, sitting in the same pew where old Grandfather Robsart had snored his way through the sermon, and watching the sun shine through the same stained glass window so that colours puddled the floor.

During the prayers Amy liked to peep through her fingers at her grandparents' grave in the chancel, though she could not read the Latin which told of their lives together. It gave her a feeling of continuity, of the slow reliability of country living where generation after generation of Robsarts had worked this land, worshipped in this church, and finally been laid to rest somewhere in the building or in the graveyard outside.

Her strong feeling for the church was partly due to the fact that the church was almost part of the manor. It was so close

15

that she could see every detail of the leaded roof and each round flint from her bedroom window. She saw the doves from their own dovecote flying round the church tower and being driven jealously away by the rooks which lived in the tall clump of elms. Even the grave mounds were friends; she had known their familiar shapes ever since she could remember, and they held no terrors for her.

The villagers knew Amy loved Syderstone, and they responded by loving her. When he was old enough she trotted daily to the vicarage to learn her letters with the children of the sturdy yeomen and peasant farmers.

'I like to read,' she told her mother, 'but writing is very hard. I don't believe I shall ever write like Johnny Carter—all neat and small except for the capitals, which are very great and proud and curly.'

Laughing, Lady Robsart said, 'Why then, you had better marry a rich man, and have Johnny Carter as your clerk to write letters for you. But you must learn to reckon up accounts and to spell out "apple" and "strawberry", for you must be able to keep house properly.'

'Johnny already does some of my writing for me,' Amy confessed thoughtlessly. 'He says he does it because he likes my dimples when I smile at him.'

'There! I knew no good could come of sending the child to learn in a country parsonage,' exclaimed Lady Elizabeth, greatly vexed. 'She should mix with gently-bred children and not these village clods.'

'I'm quick to reckon up numbers though,' Amy told her, thinking it was her lack of knowledge that made her mother frown so. 'That's because I help old Tom count the sheep when they come in for shearing. He can only count up to ten and he gets muddled in his poor old head, trying to keep a tally of the tens.'

'What more learning should she need?' protested Sir John. 'She's a country girl. Our little maid will have no need of learning.'

He put his arm round her shoulders and Amy, entranced by his masculine smell of horses and sheep and sweat, rubbed her

16

fluffy head against his jerkin and almost purred with pleasure.

'Nevertheless, John, I think it's time that Amy knew a different sort of life. What has Syderstone to offer besides sheep, and an occasional visit to the market at Lynn? As for Wells, when you take her there you allow her to behave like any ill-taught peasant. I had it from one of the serving girls that the young mistress ties her skirt above her knees and gathers samphire in the marshes!'

'I enjoy a dish of samphire,' objected Sir John, reddening guiltily none-the-less. 'Especially when my girl has gone to the trouble of picking it for me.'

'Ugh, John! Fancy eating *seaweed*,' protested his wife.

Sir John knew that it would be useless to remind her that samphire was a herb, and not seaweed. Elizabeth had been brought up in Camberwell and when she married Sir Roger Appleyard they had lived in Wymondham. It was not until she came to Syderstone that she heard of the samphire which grew so prolifically in the marshes surrounding Wells.

'Amy thinks it delicious, don't you, love?' Sir John said, but Amy had stopped listening to the argument.

Gazing unseeingly before her, she was reliving her visits to the marshes. The strong wind blowing, salt and cool, off the sea. The sky blue above, and the marshes stretching all round her for miles, with their pools of water ranging from light, cloud-reflecting blue to dark, ominous black. The stretches of mud, where the clumps of grass grew brighter than any emerald; and delicate harebells, patches of purple heather, wiry sea-pinks and yellow lichen made the place a paradise of colour.

The samphire was really a good excuse for her to tie a string round her waist so that her skirt barely covered her knees, cast off shoes and stockings, and paddle through the delicious squelchy mud and the clear water, pulling handfuls of samphire until her basket was laden and she must turn back to her father and become a young lady once more.

'St Peter's herb, that's what the old folk call it,' she said dreamily. 'I dunno why, it's growed there for ever though, and doubtless there be some story to account for a queer old

17

name like that.'

'Listen to her,' said Lady Elizabeth sharply. 'She sounds more like one of the village children than the daughter of Syderstone manor. John, it's time we went to live at Stanfield Hall. In Wymondham she will be able to widen her acquaintance. Both Frances and Anne have married into good families and they met their husbands in Wymondham.'

'But Amy's not husband-high yet,' protested Sir John, half-laughing.

'No, of course not. But she needs to mix with her own kind instead of your tenants and a few business acquaintances. *Gentlefolk*, John. Then when the time comes for our girl to wed she'll be on equal terms with any lass in Norfolk.'

Amy gazed from one to the other with frightened eyes. She knew of course that her mother felt far more affection for Stanfield Hall than she ever could for Syderstone. When they visited Wymondham then Lady Elizabeth was happy, but Amy felt only homesickness for her father's broad, flat acres. Never before had it been openly suggested that they should make their home in Wymondham.

Stanfield Hall is only for *visiting*, Amy thought, panic-stricken. Here, at Syderstone, was where she belonged. Her life was here, her friends. She fled from the house and went and sat by the great well in the courtyard. If she leaned over she could see it going down and down until far, far away in the blackness shone a pinprick of light that she knew was water. From the sides of the well small clumps of fern grew, and soft spongy mosses. Amy shut her eyes, pressing the tears back, and listened for the drops falling from the wooden bucket that hung above her head. She could see them in her mind's eye, forming quickly—for the bucket was leaky—and the gathering momentum as they fell so that they hit the far-off water with a shrill plop, which was magnified by the walls of the well so that it echoed and re-echoed back to Amy's ears.

She listened to the other sounds she knew and loved so much: the soft cooing of the doves in the dovecote, the scrabbling of their pink feet on the thatch of their home; the faint bleat of a sheep calling its young and the never-ceasing sound of the flock cropping the close turf, as they grazed up to the very walls and hedges of the manor garden.

Consciously straining her ears now, she could even make out the soft blowing breath of the horses in the nearby stables as they investigated their mangers, and the occasional clop of hooves as one of the animals changed its position.

Was it true? Would she really have to leave all this? At present she was feeding a motherless lamb from a bottle, and it followed her wherever it could. She could hear it now, scrabbling with its sharp little cloven hooves at the gate into the yard and bleating plaintively.

We *can't* leave Syderstone, we *can't*, Amy thought vehemently. There have always been Robsarts at the manor. Surely her father would not leave the peace and quiet of the home they both loved, for the bustle and busyness of Wymondham?

Then she heard the bleats of her lamb become quite desperate and opening her eyes, Amy saw it squeezing and wriggling its small body under the gate.

Laughing, she ran towards her pet and let it into the yard, where it butted her knees with its hard little head and nudged her caressing fingers, telling her that it would like some milk.

Amy forgot leaving Syderstone. Such a thing was incredible, impossible: as impossible as that the sea should ever forsake Wells. She and the lamb went towards the dairy, to beg some milk from Moll, the dairymaid.

2

Love thy neighbour?

'Now you're almost sixteen, aren't you glad we left Syderstone and came to Stanfield Hall?' Elizabeth Robsart asked her daughter. Surely, she thought, after the pleasant years spent in Wymondham, Amy could have no regrets for the dull life they had left behind them.

Amy looked thoughtfully round the rose garden. The two women were sewing out of doors, taking advantage of the glorious June weather. It was true enough that she was fond of Stanfield Hall, even though it could never replace Syderstone in her affections. But she liked the odd-shaped house, like a capital E with the middle stroke left out, and the moat where the ducks and swans swam and the waterlilies spread their broad, flat petals. This part of Norfolk too, was different. It was good barley-growing country, though there was plenty of fine pasture land for sheep grazing, and it was wooded, so that she grew as familiar with the shy woodland flowers as she had been with the blooms of moor and marsh.

'It's very pleasant here,' she admitted. 'But I don't really compare it with Syderstone, Mother. They're quite different. I'm thankful that I had those quiet years in North Norfolk and really, it's better that I should have done. After all, sister Frances married into the Flowerdew family when she wed her William, and it was her brother-in-law, John, who caused all the trouble over the pulling down of Wymondham Abbey. We were lucky not to be living here then, or he would have been our guest since he stayed in this house, and we should have shared the hatred which came his way from the common people. As it is, we worship beside the townsfolk of Wymond-

20

ham in that part of the abbey that remains, and are at peace with our neighbours.'

'Yes, but now that we are settled here, you're happy, aren't you?' asked Elizabeth.

'Yes,' said Amy with a laugh. 'You were right, Mother. It's best for a maid to meet a variety of people and be at ease in a crowd. I enjoy having the bustle of Wymondham near at hand and as for Norwich—I can't imagine why the city ever frightened me! The people go about their business merrily, with a good word for most. I love watching the Flemish weavers at their looms, and the sellers selling and the buyers bargaining.'

'You love the strolling players, and the vendors of silks and satins too, don't you?' teased Elizabeth, knowing how her daughter would watch open-mouthed as actors pranced in a cleared space; and of how diligently the girl searched for material for that very special dress.

'Yes, I'm incurably light-minded and love all frivolity,' Amy said, dimpling at her mother. 'I even love our neighbours—or most of them.'

She knew that Lady Robsart harboured a secret wish to have her youngest child married to one of the eligible young men living near Wymondham—Richard Gresham, or possibly his younger brother Harry, would have been eminently suitable.

The Greshams were a large and prosperous family with a magnificent house at Intwood, scarcely three miles from Stanfield Hall. Sir Richard had a son, Thomas, but he was grown-up and married. However, Sir Richard had two nephews in his charge most of the time and their sister Mary Gresham lived with him always, so the four children had grown very close. Richard, named for his rich uncle, was by far the better match, but Elizabeth realised with a sigh that Amy could scarcely fall in love with Richard's sober righteousness when Harry's effervescent personality was so much more akin to her own.

Looking at her daughter now, Lady Robsart thought that she was becoming a very lovely girl. Her dark blue eyes were set wide apart in an appealing, heart-shaped face, and her thick, glossy hair was the colour of ripe wheat.

She should marry well, thought Elizabeth with pleasure. After all, though John Robsart was not rich, he owned good country property. Syderstone alone grazed three thousand sheep, and though only country people, their blood was good enough for most. There was Arthur of course: but Arthur had inherited his father's good looks combined, fortunately for Amy, with the lazy good nature of his peasant mother. He idled his time away, and at the moment was in hot pursuit of a rich widow some years older than himself, who showed every sign of succumbing to his charms. Sir John tolerated his bastard son, and loved his only daughter. It seemed unlikely to Lady Elizabeth that the Robsart money and lands would be left to Arthur unless he mended his ways and somehow worked his way into his father's good graces.

Elizabeth looked again at her daughter and reflected that even if Sir John were to turn the child penniless from the door, she would not remain unmarried for long. It wasn't just that she had beauty—many girls had that at her age, to fade into plainness within a few years. Amy had charm, and some other, indefinable, quality of character that could not go long unnoticed.

The year that followed lived up to all Elizabeth's expectations for her child. Many young men rode up the avenue of oaks which led to the Robsarts' front door. Amy was admired for her beauty, her gaiety and her charm. But she showed little interest in any of her admirers except for Harry Gresham, who was her most constant escort and closest friend.

Elizabeth would have liked to present her daughter at court, but she had no friends amongst the 'new nobility' who had sprung into prominence at the coronation of young Edward VI. However she and Amy had paid visits to London, for they were both extremely fashion conscious and well aware that only in the great city would they see for themselves the newest and most daring of fashions, both in style and material.

And at home in Norfolk it seemed that monarchy and politics touched them very little. Amy had been brought up, so to speak, with the fall of the monasteries crashing in her ears; so

22

any sorrow she might have felt on Henry VIII's death had been dutiful and perfunctory. In truth, she felt more curiosity at the thought of the reception awaiting the dead King in Heaven, faced with four wives all longing to give him a piece of their minds.

'Of course I know the Duke of Somerset is Protector,' she said to Harry. 'But in truth, Hal, if one follows the faith that is taught in the churches, and does not go against one's own conscience, what difference does it make who sits on England's throne? The price of wool and barley mean more to us, than whether the late King's wishes are being properly carried out.'

'Amy my girl, you'll never be wife to a great courtier if you talk like that,' Harry told her. But Amy only laughed. He knew as she did, that her mother was the one who desired an important marriage for her. She was quite content to hear and heed little of London matters, which scarcely affected anyone in East Anglia.

Then, quite out of the blue, something happened that touched all of them, and Amy most of all.

It had begun, folk said, with the dissolution of the monasteries back in King Henry's time. The townspeople of Wymondham had bargained with the King for a part of the abbey to be left to them so that they could worship there as if in a parish church. The King had agreed, selling them the part of the abbey they wanted and granting them certain other materials to help towards the building of the new south aisle, which had already been destroyed. These materials, which included the timberwork of the roof of the chapter house, a quantity of stone, glass and old windows, were to be handed to the parishioners of Flowerdew, together with lead for the roofing of their future place of worship.

But the Flowerdews were a greedy family. Seven brothers, one of whom was an eminent lawyer, could wield a lot of power in a semi-literate community. There were delays, contrived accidents, and outright dishonesty. The people of Wymondham got part of the abbey, it is true, but only after the Flowerdews had stripped it of everything they could lay their hands on. As for the lead, that was never seen again and the Flowerdews waxed fat on their gains.

In time, of course, the grumbling died down. It had to, because those who were heard to speak against the Flowerdew family always seemed to suffer some sudden calamity: to contravene some law of which they had never heard; to lose a beast in the woods; to be set upon by beggarly ruffians. So, however unwillingly, the people ceased to talk of the losses Wymondham had sustained. But they did not forget.

Funnily enough, it was another abbey that started the rumblings of more trouble. When Henry had sent the monks packing, he had granted to John Dudley, now Earl of Warwick, the Abbey of Choselee. Warwick decided to sell the abbey, and knowing Flowerdew to be a canny lawyer, put the sale of the property into his hands. It was bought by a respectable Wymondham man, Robert Kett, who already owned several parcels of land around Choselee Abbey including Gunvile Manor, where he lived.

Perhaps because Edward Flowerdew was acting for someone else and not in his own interests, the sale went through without a hitch, and Edward Flowerdew was loud in his praise of Kett's good sense and amiability.

'No lofty manners from the Earl of Warwick,' he told his family, savouring the word 'Earl' on his tongue. 'Just a desire to see the business settled to everyone's satisfaction.'

Whilst these events, apparently so harmless, were taking place, all over the country manor owners began enclosing the common land for grazing their sheep. It happened in Norfolk. The Flowerdews began to extend their boundaries. Whether it was because of this or not, Kett and Edward Flowerdew quarrelled. Amy no longer heard her half-sister's family sing the praises of the Ketts. But at that time landowners were more concerned about the discontented peasants grubbing up fences than with quarrels between neighbours.

Harry had come over from Intwood to take Amy to the fair in Wymondham. It was the sixth of July, and a hot day. His horse had stirred up the white dust as he cantered up the drive, and his long boots were chalky with it.

'It's awfully hot to go to the fair, Amy,' he said, when she

24

came out of the cool of the house. 'Wouldn't you rather stay indoors? Or perhaps we might walk in the woods, where it is shady.'

'You may be right; the streets will be terribly crowded with all the people from the country who have come to visit the shrine of St Thomas,' agreed Amy. 'But we need not go right into the town if it's too crowded and hot. Shall we just ride slowly in that direction?'

Harry agreed, and the young couple walked their horses along the narrow, leafy lanes. But the heat seemed trapped there, so they were glad to emerge on the outskirts of the town.

As Amy had foretold, people thronged the streets and spilled onto the squares and common. They had expected to meet folk out to enjoy themselves, but instead they found themselves gazing at angry faces. Speakers thrust themselves out of the main throng and harangued their fellows furiously, the sweat dripping down their bearded cheeks.

'I don't like the look of this, I think I ought to get you away,' Harry muttered, but Amy said impatiently 'Hush! What is that big fellow saying, Hal? The one in the blue smock with the great tawny beard.'

The man's loud voice rose above the surly muttering of the crowd: 'I say that common land is common land, and meant for the likes of us to graze our few poor cattle and sheep,' he roared. 'I say as this here putting up of fences is wrong and wicked. Shall we stand by and gape wordless whilst our children cry for bread? Shall we nor act when we see rich men with a fortune on their backs and rich food in their bellies grabbing more land from our meagre commons?'

There were mutters of assent from the crowd and one woman called shrilly: 'I seen my man lose his job, when lord of the manor put down more pasture for them dratted sheep. Yet soon there will be nowhere for us to graze our cow, for our cottage was close up against the manor, for *their* convenience.'

'Aye, lose your jobs, lose your pasture and lose your lives if you like,' roared the man. 'But me, I won't stand for it. I'm going to show 'em, that's what. Root out their greedy, groping fences I will, with my own hands.' He held up a pair of black-ened, calloused hands the size of shovels. 'Who's with me, I say?'

There was a roar from the crowd and Harry unceremoniously grabbed hold of the reins of Amy's mare and they moved quietly away. The crowd surged towards the speaker, all anxious to tell him how they had suffered, but would suffer no more.

As soon as they were out of sight they allowed the horses to break into a trot.

'That was the beginnings of a rebellion, Amy,' Harry said gleefully. 'About time too, if you ask me. Let them pull up a few fences so that their skinny cattle can feed—and their skinny children too. I know sheep have led to unemployment but land enclosures have gone far enough.'

'I'm not saying anything to Father,' Amy said, her brows drawing together and her lips tightening. 'He's done no enclosing of the common land, nor would he. But he might feel it his duty to warn other landowners and that might lead to bloodshed. Don't you tell your Uncle Richard, Hal.'

'As if I would! No, they'll pull up a few fences and the landowners will mutter and perhaps Parliament will take notice. Here's your drive, Amy. Is your mare tired, or shall we race round to the stables?'

Amy's mare had already pricked up her ears at the sight of the familiar buildings which to her meant rest, and food and drink. So the two youngsters galloped down the drive and into the stableyard, where they handed over their mounts to the waiting groom.

They told their elders that it had been too hot and crowded to stay long at the fair, and then thought little more of the matter, expecting to hear casually from some landowner that 'his' newly-fenced land had been invaded by rough peasants who had taken themselves off on receiving some money and food.

The news, when it came, however, was very different. Sir Richard Gresham rode over to Stanfield a couple of days later, purple-faced with indignation, to tell the story so far as

26

he knew it. 'An unruly bunch of ruffians, drunk no doubt, attacked Flowerdew's new fencing, down by the common land,' he told Sir John. 'Then Flowerdew came out, thinking to scare them away with threats, but there were too many of them. So the cunning fellow gave them money to leave his property alone and attack Kett's new place, Choselee Abbey. "For abbey land should be common land," he told them.'

'That was a typical Flowerdew trick,' Sir John said drily, but Sir Richard hardly paused in his excited speech.

'Over to Choselee they went, the whole ill-fed, stinking rabble,' he went on. 'And what do you think happened then? That rascal Kett came out of his fine new house and joined them in pulling up his own fences! The man's mad, I tell you. Now they say he's their leader, and is going to stop land enclosure throughout the length and breadth of the county.'

Amy, sitting by the low window to get what breeze there was, said quickly, 'Surely you mean that Robert Kett will *speak* for the rebels, Sir Richard? We've known Mr Kett ever since we came to Wymondham and have always found him a most pleasant neighbour and a gentle and kindly man.'

Harry, watching his uncle, saw his eyes pop with indignation, but he merely said, 'What, Miss, what? I tell you the man's a rogue, and has promised to lead the rebels to stop land enclosure by force if necessary. You mark my words, Kett won't find a friend amongst the landowners of Norfolk when he realises what a fool he's been, and returns to his home.'

Amy got up, curtsied slightly and went out of the room, closely followed by Harry. In the quiet of the garden, with the scent of summer flowers around them, she looked enquiringly at her friend.

'It's true, he *is* leading the rebels,' Harry said. 'He and his brother William, the one who used to be a monk. I've never valued Robert Kett so highly as I do now, Amy. He's that rare combination—a rich man with a strong social conscience, who does not only *think* all men have equal rights, but is willing to fight for what he believes. Lord, you should have seen Uncle Richard's face when he was told that his fences were being pulled down—and by Kett! It was the worst blow of all, that

27

a *gentleman*, as he would say, would stoop so low.'

'I wish them luck,' Amy said, a trifle defiantly. 'I know sheep bring in good money and it pays us to keep them, for one good shepherd can take care of an immense flock; but no one has done anything to stop the enclosing of common land and that's going too far.'

'I say, Amy, you're really *in* this thing, aren't you?' said Harry suddenly. 'Your sister Frances is married to William Flowerdew, your father owns some of the largest flocks of sheep in the county.'

'Frances is my *half*-sister, and no Robsart has ever enclosed common land,' Amy said stiffly. 'But I do see what you mean. We'll be forced to take sides, I suppose, and naturally land-owners will stand together. Oh dear!'

And as the days passed, Amy realised that this was more than neighbours falling out. Her parents, usually of one mind over family matters and politics, were deeply divided. Sir John knew Robert Kett well because they had mutual interests in their land and their stock. He liked the man and his friendly wife and well-mannered, intelligent children. On the other hand, despite a fondness for his step-daughter, he found he could only dislike and fear the Flowerdews.

Elizabeth for her part, had never really known the Kett family well. They were younger than she, and she bitterly resented a man of property standing up for the rabble, especially when he was her son-in-law's enemy.

So for the first time in their married lives together, John and Elizabeth found themselves at odds. Not that either *said* much; it was more the silences that spoke, Amy thought. Where once they would have discussed the news eagerly, now a remark about Kett and the rebels would fall flat, leaving only a conscious guarding of tongues on both sides.

'The Ketts and the rebels are gathered on Mousehold Heath, above the city of Norwich,' Sir John told his daughter. 'They say that unless an Act is passed by Parliament for-bidding enclosures of common land they will capture the city, and hold it against all who oppose them. They are strong, both in numbers and resolution.'

'Somerset will send an army against them,' Elizabeth said with cold triumph. 'A disorganised rabble like that won't stand for long against trained soldiers.'

'Maybe you're right and maybe you're not,' said John as peaceably as he could. 'But whatever happens, there will be no markets held at Norwich, nor at Wymondham either, for many days. Do you agree, Elizabeth, that now would be as good a time as any for me to visit Syderstone? Amy could accompany me and see to the household.'

Elizabeth agreed that this was a good idea. Whatever the rights or wrongs of the rebels' cause, both Amy's parents were aware that their daughter was emotionally involved with the country folk she knew. It would break her heart to see them cut down by foreign soldiers.

Elizabeth bade her husband and daughter goodbye, convinced that by the time they returned all the trouble would be over. It was a long journey to Syderstone and they would take two, perhaps even three, days to reach their destination. Several days of hard work awaited them there, and then the journey home to Wymondham had to be accomplished. With luck, Lady Elizabeth reasoned, the army from London would have descended on Kett and the rebels and sent them packing, and life would be back to normal again, long before John and Amy came riding home across the moat.

3

Country girl

'Well, whatever may be happening in the rest of the country, Mrs Yalding doesn't change much,' commented Amy as she and her father approached the small wayside inn where they usually broke their journey. 'See, Father, she's feeding her poultry in the orchard. As fat as ever—and as noisy! It would have to be a very ancient bird that wasn't roused from dreaming by the racket.'

They dismounted outside the inn and a servant led the horses round to the stables whilst the landlord, even fatter than his wife, came wheezing out to greet them.

'Why, Sir John, it do be a pleasure to see you and your lass at my humble tavern,' he said, beaming all over a face red as a Dutch cheese. 'Come you in, my dear, and sit down, whilst your father and I see to your luggage and them fine horses. My old woman she's a-hollerin' to the poultry in the orchard, but she'll come running when I tell her who's come riding by!'

Sure enough, Amy had scarcely settled herself in the parlour when Mrs Yalding came in, pushing her hair under her cap and exclaiming rapturously how time flew. Amy recalled other visits, when she had stolen into the kitchen for a handful of sweetmeats or an apple.

'But now you're a woman grown, smart as paint and pretty as a picture,' Mrs Yalding said. 'I've a fine dinner in the oven and the fire roaring away despite the weather, almost as if I'd guessed visitors were a-coming.'

She chuckled, rolling her eyes at Amy, who laughed too, knowing that quite probably news of their progress had indeed reached the inn some time before their small party.

30

'You and your husband don't change much though, Mrs Yalding. You don't look a day older than when Father first brought me here as a child. It's lovely to be back, and I'm looking forward to seeing Syderstone too, of course. You've not suffered from land enclosures in these parts, I trust?'

'Well, I wouldn't say that, my dear, for trouble anywhere means less trade for the tavern,' Mrs Yalding pointed out. 'Howsoever, that isn't to say we've had trouble locally, 'cos we haven't. We still graze a few beasts on the common land and none try to say us nay.'

She went briskly out of the room and came back with a tray bearing cups of wine and a platter of small, rich cakes.

'Help yourself now, love, for you've had a warm ride and could do with refreshment. Don't stint for fear of spoiling your dinner, for that'll be some while yet. I've heard that there's trouble your way though, and no mistake. Father, he went into Norwich with a waggon full of plums to sell in the market and came home with a tale of an army up on Mousehold, drilling an' all like proper soldiers. They took his plums—and paid up like gentlemen, or would have, but Father wouldn't hear of it. Said he was too old and too fat to fight, but he'd feed 'em and welcome. Aye, 'twas the enclosure rebels right enough, and more power to their elbows, say I. 'Tis difficult enough for a yeoman farmer to scrape a living from his soil now on account of the rents and taxes he has to pay, without stealing the common grazing.'

'I know,' said Amy unhappily. 'The trouble is, we're mixed up in it ourselves. Of course, *we* would never enclose common land, but my sister Frances married William Flowerdew, and that family ...' and out came the story of Robert Kett and Edward Flowerdew, which had not yet reached Mrs Yalding, so far from Wymondham.

'But Mother says the real trained soldiers from London will soon send the rebels packing,' she ended miserably. 'She says they'll hang the ringleaders and those that aren't killed by the soldiers will have to go back to their cottages worse off than before.'

'Don't you worry your pretty head,' Mrs Yalding said com-

31

fortably. 'They say men are marching against the enclosures in
Kent, Wiltshire, Oxfordshire—even outlandish places such as
Devon and Cornwall. Now the Duke can't tackle 'em all, can
he? They call him the Good Duke you know, them as knows
him. And the little King, now, he'd not want to see his subjects slaughtered. They'll put all to rights without any help
from us. Quite probably they won't bring the military into
such a small matter. Now let's see you smile, for your face is
enough to turn every pan of milk in my dairy into curds, so I
tell you!'

Amy was heartened a good deal by the conversation. She
wanted everyone to be happy, as she was. But she knew it was
easier to be happy with a full stomach and pretty clothes on
your back than when you were starving and clad in a few
wretched rags. But Mrs Yalding was a sensible woman. She
put her trust in the Duke of Somerset and in King Edward VI,
and she was probably right. Immensely reassured by this
simple countrywoman who had eased her fears in a way her
own parents had been unable to do, Amy slept well that night.

They arrived at Syderstone in the late afternoon, riding along
the flat road with the verge starred with meadowsweet and
moondaisies, with here and there a scarlet poppy drooping its
head in the heat.

'Is it good to be back, little woman?' Sir John asked softly,
seeing the eager look on Amy's face as her eyes fell on the
manor house, serene in its sea of sheep. Amy nodded, smiling,
as they rode between the avenue of tall trees that led to the
front door. Mrs Beckett, trim in her grey gathered gown and
white frilled cap, the house-keys jingling at her waist, stood
waiting to welcome them.

Amy greeted her fondly but lost no time in flying through
the house and out of the kitchen door into the cobbled yard,
where already one of the farmhands was leading their horses to
the stable.

Pretty Moll, plumper now and always delighted to see Miss
Amy, confided that she was expecting again—and pray
Heaven it might be a boy this time, for her Ned had not been

32

overpleased when she had presented him with a second daughter last year.

Amy listened, and laughed at Moll's jokes, filled with the warm sense of contentment, of *belonging*, that always came over her when she returned to Syderstone. She supposed it was because this was her birthplace. Here she had first opened her eyes and seen the wide Norfolk sky, unbroken by hill or mountain. Here she had learned how to value simplicity and quietness.

As Amy went back through the kitchen, she was unable to resist peeping into the stillroom and opening the milk book, which told how many cows they had, and when they had calved. She thought a trifle wistfully that, young lady though she might be, Mrs Beckett's handwriting was better by far than her own. Then she noticed a mistake in the figuring and felt happier.

At least she was quick at adding and subtracting, even though she had never mastered a handsome handwriting, she reflected. She could work out a price and make a fair guess at the yield per acre whilst others were still scratching their heads and wondering. She could imagine Mrs Beckett, by the light of a tallow candle, laboriously scratching out the figures and writing them down again and again, until the page was grimed and the quill broken.

After she and Sir John had eaten, they went round the estate together, noting with pleasure how healthy the stock was, particularly the sheep. Old Tom, incredibly ancient and more bent than ever, smelling more like a sheep than most of his flock, was still a skilled shepherd. The lambs born that spring were well-grown and that night she and her father would decide how many lambs to sell at the market and which of the old ewes were no longer worth their keep. The ewes would be slaughtered and their meat salted for the table, though it would be pretty tough. Even with the size of the flock always increasing, they did not retain above a dozen fully grown rams, so most of the young males would be sent to the market at King's Lynn.

When they returned to the manor, Amy sat down at the

33

table in the small, cool study and pulled the books towards her with pleasurable anticipation. She might be no scholar, with only a smattering of halting French and Latin, but she was a good businesswoman. Her father often told her that he was glad she would inherit his property after his death, for she would manage it all so well.

'Though of course Arthur will be well provided for,' he would add, with a rueful smile. Most people liked Arthur and Amy certainly did. But she was aware as her father was that poor Arthur had no liking for work, and had he been given the most magnificent of manors would either have sold the property or put it in charge of a bailiff, who would have gleefully cheated him. Naturally it came as an even deeper joy to Sir John when Amy showed every sign of becoming as keen and intelligent a landowner as he was himself.

So whilst Amy's mother yearned to see her daughter at court, being sought after by rich noblemen, and spent most of her happiest hours dreaming of her daughter's marriage, Sir John patiently taught a most willing pupil all he knew of estate management. And Elizabeth taught her the intricacies of running a big household, how to manage servants, how to preserve, and salt, and bake and make.

However, she had not seen fit to teach her daughter a dairy-maid's craft, not foreseeing that she would need such knowledge. But Amy wanted to know both sides of everything, and always took advantage of her stays at Syderstone to work side by side with the women until she was as knowledgeable as they.

Nevertheless, next morning as she ran lightly downstairs, she felt a pang of guilt at the thought of what her mother would say could she see her now. Her blue stuff dress was plain and serviceable, the hem an inch above her ankles so that she could work outside without soiling her skirt. An apron, of coarse unbleached linen, protected the gown, red woollen stockings kept her ankles warm and a full white cap covered her curls. On her feet she wore heavy wooden pattens, ideal footwear for muddy or dusty yards.

Sir John also suffered from guilt when he saw Amy so sensibly dressed, because he knew he would never mention the matter to his wife. So he insisted that whilst she might dress as she pleased during the daytime, in the evening she must become once more a fashionable young lady, even though they might spend several hours scarcely exchanging a word as they pored over the account books.

Time passed all too quickly for them both, but at last they could linger no longer. The work was all finished, the servants and outside workers had their orders. After many goodbyes had been said, father and daughter rode slowly back to Wymondham, both thinking that whatever awaited them there, they would be better able to face it because of the quiet interlude they had enjoyed at Syderstone.

4

Enter a dark stranger

'The Earl of Northampton and a body of horse have attacked the rebels,' Elizabeth told them as soon as they had tidied themselves after the long ride. 'And what do you think? Kett and his men drove them off! It's said the yeoman fought like trained soldiers and scattered the royal troops like chaff before the wind. I declare, I felt proud to own myself a woman of Norfolk.'

Amy stared at her mother in amazement, then smiled faintly. Kett had won a victory over her mother's prejudices as well as over the army, evidently!

'What will happen now, Mother? Will the Duke accede to Kett's requests? They seem sensible enough, after all. No idealistic demands that would be impossible for the Duke to meet with honour.'

Elizabeth's pleasure faded a little. It seemed to Amy that her mother drooped at having to face the unpleasant possibilities ahead.

'Who can tell, poppet? I know you think Robert Kett is a worthy man, and now—well, I agree with you. But it seems that a rebellion, even in a just cause, must have a scapegoat. Someone will have to be found to bring Kett to his knees, just to show the country that rebels can never prosper, however honest their cause. I'm afraid that even if their requests are granted, the leaders of the rebellion will suffer for their part in it. The most we can hope for is that the peasants will be allowed to go free.'

Amy looked hopefully at her father, but his grave face said more than words. So all Amy could do was wonder and worry over what would happen next. Kett's men were upon the heath but also in the city of Norwich, where they had descended when the army marched and attacked their force. So with the inner knowledge that there must be another attack to save the Lord Protector from the ignominy of a defeat, however small, Amy waited as patiently as she could. She knew that all up and down the country there were women as young as she who waited in fear and want, while their children cried for their fathers and for good. And those young women could give their children nothing, until the troubles were over and settled for better or worse.

The day after their return, John Appleyard came back from a visit to one of his properties at Hales. He walked towards the house, whistling under his breath, enjoying the thought that one day this fine house would be his own.

As he passed the rose garden he saw Amy standing with her back to him, cutting blossoms. He tiptoed across the intervening lawn and when he reached her, ran his fingers down her spine, making her jump and squeak. As she jumped, the roses she held pricked her fingers and she spun round and pinched John's arm with sisterly venom, scowling at his smirk.

'What do you think you're playing at, frightening me like that?' she demanded crossly. She flourished the small pointed knife which she was using to cut the roses. 'You might have got this stuck in your ribs if I'd thought you were a wild foreign mercenary from the army, sneaking up to dishonour me.'

'I'm the bearer of good tidings,' John told her, his eyes gleaming maliciously at his half-sister. 'The Lord Protector is sending another army into Norfolk. It will be led by the Earl of Warwick and his sons. The Dudleys are famous soldiers, they'll soon teach your precious Kett a lesson; he'll think twice about standing up to his betters after this, I'll be bound.'

'You're no better than Kett, and nor am I,' snapped Amy. 'Until the troubles started you were proud enough to stand beside him at market, to hear his opinion of the stock. No one called him "Kett, the tanner", then as they do now. Why do you want to pretend that he's a simple tanner, who is doing what he has done through ignorance? Do you realise, half of us never knew he owned a tannery until people began to look round for some label other than "honest landowner" to tie round his neck? Oh, go away, John. It's silly to get into a temper in this heat.'

'I'm sorry,' said John, startled to hear such an outburst from his usually sunny sister. 'But speaking of heat, why are you out here cutting roses instead of enjoying the cool in the house?'

'Our mother isn't well. She has a fancy for a jug of roses to stand by her bed. Why don't you go indoors and talk to her? It would cheer her up.'

'Mother, sick?' said John, his protruding blue eyes widening. 'Why, of course I'll go to her. It's strange, our mother is such a healthy person that it sounds worse when you say she isn't well than when Frances or Anne take to their beds, because they do it so often.'

'I know what you mean, and quite honestly, I think she's not as ill as she believes,' Amy said with a half-smile. 'She fears she won't see another summer, and so has asked for roses by her bed. When she feels more herself, she'll laugh at her whims and fancies.'

'What is the illness? Not the sweating sickness or some such thing?'

'Don't be anxious,' said Amy hastily. Though she and John often argued they were fond enough of each other, and both were staunch admirers of their handsome mother, who had raised four children out of five to maturity.

'Of course I'm anxious,' growled John. 'It's this confounded rebellion that's caused it, I suppose, and the hot weather. Worried by the first, and worn out by the second. Can I go and see her?'

'I told you to do so,' Amy pointed out. 'It will do her good, take her mind off herself. I'll follow you when I've arranged the roses.'

When Amy took the flowers into her mother's room, she found Elizabeth sitting up in bed, still pale but listening somewhat fearfully to John's tale of the army coming to Norfolk led by that redoubtable soldier, John Dudley, Earl of Warwick.

38

'He has nearly nine thousand men and many of them are the Lanzknechts—German mercenaries, Mother. More like machines than men I've heard tell, so now we'll see something *like* a battle,' he was saying triumphantly as Amy entered the room.

Amy frowned at John, seeing her mother's apprehension. The talk of the German mercenaries would frighten a fit woman, let alone a sick one. She could see that Elizabeth was already imagining those almost legendary troops butchering the stolid Norfolk peasants.

John, she knew, would not mind seeing the peasants slaughtered by foreigners. He disliked Kett for his sister's sake, and was all in favour of enclosing the land, so he would have no objection to blood being spilt in order to quell the rebels. But we women are softer, thought Amy. She knew many of the men amongst Kett's band: cheerful countryfolk who tilled their bits of ground and grazed their sheep and cattle on the common land. She knew the frightened, white-faced women who would be waiting for their men in the damp, dark cottages—and how many, now, would wait in vain?

Fortunately John had been shaken enough at the sight of his mother's pallor to heed Amy's warning frown, and after he left, Amy sat with Elizabeth, talking cheerfully of the potpourri of rose petals which would scent the house all winter, after such a magnificent summer.

When at length she left the room it was to speak to the cook about preparing a light broth for the invalid. As she walked back across the rush-strewn hall a servant hurried to the big front door and when it opened she saw Harry Gresham on the threshold.

'Hey, Amy, don't hurry off, for it's you I've come to see,' he called cheerfully. 'You and your parents are bidden to dine with us tomorrow. Will you come? Say yes, for we have important guests.'

Amy smiled and walked towards him. 'Harry, how nice. But I'm afraid Mother isn't well. I don't suppose we shall be visiting for a while. You know what Father is; he'd not enjoy an outing until she's herself again.'

Harry's face fell. 'Intwood will seem a poor place with no

39

lovely ladies to grace our table. Do change your mind,' he wheedled.

'If your sister Mary heard you say that, your ears would be ringing,' retorted Amy. 'Who is so important that you need us to help you entertain them, anyway?'

'The Earl of Warwick and his sons,' Harry told her gloomily. 'Don't think I had a hand in bringing them to Intwood Hall, because I had not. It's my belief Sir John Dudley comes mainly to see Thomas. When Uncle Richard's heir honours us with his presence there is usually something behind it, believe me. But couldn't you come by yourself, Amy? Mary can't be expected to entertain three London lads alone—and I believe Dudley's sons to be exceptionally handsome.'

'I would like to come,' admitted Amy. 'Even if the Dudleys are as ugly as Satan I'd like to see them and hear all the London gossip. But Father wouldn't hear of it at the moment. However, perhaps your uncle might invite us in a few days; I'm sure Mother will be better by then. The Earl may still be in the district—especially if he finds Kett as difficult to tackle as Northampton did.'

Harry shared her laughter. He was a loyal member of the Gresham family, of course, but despite his uncle's righteous indignation against the rebels he was secretly in sympathy with Kett and his men. Indeed, what young person in the county was not? At heart the young are natural rebels against established order and they love vain battles and lost causes. So the romance of Kett and his humble followers encamped on Mousehold Heath and winning the city of Norwich had found its place in the hearts of many youngsters.

'Come in anyway, Harry,' said Amy, belatedly remembering her manners. 'Dear John has been sitting with Mother worrying her with his foolish talk. He's gone now, though, so I thought I'd leave her to sleep for a little, and take her some broth when she wakes. Father is supervising the cutting of the barley in Five Acre—or so he says.' She giggled, sitting down with a swish of many petticoats. 'Really, I think he's after a few rabbits,' she confided. 'Only he won't admit it in case his aim with a cudgel isn't what it used to be. But in any case,

40

he'll bring some rabbits in this evening, even if he's had to part with a groat to persuade some urchin to give him a couple.'

They laughed together indulgently over the foolish simplicity of adults, who could be capable of such transparent deceit.

'Sir Richard sends his regards,' remembered Harry. 'And so does cousin Thomas. As a matter of fact he was very keen that you should dine with us. He obviously wants to impress the Dudleys.'

'I *think* you meant that as a compliment, but I'd far rather do something for Kett, something to show whose side we're on,' Amy said, eyes shining. 'I'd like to prove to him that all well-born Norfolk people aren't narrow-minded and selfish.'

'I know what you mean. Why, I'm at Uncle Richard's to learn the manners of a gentleman, but if Warwick's a gentleman I'd do better learning to be a knave.'

'Isn't he very *Earlish*, then?'

'No—yes—hang it, I don't know, really. He's smooth as they come and pleasant enough in his manner. But you can sense his sheathed claws.'

'Well, Harry, Warwick's father was a prince amongst rogues. Remember Edmund Dudley, chief money grabber for old Henry VII? I don't recall him of course, but I've heard him spoken of—and never with anything but dislike. But this Dudley is said to be handsome, and they say his wife is beautiful still, even after bearing him thirteen children.'

'I haven't seen Lady Dudley, nor the sons yet,' admitted Harry. 'Though the father is handsome, I suppose. But why not come and see for yourself, Amy? The Duchess is not with the Duke but you'd meet him, and his three boys.'

Amy looked wistful, but seeing Harry off at the door, could only repeat her promise to pass his invitation on to her father. However, as she suspected, Sir John would not take advantage of the most pressing invitation during his wife's illness.

In the circumstances, Amy thought she would simply have to nurse her curiosity. But when her mother expressed a desire for honeysuckle to mix with her pot of roses, Amy told her

41

promptly that she would take a walk in the cool of the evening, and bring home a posy of honeysuckle from the hedgerows.

'How unselfish of you, darling,' Elizabeth said with weary sarcasm. 'It *is* today that we were to have dined at Intwood, is it not? I thought so. Well, if you should chance upon any of the noble soldiers of the crown, bring me the latest gossip.'

So that evening, Amy slipped out of the house into the cool air, and set off purposefully in the direction of Intwood Hall, not forgetting to climb into the leafy hedges to pluck every pinky-gold sprig of honeysuckle that she passed.

She had climbed a grassy bank and was well into the hedge, her hair falling down but her arms full of the coveted blossoms, when she heard someone approaching. She turned, blushing, and looked down on a young man, striding along slashing moodily at the tall meadowsweet with a stick he had cut from the hedge. Just as she was thinking, 'if I keep still he may not notice me', the young man glanced up to the top of the bank and saw her.

His initial amusement slowly turned to appreciation as his eyes took in the tumbled fair hair, the shapely figure and the flushed face of the girl poised on the bank above him. For her part, Amy saw a tall young man with bright dark eyes which were fixed on her face. His black hair curled thickly on his head but he was beardless, and his skin was tanned a golden brown by the sun.

'Let me help you down, mistress,' he said in a deep young voice which held a hint of laughter.

Amy, accepting his proffered hand, laughed outright and he joined her, so that they stood smiling into each other's eyes like old friends instead of strangers.

Amy curtsied, beginning to thank him for his help, when he said suddenly, 'Why, would you be the maid who was to have dined with Sir Richard Gresham this evening? Would you be mistress Amy, daughter of Sir John Robsart?'

'Yes, I am. His only daughter,' admitted Amy, feeling even more at ease now that she knew who this gorgeous young man was. 'You must be one of the Earl of Warwick's sons.'

'Yes, I'm his third son. Robert Dudley at your service,

42

Mistress Robsart,' answered the boy. 'Are you turning for home, now? May I accompany you?'

'I think I had better be going home,' agreed Amy. 'My mother is ill, and wanted some honeysuckle for her bedside, but I've gathered more than enough already. However, it's so sweet that I can always use the spare blossoms about the house.'

The two of them turned and walked slowly towards Stanfield Hall.

'Why are you walking—alone, too—through our country lanes when there must be so much of interest going on at Intwood?' Amy asked presently.

She thought the question must have been a tactless one for the look of gaiety left his face to be replaced by a scowl, and once more he switched at the flowerheads with his stick.

'My father doesn't need *me* when he and Thomas Gresham discuss finance, and the best way to treat for peace with Kett,' Robert said sullenly. 'I've got my own ideas of why they want me out of the way, but I don't care to be treated as a child.'

Amy stole a look at him. She thought with wonder that surely a creature of such godlike beauty should never be lightly dismissed. He was so tall—taller than any man of her acquaintance. His broad shoulders appeared even broader in his padded doublet, and his hose, of finest material, showed off his long, athletic legs.

Robert, aware of her scrutiny, remembered his host's description of the girl as 'a veritable diamond, sir. One of our real country beauties, fresh and sweet as nosegay.' Robert thought Sir Richard had been right. His eye, experienced in the ways of women though he was only seventeen, saw she employed none of the artifices of the ladies of the court to enhance her beauty. It did not occur to him that her eyes seemed twice as large and bright because of the admiration that shone from them. He thought only that here was a girl who seemed totally unaware of her own charms, and delightfully conscious of his!

But Amy was not only unaware of her own charms; she had no idea that she was rousing feelings in the susceptible breast of her companion.

'Will you spend much time at Intwood, sir?' she said at last.

Robert considered, whistling softly between his teeth. 'Oh, two or three days. There are matters—but I'm not sure I ought to burden a child like you with such things.'

Amy tightened her hand round the honeysuckle until she felt the woody stalks prick her fingers, and lowered her lashes demurely so that he should not see the annoyance in her eyes.

'I'm past sixteen, going on for seventeen,' she said severely.

'Yes, I was only teasing you—I'm seventeen myself,' Robert admitted, giving her a sudden, disarming grin. 'The truth is that my father feels seventeen is not much of an age and I'm annoyed at being kept from his councils with Gresham.'

'I'd dearly like to meet your father,' Amy ventured. 'But I don't suppose I shall. I've heard a great deal about him, of course.'

'You *should* wish to meet Father, for he is a great man. He's proved himself on the field as a soldier, as I wish to do one day. Sometimes he may appear harsh, but you should see him at home.' He laughed. 'He's absurdly in love with my mother and she with him, despite their age. But in the house my mother has absolute rule and her "dear John" who roars out his orders on the battlefield obeys his "dear Jane" like a lamb.'

'They sound very nice,' Amy said thoughtfully. 'My parents, like yours, are everything to each other. But fond though they are, often my father only pretends to do as he's bid for the sake of peace. However, I must leave you here, sir. I'll tell my mother I met you, and only wish I might do so again.'

This artless speech pleased Robert. Perhaps her very lack of dissimulation after the tortuous affairs of court added to her attraction. At any rate, when they parted he had gained her promise to walk the same lane at the same time the following day. He would come unless his father had decided to march, he told her seriously; but if such a thing did happen she would surely hear of it and know that he had not deliberately failed to keep the tryst.

Amy went to her mother's room quite breathless with excitement. 'He's very handsome, Mother, a most gallant gentleman,' she concluded when she had told Elizabeth of her meeting. 'I wish with all my heart that you were well enough to meet him. He spoke of his parents in such glowing terms—it's easy to see they're a happy family—and his look when he called his mother his father's "dear Jane" was so gentle and affectionate! Why, I began to believe the Dudleys were a more devoted family than the Robsarts, and *that* would never do!'

Elizabeth, holding a sprig of honeysuckle in her hands, replied thoughtfully, 'My love, he's a young man of the world, the first you've met. You are a country beauty, perhaps the first he's met. Don't expect too much to come from such a brief meeting. That way heartaches lie.'

'I have my fair share of admirers,' said Amy indignantly. 'I'm not likely to pine and fade because one young man speaks sweet words and goes away. There will be others.'

Elizabeth smiled. 'Good girl. Never let any man think that he's your one hope, because he won't respect you for it, and may even ill-treat you as a result. Now go to your father, and talk about sheep! I dare swear they still interest you more than talk of love and marriage.'

But Amy, going obediently downstairs, thought that this time her mother was wrong. *One* young man at any rate was going to disturb her dreams for some nights to come.

For the next two evenings, Amy met Robert in the lane and they talked their thoughts out, each discovering in the other something pleasant and new at every meeting. But on the third evening, Robert was accompanied by an older gentleman, whom Amy guessed at once must be his father. The Earl was not as tall as his son, nor did he have his air of swashbuckling charm, but nevertheless there was a strong family likeness. Despite medium height and slender build he had tremendous personality, though Amy was not sure at first that it was an altogether pleasant personality. However, she had to admire his clothes, which he wore with an elegance that matched the garments themselves. He seemed to have no particular love for the vivid shades that made so many courtiers look like fine-feathered parrots; his doublet and hose, and his short, swirling

45

cloak were of a material dark and rich, exquisitely cut yet without ostentation.

Amy was aware that his eyes, half-hidden by heavy lids, were regarding her with amusement, but nevertheless he at once engaged her in conversation. Amy, on her mettle, answered him decidedly and frankly, determined that he should not think her a spiritless country girl, who had caught his son's eye by her pretty looks.

Presently the conversation turned to the rebellion, and Amy told him without mincing words that in her opinion there was much to be said for the good sense and ideas of Kett and the men holding Norwich. She saw his eyes gleam with interest quickly veiled.

'Perhaps you're right, Mistress Robsart,' he said languidly. 'Indeed, my orders are to sue for peace and to tell the good people that if they will give Kett into my charge to stand trial they can go back to their land with a quiet mind, for the Duke of Somerset—I should say the Lord Protector—intends to stop the enclosing of common land.'

'How could they give up Kett, who has given up so much for them?' asked Amy, staring at the Earl. 'Why, Norfolk memories are long, sir. People still murmur about the rebellions in the north during King Henry's reign; you will recall how the King pretended to pardon the leader of the revolt, and brought him to London to honour him. Yet he was killed for his part in the rising. How can the peasants hand Kett over to London justice? It would be a treacherous act, sir, and one to which the people of Norfolk would never stoop.'

Robert looked anxiously at his father, afraid that Amy might have proved over bold, but the Earl was eyeing her with something akin to respect.

'You have faith in the people of Norfolk? You believe they will fight—and die—rather than give up their leaders and go home in peace?'

Amy nodded so vigorously that her curls danced. 'Why, and how could it be otherwise?' she asked. 'I've lived over sixteen years in this world and all of them have been spent in Norfolk, except for trips to London, which don't really count. My experience is that the people stick together. They are stubborn, I admit that. Have you never heard the saying "Norfolk born and Norfolk bred, strong in the arm and thick in the head"?'

The Earl threw back his head and laughed. 'It seems I shall meet opponents worthy of my steel,' he said, smiling at her. 'A green girl who is not afraid to speak her mind, and yeomen who will take up my challenge and fight for what they believe to be right. Well, I've been forewarned not to expect an easy meeting, at any rate. I must turn back now, Mistress Robsart, for I suffer from gout and the evening chill adds to my discomfort. But Robert will see you home—and perhaps he could see your father, although I am sorry to hear your mother is ailing?'

Realising the importance of the remark, Amy coloured to the roots of her hair and stammered, 'Yes, I'm sure—yes, certainly my father will be glad to meet your son. I—I hope nothing I've said has offended you, Sir John?'

Smilingly shaking his head, the Earl turned and began to retrace his steps whilst Amy and Robert almost ran back to Stanfield Hall.

Since Elizabeth pleaded so urgently, Robert was taken to her room, where afterwards she gave her unqualified approval of someone with a smile so open and a disposition so sweet. Sir John Robsart also liked the young man, and when Robert told him they would be marching on Norwich the following morning, he bade the lad to take care of himself and to come and see them whenever he found himself in the district.

Robert left the house at last, with two exciting thoughts in the forefront of his mind. He was seventeen and going to fight his first battle, and he had found the prettiest girl in the kingdom to pay his addresses to. Her parents liked him, his adored father had not tried to hide his admiration for a spirited and lovely lass.

Robert Dudley was well content.

5

Rebellion

'All might have been well but for the affair of the herald,' Robert Dudley told Amy darkly.

Amy knew now that the fighting was over, the survivors had returned to their homes and Robert and William Kett had been caught and taken to London where they would be tried—and no doubt hanged. But instead of going off with his father and brothers to the capital Robert had lingered, knowing how eager Amy would be for news.

'What did the herald do? Insult the rebels?' demanded Amy.

She was sitting on a low stool gazing up at Robert, who lounged in the big easy chair, very much the triumphant warrior.

'Lord, no. Father sent the herald ahead with a pardon for all who laid down their arms and returned home peacefully, provided they gave up their leaders to stand trial. That meant the Kett brothers of course. Robert Kett was in favour—more praise to him—and all might have been well. But a foolish boy in the crowd made—made—well, a very rude gesture, let's call it. One of the men escorting the herald—more foolish than the lad if you ask me—shot the youngster and killed him.

'I wasn't there of course, but you can imagine the scene. A bullet is no answer to a gesture, however obscene. The herald told us that only Robert Kett saved him from being torn to pieces by the maddened people. The lad had been shot in the stomach and didn't die easy. But though Kett managed to save the herald's life, he couldn't get him a hearing. In fact he had to more or less smuggle the party away from his own men. So

48

as you foresaw, the rebels obviously had no intention of giving up their leaders and returning to their homes.'

'This was in the city, was it? Kett made good his promise of taking over the city should their demands not be met?'

'Yes, Amy. Kett still had his camp up on Mousehold overlooking us, but he had occupied the city as he had promised. For a day or so we prowled round that city of yours like a crowd of cats round a mouse-cage. But though there are city gates in plenty they had all been well barred against us.

'Then Father bade the pioneers to dig and tunnel their way under the walls near one of the gates. The plan was that Northampton should lead a force through that way, secretly, whilst Father and his men—me amongst them of course—created a diversion by trying to enter through one of the other gates.'

'Can't you remember the names of the gates?' asked Amy despairingly. 'It would make it much clearer, you know. Was it St Stephen's gate? Or St Benedict's? Magdalen's? Bishopsgate?'

'Stop, for goodness' sake,' pleaded Robert, laughing. 'There are twelve gates into the city, and we got in by one of them. Don't you want to hear what happened when we finally got inside?'

'Yes, of course, I'm sorry,' Amy said remorsefully. 'You got in. What happened next?'

'Well, we had to fight of course. I'd never been inside the walls before, so it was very confusing at first. It's said that Norwich is a fine city, but the streets are cursed narrow for fighting in—and then when you least expect it, there is a big gap in the houses with a fine tree-grown space. So naturally the rebels knew where to manoeuvre, so that they could use their sword arms freely, and we were in the dark.'

'Those are plague spots and fire damage,' Amy said quietly. 'The Flemish weavers live under very cramped conditions, and the plague they have brought with them has flourished. When a house is infected by people who have died from the plague, the neighbours soak the timbers and thatch and set fire to it.'

'Oh, is that the reason?' said Robert, mildly interested.

'Yes, but despite all that, we hanged sixty rebels in the market-place that night.'

'How did you know they were rebels?'

'Don't get worked up, of course they were rebels. At any rate, they had been fighting to keep us out of the city, so what else should they be? Yes, they were rebels for sure.'

'I take it they didn't have the word "Rebel" branded on their foreheads,' Amy said with withering sarcasm. 'So how do you know they weren't just honest citizens, caught up in the street fighting?'

'Well, as to that, any "honest Norwich citizen" who helped to keep us out of the city was a rebel, whether he was one of Kett's men or not,' Robert said, stung.

'Then we're all rebels, for no one wanted your foreign soldiers rampaging through our peaceful shire, very likely committing rape and murder just for sport,' retorted Amy.

They stared at each other angrily for a moment, then Robert's lips twitched and Amy, always quick to want peace, smiled back at him.

Resuming his tale, Robert went on: 'So there we were, in the city at last. We stayed at a tavern called the Maid's Head, and very well they looked after us, too. But then the fun started. Kett's a clever man—a darned sight too clever to be on the wrong side, as Father said. Through some mismanagement our food and munitions had been left unguarded outside the city walls whilst we fought in the streets, and Kett had the good sense and foresight to realise something of the sort might have happened. So whilst we were licking our wounds and thinking the battle won, Kett nipped out of one of those accursed gates and carted off all our gear. Then he blockaded us into the city—quite a change from the conquering army stuff, I can tell you!'

'How did you escape?' asked Amy, her eyes alight with excitement.

'Fought, and fought again. By then, of course, the rebels who had escaped hanging had withdrawn from the city, so we knew friend from foe. The people of Norwich were no more

50

anxious to have hungry troops billeted on them than we were to be in a state of siege. So they helped get a body of men out of the city under cover of darkness and they recaptured most of our munitions, which had been too heavy and cumbersome for the rebels to take far. Then, having got out of the city, we had to think again.'

'Why? Surely it's easier to fight men in the open than when they are defending a city?' asked Amy.

'Not when they have a position such as Kett had acquired. Lord, that man's a strategist! He had camped on some heath —you probably know it—Mousehold. About the only hill there is in these parts, I'd say. He had every advantage, Amy. Our men would have had to attack running uphill; we couldn't see his forces very well, but our army was laid out like a map before him, so that he could choose where and when to attack our weakest point. Our heavy guns were useless, we couldn't aim them properly at the enemy; and by the time our swordsmen and bowmen had climbed that hill they would have been an easy target for the men at the top.'

'Yet you attacked? That was brave, in the circumstances.'

'No, not really. You see, Father circled Kett's camp, but we felt sure it would be certain disaster for our forces if we attacked there. But Father knows something of men: he decided to hold back, hoping that our inaction would worry the peasants so that they would become nervous and decide either against fighting, or to attack us. Father was right, as usual, for after a while Kett led his men down from the heath-top into a place called Dussendale. There seemed no rhyme or reason in the move, but is was greatly to our advantage.'

'No rhyme or reason, why that *is* the reason,' cried Amy. 'They are only uneducated peasants after all, and I suppose they remembered the old rhyme about Dussendale.' She closed her eyes and recited the lines in a voice that faltered a little.

'The countryfolk, Job, Dick and Jack,
    With clubs and heavy shod,
    Shall fill up all of Dussendale
    With bodies and with blood.'

51

'So that was it!' Robert exclaimed. 'Father will be interested, for our spies said that Kett seemed to be persuaded into taking that course only after long talks and many arguments. He must have known it was suicide, militarily speaking.'

'Poor, simple fools,' said Amy sorrowfully. 'They thought the prophecy would be fulfilled and they would fill Dussendale to overflowing with the foreigners' blood. Instead, they spilt their own.'

'Aye, three thousand five hundred men were slain on the field they say,' agreed Robert. 'But when you say *foreigners*, there were not so many mercenaries as there were English.'

'You were all foreigners to us Norfolk folk,' explained Amy stiffly. And then, seeing the handsome forehead crease into a frown, added hastily, 'I said *were*, Robert. You've been a good friend to me, and from what I've heard your father saved the lives of many he might have slain, by stopping the battle when the rebels threw down their arms.'

'Yes,' agreed Robert with a reluctant grin. 'But I'm bound to admit, they were stubborn until the very jaws of death gaped before them. They fought on long after they must have realised they had no chance of success. They refused to give up their leaders and go peacefully home, even when we outnumbered them ten to one: they with their billhooks and scythes, and us with our guns. They said they would rather die fighting than be slaughtered by the foreigners when they were weaponless. But when they had arranged for their leaders' escape and were surrounded, with our guns pointing death on every side, then they threw down their arms. As you know, we found the Kett brothers, hiding in a barn in some god-forsaken spot. The farmer denied any knowledge that they were there and they swore he spoke the truth, so maybe he'll not pay the price for succouring enemies of the King. But the Ketts . . .'

'The "god-forsaken spot" was Swannington. And you don't have to tell me the Ketts will die,' said Amy. 'We shall grieve for them, Robert. Even those people who did not fear the Flowerdews before will think twice before trusting them now. But for them, none of this might have happened. Even our family has been touched by it. Mother's health grows worse.

She worried over the rebellion, now she worries over her daughter, Frances Flowerdew. It is not a popular name in Wymondham at the moment, especially amongst those whose men did not return from the camp on Mousehold heath. To think, I laughed with my brother John when she said she feared she would not live to see another summer. Now I believe I see it in her eyes. I don't think she'll live to see Christmas.'

'I expect it's just the hot weather, and her worries over the rebellion,' Robert said comfortingly. 'It is natural enough that she should be distressed, for she must have known personally many of the men who died. With careful nursing she'll soon recover her good spirits. I'll come down to visit you whenever my duties permit me to leave London, and I'll bring Lady Elizabeth some little comforts to cheer her—my own mother will advise me what will do your mother most good.'

When the time came for Robert to leave, Amy walked down the dusty country road beside him. Overhead, the leaves drooped on their branches, as if they were tired of summer and longed to fall. Robert led his horse, the reins looped over his arm, and wondered whether he would get his ears boxed by his companion if he tried to kiss her farewell.

He need not have worried. Amy feared that once Robert was back amidst the gaieties of London he would not think of her again, but she remembered her mother's words and did not press him for the date of their next meeting.

But when he put his arms round her, she put into her kiss the feelings she would not put into words. His tentative lips met a warm, eager mouth that changed the embrace from a parting gesture into a world-tilting experience that made him drop the reins so that his horse wandered off. He forgot everything for the moment except the feeling in his arms as they tightened round a youthful, yielding body, and his mouth crushing hers.

When they drew apart, they looked shyly at each other, reluctant to speak of their feelings. They were glad of the diversion of chasing Robert's horse, laughing as they untangled the reins. Amy waved and smiled as Robert mounted his stallion and trotted off down the road.

Amy, returning to Stanfield Hall, no longer doubted that Robert Dudley would return. She had discovered that his power over her was equalled only by her power over him. She knew for certain that no matter how many men she met they would never compare with Robert: something within her, some feminine instinct which had awoken in his arms, told her that he was similarly caught up in their relationship.

Then, for a while, all her thoughts were turned in one direction. Day and night, she nursed her mother. It seemed as though Elizabeth was gradually wasting away, growing paler and thinner before their very eyes, despite everything they did. She suffered pain but complained little; only when she dropped into an uneasy slumber did she moan and cry out in her sleep that the pain was growing stronger, until it seemed that it would devour her.

Amy sometimes suspected that her mother's sudden death in her sleep was not as natural as it seemed. She had seen her father, his face drawn with worry and his eyes sunk into his head with tiredness, searching old books for remedies against the pain Elizabeth suffered. But if he had, by accident or deliberately, administered a dose of something fatal to Lady Elizabeth, Amy could only be glad for her mother's sake.

Before Christmas, as Amy had foretold, the Robsarts were in mourning—and Elizabeth Robsart was at peace. They buried her where she had wanted to lie; in the soft rich mould beside Wymondham Abbey, where once the monks had tilled the soil but where now, every Sunday, the people of Wymondham went to worship. Amy was proud of the number of people who came to her mother's funeral.

As everyone had guessed, the Kett brothers had been tried and condemned to death. The trials had been something of a farce—one of the Flowerdew brothers sat on the jury that convicted Robert—but no one had expected anything else. What the people of Wymondham and Norwich had *not* foreseen, however, was that the brothers, having been hanged, would then be tarred and hung in a public place, where the sight of their mutilated bodies and the smell of tarred and rotting flesh would remind others that the arm of the law was long, and its blow swift and terrible.

Robert Kett was hung in chains from Norwich Castle, but William was hung from the tower of that part of the abbey now used as the parish church, where it was impossible for his fate to be forgotten. Robert Kett's wife and her many children, who had formerly been consistent churchgoers, now attended services elsewhere; rarely, now, did the Ketts come to the abbey. But they came for Elizabeth's funeral and Amy was grateful, and said so.

'We come to show her our respect,' the eldest Kett boy, also called Robert, told Amy a trifle stiffly. 'But in time, we shall worship here again. In time.'

The widow herself was more forthcoming. 'Your mother never knew us very well, but she was kind to me when my husband first left home to lead the rebels. Law and justice have taken from me the man I loved; but in their way, I suppose, they were merciful. Our lands should have been forfeit, but young King Edward has seen fit to grant most of them to us again. We feared at first that people would shun our company; but time has proved us wrong, thank God. Those who were our friends, are friendly still. Now I am determined that the past must be forgotten. Indeed, Robert would be shocked to know that we have stopped attending the church he worked so hard for. If I could tell him that I do not come to services here any more because his younger brother's body is hanging over our heads, his chains clinking when the vultures and crows swoop, he would say "That is only a shell, my dear. William and I have deserted the shells of our bodies and our souls are in Heaven". So now I must put aside grief, and dark thoughts of vengeance, for fear they touch my children. Your mother's funeral will lead us naturally back into the life of the church, and we will worship again amongst friends.'

With his mother dead, John Appleyard seemed to forget how much he owed to his stepfather. John had married an East Bradenham girl, Elizabeth Hogan, and though they had a pleasant home and manors enough, none of them compared with Stanfield Hall. Because Stanfield Hall had been Elizabeth's dower house from her first husband, on her death it automatically reverted to John Appleyard, as her husband's heir. Sir John Robsart was uneasily aware that he was living in a home that really belonged to his stepson, and though he paid him rent and looked after the farm as though it had been his own, he would willingly have returned to Syderstone.

He lingered only for Amy's sake. In Wymondham she was more accessible to her lover than she would have been living out at Syderstone. For Robert Dudley had been true to his word. He had visited them constantly, even during the weeks of hardest trial, when they knew that Elizabeth was dying, and had gone too far for them to be able to comfort her.

However, when spring came again and John's veiled hints and insinuations were becoming more difficult to bear, Robert came on a flying visit, and to the Robsarts' relief, suggested that they should move back to Syderstone.

'For I know, sir, that you've only stayed on here for my sake and your daughter's,' he said frankly to Sir John. 'But now we are betrothed, and both have work to do in preparation for marriage. I shall visit you at Syderstone just as often as I have visited you here, for my father says he will give us Cockisford Priory as part of the marriage settlement, and it lies near Syderstone. Amy can sew her bride-clothes as easily at Syderstone as she could here.'

'Cockisford Priory?' said Sir John, his eye kindling. 'Then you and Amy will be near me, and whilst the child lives under my roof she will be within a short ride of her new home.'

'There will be a great deal to set to rights; it will be fun making the old priory into a home,' said Amy, visualising the great grey pile which had been pillaged considerably before it came into the Earl of Warwick's possession.

'Hard work will keep your mind off our separation,' Robert told her, laughing. 'I don't suppose we shall be able to live at the priory ourselves for several years, as I believe it needs almost total rebuilding. But I have arranged for the farm buildings to be reconstructed, and you, my love, can be close at hand to supervise the bricklayers and carpenters who will move in during the course of the next few months.'

He drew her aside and said in a lower tone, 'Come, Amy. You must see that it is for the best if you go back to Syderstone. Your father is not wanted here, and John Appleyard doesn't mind letting him know it. Anyway, why should your father be bailiff for an Appleyard, when he has his own good acres to mind?'

'You're right, of course. I'll be happier at Syderstone too, out of reach of John's malice. Lately he has been quite unpleasant to Father.'

But before they set out on their journey back to Syderstone, Amy went over to Intwood to say goodbye to her friends.

'We're to be married on the fourth of June, when Rob is eighteen,' she told Mary and Harry Gresham. 'Guess where we are going to be married, Mary?'

'At St Peter Mancroft, in Norwich? Many big weddings are held there.'

'No, nor at Wymondham, though that would have suited me better than St Peter Mancroft. Rob didn't want to get married in Syderstone church—too small for his grand relations and friends, no doubt. Instead, we are to be married at the old Palace of Sheen, which is the new Palace of Richmond!'

'Gracious, Amy, you'll be too important to know us,' laughed Mary.

Harry was silent, frowning at his hound, Jericho, who lay at his feet.

'Wait, you haven't heard the best bit yet. The King will be present,' Amy said with simple pride. 'Not only the King, either: his sisters, the Princess Mary and the Princess Elizabeth; the Lord Protector and his wife and sons—oh goodness, it will be a day to remember.'

'It will indeed,' said Harry drily.

'Oh, yes, and you'll both come, won't you?' said Amy hastily. 'Dear Sir Richard will bring you, I'm sure. Your cousin Thomas will be amongst the distinguished guests, though I've never cared a straw for Thomas. But you and Harry have been a part of my life ever since we came to Wymondham. I shouldn't feel I had been properly married if you weren't there.'

'Of course we'll come, silly goose,' Mary assured her. 'Wild horses wouldn't make me miss your wedding and when the King is thrown in as a special attraction I daresay even Harry will put on his best doublet and go to London.'

'I might. Your new father-in-law could do me a good turn if he would. I want to be a soldier and he's in a position to advise me. I suppose that now the disagreement with Somerset has become open knowledge, the Earl of Warwick will appoint himself the new Lord Protector?'

The girls exchanged bewildered glances. They knew that there had been trouble in London; Somerset had kidnapped the young King to try to assure his own safety. They gathered, in a confused way, that the Protector had been overbearing to some of the Lords, who were supposed to share his duties on the Council. That he had enemies was obvious; everyone who has power makes enemies. But his time in the Tower had been of short duration; the King had seen to the safety of his uncle, people said. And the Earl of Warwick, far from appearing to want the job of Protector, had been the one who had arranged for Somerset's release.

'The Earl would certainly help you to become a soldier, if only for his friendship with your cousin Thomas,' Amy said slowly. 'But, Harry, what makes you think he wants to appoint himself Lord Protector? He has gone to some pains, has he not, to clear up the trouble the Duke of Somerset was involved in?'

Harry glanced with mocking affection at the wide-eyed bewilderment which showed plainly on Amy's guileless countenance.

'Amy, you're *marrying* into the family,' he said incredulously. 'Has it never occurred to you that the Earl is a very ambitious man? When a man rides ambition, my girl, he'll not be content with second place for long. It's top dog or nothing for him. He is slowly draining Somerset of his power; he is making the Council scratch their heads, and the young King glance sideways at his uncle. Then, when the time is ripe, he'll act—and rise or fall, according to his wisdom in choosing the moment. Come to think of it, Robert could have told you all

58

this, if he had wanted to. Or is Robert like his father, Amy? Does he ride ambition?'

'Robert has ambitions, I suppose: to marry me is one of them. But he gains nothing by such a marriage. I may be my father's only *legitimate* child, but Arthur has just married, and his wife may well give him a son which would bear the name of Robsart. I believe then that Father would perhaps make Arthur his heir, although I know he would not leave me penniless.'

'I meant nothing like that,' Harry said hastily, reddening. 'And don't underrate yourself, girl. Any man would be glad to marry you for yourself, and not want a penny piece in exchange. No, I merely meant that if Robert was as ambitious as his father, he might not want you to know all the family secrets, in case he lost you.'

'I am marrying Robert, not his family,' Amy said coldly, though the colour burned in her cheeks. 'If his father is really planning against Somerset perhaps he believes himself truly the better man; I don't know. But I'll not have my best friends thinking that Rob is as—well, *calculating*—as his father.'

'The Earl can't be *so* calculating, Amy, for as you've said yourself, you have no great dowry to attract a husband,' Mary said hastily. 'But this is foolish talk! We in Norfolk know very little of affairs in London and Harry may well have picked up some idle gossip about the Earl. We all know that you and Robert are marrying for love alone—look how he has come riding to Wymondham in the worst of weathers, just for a few hours with you. Come, tell us what you'll wear—and also what *I* should wear, for I've never been to a grand society wedding before!'

'Neither have I,' confessed Amy, and the dangerous subject was changed to the fascinating topic of clothes. But as Amy rode home with Harry politely escorting her, she thought despairingly that the conversation had changed things, because like the serpent in the garden of Eden, doubt about the Dudleys had been put into her heart.

She glanced sideways at Harry and caught him looking at her. Quickly she turned her head once again, to gaze unseeingly at the road ahead. So that was it! Harry really did like her, and not just as a brother might, either. He looked like a person who knew the extent of his loss but was powerless to remedy it.

Harry still had his way to make in the world. He had a father who was fond of him; but he had many brothers and sisters and his parents had little money and less influence. Amy knew she would not have married Harry even if he had asked her. There were too close; she had never been swept off her feet by Hal, he had never even kissed her.

Amy sighed to herself. So much lost, she thought. Friendship, because she could never act naturally again with Harry, knowing how he felt about her. Trust, because she would never know whether Harry spoke from his heart or from jealousy. Then she remembered Robert and her heavy heart lightened. She had what she most wanted from the world: the love of Robert Dudley. The rest was like losing a candle, when the sun shone hot in the heavens.

She knew, when they reached Stanfield Hall and she said goodbye to Harry, that it really was goodbye. They might meet again, but they would be different people. Yet the knowledge no longer gave her more than a passing stab of disquiet. She was the darling of Robert's heart, and in a short time their lives would begin together and they would go on together, until death parted them.

It was enough.

6

Marriage

The weather was pleasant, fortunately, when the Earl of Warwick came riding through the countryside to decide on the marriage settlements. He rode along through the whispering green of May admiring the blur of bluebells amongst the trees, thinking of the pleasure he was giving to his son who rode at his side.

He knew the extent of the Robsarts' land and money, almost as well as did Sir John. He knew all about the charm of Arthur Robsart, who had married Alex Chapman's handsome widow, so that even the paltry lands and manors Robsart meant to will to Amy might never be hers. The knowledge that he was being absurdly generous to Robert and this pretty lass warmed his heart. It was good to be generous—especially when people knew about it. They would say, 'He could have had a Duke's daughter for the lad, yet he gave him his heart's desire and let him marry an unknown country girl.'

He smiled at Robert and was rewarded by a look of pure affection. The boy knew he was lucky. His elder brother, John, was to marry Ned Seymour's daughter. Her name was Anne, and she took after her mother. Probably one day she would have that lady's sharp tongue—already she had the Duchess's fine profile and thin, determined lips. His other children were all going to marry where it would profit him best—but then none of them had ever fallen deep in love, as Robert had.

'Well, Robin, nearly there.'

'Yes, Father.'

'You're a lucky dog, my doy. Know it, do you?'

'I do. She's not only beautiful, she's got spirit and gaiety. A

61

quick foot in the dance and a merry laugh for a joke. She's gentle too, and very practical. She's been well-taught in household matters and she knows more about estate management than I do!'

Warwick smiled to himself. The boy might not have taken his meaning precisely, but then what did lovers know of marriage settlements, and dowries? Or, for that matter, of political intrigue; the fascinating task of gently steering minds until they saw things the way you wanted them to see things?

They rode up the drive to Syderstone Manor and he knew a moment of misgiving. These broad, flat acres dotted with the grazing sheep and cut about by marsh—what sort of inheritance was this? And the girl was one of your golden-haired beauties. Her looks might fade early, and Robert might find himself married to an insipid woman with a cluster of children demanding all her attention. He gave himself a shake. He had married to the best advantage himself, yet he had loved Jane Guildford truly long before their wedding and still he loved her truly. He knew she was no longer the slender little creature he had loved when he was in his teens—the daughter of Sir Edward Guildford, who had adopted him and looked after him when his own father had been hastily executed by Henry VIII. Yet though she had borne him thirteen children, she still had the power of fascinate him, making him indifferent to the charms of other women.

They dismounted and the girl came running out of the house to greet them. She was much as he remembered her: slim, strong, with her hair tucked out of sight beneath her coif but her lashes shining gold in the sun, and her eyes blue as the flowers they had passed. She turned to lead them indoors and he saw the long wheaten hair curling down the length of her back until it reached where he judged her knees must be under her gay taffeta gown. Her step was swift and confident, she neither blushed nor sidled past him. In the house she introduced her father and then caught Robert's sleeve to lead him from the room. The Earl saw Robin's eyes kindle with desire as he touched her hand, and he smiled again to think that so light a touch could turn Robin from a boy into an eager man.

This marriage is right, he thought abruptly. The girl is innocent and beautiful, yet she has strength of character. If she had not, Robert would have seduced her months before.

He turned his charming smile on Sir John. 'The lovebirds have left us, sir, so let's to business.'

Laughing, Sir John led his guest over to the table where he had plans of his land drawn up. The two men began their talk.

'My father is giving me twenty pounds a year, Rob. It's not much.'

Robert leaned over the well, and dropped a small stone down into the depths. It fell straight, and he counted to five before they heard the echoing splash.

'We shan't need money, Amy my love. I shall be a Gentleman of the Ordinary on the King's household, which carries various rewards, and you'll live either at court with me or in one of our manors. But it will give you a little independence, which is no doubt what your father wishes.'

She nodded, then bent to stroke a tabby cat which pressed against her skirts. Robert saw her hair fall forward to show the nape of her neck, white and slender. It was somehow vulnerable and childish, making him want, foolishly, to seize her in his arms and squeeze her until she cried out, or to stroke her neck, very gently, as she was caressing the cat.

He shook himself impatiently. What a fool he was over this green girl! He wanted her more than he had ever wanted a woman before, yet he could never bring himself to risk a rebuff. Sometimes her very gentleness made him want to grip her too fiercely, so that his fingers left bruises on her arm. But she was no well-brought-up young lady to wince quietly and tremble under his hand. She never troubled to dissemble.

'That *hurt*,' she would say in a shocked voice, and more than likely, before he could so much as apologise, her small but capable hand would come up and give his ear a good clout, so that his head sang.

He had no idea what she might do if he tried to make love to her. He sometimes told her teasingly that she could give him lessons in self-defence, but that was when he had been rough and she had paid him back in his own coin. When they kissed, he could feel her responding wholeheartedly, but it was always she who broke away from the embrace first. He thought it was because like him, she distrusted her own will power. She is afraid of her own desires, he told himself.

'You're coming back to London with us, to meet my mother and the rest of my family.'

'I know, Rob. Father told me, and we're all packed.'

'Do you realise, Amy, that it's only two weeks to our wedding day?'

She straightened up, picking hairs absently from where they had clung to her fingers, pushing the cat gently away from her feet.

'Of course I know. Sometimes I get terribly excited and feel I can't wait; then I feel frightened.'

'Why do you feel frightened, Amy? Are you afraid of me?'

The thought made him feel masculine and superior, but Amy shook her head, laughing up at him.

'I'm afraid of meeting your family,' she said.

Their laughter mingled, but Robert knew she had told only half the truth. She was frightened, as he was himself, at the thought of the wedding night. Being alone together at last, each feared they might in some way disappoint the other. Robert knew it must be that way with Amy too, because she was a girl, and he knew his sisters liked to frighten each other before a wedding by tales of the pain suffered by the bride. And him? He was afraid he would suddenly fall into one of his foolish fits, when she seemed gentle and tender, too fragile to touch. A great idiot I'll look, if I can't leap over my wife on our wedding night, he thought savagely.

Of course, I can drink myself bold—but suppose I overdo it, and just roll into bed and snore all night? Or worse, suppose I get like dear old Chris did on his wedding night—he spent the night making mad, passionate love to a bolster, with his wife and her friends giggling outside the door, because he had been too drunk to know what was happening.

Then he looked down at Amy and she smiled at him;

slowly, the dimples in her cheeks peeping, her eyes narrowing into shining slits of mirth. He felt an overwhelming sense of relief. She knew how he felt, he knew how she felt, and together, somehow, everything would be all right. At that moment, he felt happier and more self-confident than he had ever felt in his life before. Taking her hand, he pulled her towards the house, saying gaily that they must see how their fathers were getting on.

Meeting the Dudley family was quite as frightening as Amy had feared. A few days before the wedding she visited them in their London home and found herself facing the enormous Dudley clan. She met Robert's eldest brother, John, with his betrothed, Anne Seymour, and she talked to the only child present, little Frances Dudley. But Ambrose, Henry, and Robert's sisters-in-law confused her by some strange resemblance; not so much physical as mental. These people were members of the great ruling class and they knew it. Robert's mother, small and fine featured, greeted her kindly, but it was plain that she was more interested in her other future daughter-in-law, Anne Seymour.

She and her father attended Anne's wedding on the third of June, and Amy said to Sir John, 'It's like a rehearsal for to-morrow!'

Then it was The Day, when Amy and Robert would be joined together in holy matrimony, under the eye of the young King and all the noblest in the land.

The wedding itself passed in a dream. The weather shone fair and lovely, but to Robert nothing shone as brightly as the pearly innocence of the girl who was now his wife.

After the wedding feast there was dancing and merry-making. Amy was presented to King Edward, a small, fair-haired boy, who was polite but abstracted. He saw many women and attended many ceremonies, but this was too much! Two of the Dudleys married on two fine summer days, when he might be enjoying himself in his own way! But he was fond of Robert, admiring his looks, merry temperament and athletic prowess, so he tried to hide his boredom.

After her meeting with Edward, Amy was constrained to whisper a question to Robert which had been haunting her ever since the wedding ceremony.

'Who is that girl, Rob? Look, she's wearing a very plain gown—dove grey, with no ornament. She's got red hair, I think, but it's all scraped off her face and tidied into a silver net. I can see she knows you, for she's scarcely taken her eyes off you, whatever entertainment has been offered.'

Robert glanced round casually. 'Who? Oh, *I* see! It's Edward's sister, Elizabeth, Anne Boleyn's daughter. I must take you to meet her. She and I have been friends since I was eight or nine. She's a queer girl though—remember the scandal over Tom Seymour, the Protector's younger brother? Of course, I don't suppose there was much truth in the rumours, but there's never smoke without fire as they say. The reason she dresses so plainly and keeps quiet and subdued is to convince everyone that there *was* no scandal.'

'She's very pale, her skin must be like milk,' said Amy. 'How glorious her hair must look when she brushes it out at night. I can see the colour of it through the net.' She thought she should have praised the other girl's beauty as she was an old friend of Robert's, but honesty forbad it. The Lady Elizabeth with her thin pale face and sandy lashes could never be described as pretty, thought Amy.

Robert took Amy's elbow and led her over to where the girl stood, watching their approach out of dark, almond-shaped eyes.

'Lady Elizabeth, you must allow me to present to you my wife, the Lady Amy Dudley,' he said, grinning at Amy's startled face as realisation dawned that she was no longer Amy Robsart.

The two girls curtsied and smiled—Amy frankly, the other reluctantly, as though smiling was not a thing she had done much of late. Elizabeth spoke a few quiet, uninterested words of congratulation on their marriage, so stilted and formal that Amy suspected the girl had learned them by heart. Then she began to talk to Robert, with animation; an attraction hitherto unseen chased across her face, making the dark slanting eyes sparkle and the tight line of her mouth relax and curve into a mischievous smile.

Amy, unnoticed, thought that this girl could be enchanting when she chose; she used her hands a lot, gesturing to point a remark, so that no one watching her could fail to notice her slim white fingers and carefully tended rosy nails—though she wore no rings to enhance them as Amy would have done.

Her voice is beautiful too, thought Amy. She wished Robert would include her in the conversation, but he had just won a laugh from his companion—a sweet, shrill sound—and it seemed to elate him, making him talk more intimately so that the reason for their laughter was lost on Amy and she could only summon up the travesty of a smile and try to appear at ease.

Fortunately her sturdy common sense came abruptly to her rescue as she stood there, feeling lost and left out. It's me he loves, common sense said firmly. He chose me out of the hordes of women who have admired him. She tightened her hold on Rob's arm, commanding his attention.

Immediately Robert looked down at her, his glance proud and possessive. For a moment Amy thought she read something in the Lady Elizabeth's eyes; was it dislike? Envy? Or merely annoyance at having Robert Dudley's attention distracted from herself?

But the look was gone as soon as it had come, leaving the dark eyes inscrutable, the face once more the pale, proud mask that told no secrets. She exchanged a few more commonplace remarks with the bridal pair and then, turning, walked to where her brother the King stood, talking to a very small girl with freckles and chestnut-coloured hair.

'Well, what did you think of Princess Elizabeth?' asked Robert, guiding her to a seat where they might talk undisturbed for a moment.

'Why do you call her "the Lady Elizabeth" one moment, and "Princess" the next?' parried Amy. 'She must be a princess, surely—you call her sister Mary princess for I heard you.'

'Oh, no one knows quite what to call Elizabeth. She was

known for years as "the little bastard". Anyway, if Edward were to die tomorrow she would not be heir to the throne; it would be Princess Mary. I think for some reason people feel safer sticking to "Lady Elizabeth". Did you like her, sweetheart?'

'She likes you. I had the feeling she didn't like me much,' answered Amy equivocally.

'Oh nonsense, of course she liked you. As for me, I *told* you, we've been friends since we were brats in leading strings. Only of course she's old Harry's daughter and she's in the succession, so I had to be respectful to her when we did lessons together or our tutor would have beaten me. But Elizabeth has always been different from other children. She never told tales, and though she could romp and be wild enough when she chose, there was always a careful streak in her. I've never known her get into trouble—she always seemed to keep a sort of verbal back door open to get her out of hot water.'

'I can believe that. She's got a mouth that tells no tales— and watchful eyes,' said Amy rather acidly.

'Come, Amy, when you think of the life she led as a little maid—God, you *can't* imagine it! Four stepmothers; and two they say died by her father's hand. He didn't cause Jane Seymour to be beheaded, but it's said he dragged her out of childbed too soon and it's common knowledge that he was chasing after a younger, prettier woman just before Edward was born. I know Elizabeth was only four or so when Jane Seymour died, but she must have been brought up on the rumours. And she was eight when Kathryn Howard died by the axe—and old beyond her years, then. She told me she would never marry, and indeed, marriage is full of pitfalls for her. Do try to like her, Amy, she needs friends.'

'She would seem to have friends enough,' said Amy lightly, nodding to where Elizabeth stood. She was talking with the King and his little friend and suddenly the two younger ones laughed at something the older girl had said. Amy hoped they were not laughing at her.

'Amy, you can't be serious! Edward's her brother and four years younger than she is. Jane is her cousin—she's Edward's age too. They're nice enough children but much too young for Elizabeth. She's a woman. Why, Edward says he'll marry Jane, and do you know why? Because she's so small and shy that she'd never bully him, or take his money to buy herself fine jewels and clothes! No, I'm determined you shall be a friend to the Lady Elizabeth. She's had a hard life in many ways, and if she *should* ever come to the throne it would be greatly to our advantage if we were her acknowledged intimates.'

Amy, instinctively stiffening, was about to tell him that she'd choose her own friends, when she realised the absurdity of the situation. Here they were, a few hours married, and heading fast for their first quarrel over the most trivial of issues!

Smiling up at Robert she said, 'Of course, love; but the Lady Elizabeth will no doubt make the first overtures if she wants to become friendly. And remember, she's brilliantly clever—even *I* know that. She would probably find me terribly boring. I don't read very much and writing is a great labour for me. Now you didn't wed me for my brains, did you?'

'Nor is it for your brains I'll bed you,' teased Robert, but even as he said the words, he gripped Amy's hands in delighted anticipation. Amy felt her heart thump. For a moment elation was swamped by uncertainty. Then she felt ashamed of herself. Everything will be all right, because it's Rob, she told herself fiercely.

So when the bridal couple were led to their marriage chamber at last. Amy laughed at the jokes, helped the young girls who were struggling to get her out of her finery, and jumped naked into bed with Rob beside her. The onlookers grew bawdy; many of the guests had drunk too deeply and were unwilling to leave the newlyweds to their sport.

In the end Robert jumped out of bed and, aided by his brother Ambrose, drove the giggling, squeaking girls and the good-humoured, pot-valiant young men out of the room by force, shooting the bolt across the door. Vaulting into bed he kissed Amy fiercely, muttering, 'I've no mind for any more interruptions tonight,' as he slid his hands down her smooth back.

Much later, they lay still at last, and Rob, laying a gentle hand on his wife's stomach, said quietly, 'Think, my darling. Perhaps already my son lies within you.'

In the dark, Amy felt the blood rush to her face. A baby! How strange to think that this morning she had been a maid and tonight she was a woman, perhaps already carrying the beginnings of a child. Then Robert laughed softly and she was laughing too, because it was so strange and wonderful to lie together, to be young and in love. Laughter made it seem more real, somehow. Still laughing, they turned into each other's embrace, the mirth dying on their lips as breath quickened.

Dawn was stealing grey across the spires of the city, when at last they slept. They lay sprawled in sleep like a couple of puppies, yet each was aware that they had achieved their desire. They had survived the first perilous assault of being wedded and bedded; now they could begin their marriage.

Three days later saw Amy and Rob riding towards the manor of Hemsby, where they were to live for the first few months of their marriage. They travelled slowly through the gentle warmth of June and arrived at their destination with hearts so full of excitement that even the first sight of the castle did not dampen them.

'It's a ruin, right enough,' Rob said, almost with satisfaction. 'My, but there will be some work needed to set it to rights, Amy.'

However, one wing of the castle had been strengthened and rebuilt to form quite a respectable dwelling, though the young Dudleys soon discovered that their roof leaked in the rain, draughts whistled in through cracks and crannies in the big blocks of stone and in really bad weather the wind off the sea swirled the rushes on the floor and lifted Amy's petticoats above her knees.

But none of these things mattered to two young people, deeply in love. It was a challenge to their ingenuity to discover ways of mending the roof, and Robert found the servants both willing and able, once they had discovered that he and his wife, though young, were not to be easily cheated.

With only Rob to criticise, and an excellent cook to aid her, Amy was able to prove herself an efficient housewife. To Rob she was already the ideal companion. The sea fascinated them both, and together they would stroll amongst the great sand dunes spangled with marram grass so tough that it could cut leather.

When the weather was warm enough Amy listened to Rob's urgings and finally brought herself to try sea-bathing. Soon she was as at ease in the water as he, though she kept close to the shore because of the strong undertow which prevailed on that part of the coast.

Yet all too soon it seemed to Amy, their idyll had to end. The Earl of Warwick was taking more and more power from the hands of the Duke of Somerset, and he needed his sons around him. Robert returned to court and Amy moved into lodgings in London, where she fitted easily into the life of a London housewife, enjoying the busy, noisy street markets where such fascinating wares could be bought, and seeing all the famous places she had heard about. But she lived for the moment when Rob came bursting in through their front door and they were together again.

In this way, the first year of their marriage passed almost before they realised it. Then Thomas Stukeley came into their lives.

Rob did not bring many visitors to their lodgings. He preferred to have Amy to himself whenever he could get away from his duties at court. But one bright morning he ushered in a man a little older than he was himself, who walked with a swagger and talked with the deep burr of the West Country enriching his voice.

Amy, studying her guest covertly, saw a man similar in many ways to Rob and yet strangely different. He carried himself with an air of jaunty freedom, as though he revelled in the fact that he was important to no one but himself. Rob was already beginning to be aware of his responsibilities as a married man, the son of the King's chief adviser. Perhaps because of their different status, Robert was attracted to Stukeley. He was a bachelor still, and would, he loudly asserted, marry only for money; he was wild to a fault, generous and penniless, handsome and witty. So Rob could see what he might have been, had he not had good parents and a loving wife.

So Tom would come swaggering into Amy's parlour, paying her extravagant compliments in his casual, offhand way, and fling himself down in a chair to sit talking to Rob until the night was beginning to turn into another day.

Amy bore with Stukeley as patiently as she could, but she thought to herself that the man was a bad influence on Rob. However, when she heard them formulating plans for a visit to France, she could no longer hold her tongue.

'You want to go off with that idle, dissipated creature and leave me behind?' she asked incredulously as soon as they were alone. 'Oh Rob, I seem to spend so much time without you. I believe you *like* leaving me!'

'No, I hate to leave you,' protested Robert; then, with his disarming smile, he admitted, 'but I've had no opportunity for travel before, my love, and there's no danger. We shall go to the court of Henry II, at Amboise, meet all the grand French courtiers and their luscious French wives,' he warded off Amy's spirited attempts to slap him, 'with whom we shall remember our manners,' he ended.

'Manners! Tom Stukeley thinks it's a compliment to try to seduce every woman he meets,' said Amy crossly. 'But you're a married man, and don't you forget it.'

The next time Stukeley entered the house he did so with more hesitation than usual, but Amy smiled placidly, determined that he should not think that Rob had a termagant for a wife. Soon at his ease, Tom was boasting of the conquests he would make amongst the ladies of the French court.

'The French know that love-making is an art,' he said. 'I'll bed with a different filly every night, and spend the next day picking a new one.'

'Very sensible,' Amy said sweetly. 'For though you may be right about the Frenchwomen, I'm right about the English, and no honest Englishwoman would have you in her bed.'

'Why, the women I've lain with . . .' began Tom, but Amy cut him short.

72

'Whores,' she said brightly. 'I'm off to bed now, Rob. Are you coming up later, or will you be returning to Richmond tonight?'

Amy left, with Tom telling Robert that he's married a lass of spirit and humour, better than any of the fine court ladies that held their noses so high.

But once in her bed, Amy buried her head in the pillow and wept.

7

Dudley's rise

Whilst Robert was in France, Amy spent a few weeks in Norfolk, first staying with her father at Syderstone and then with John Appleyard and his wife Elizabeth at Stanfield Hall. She enjoyed seeing old friends and talking to her relations, but she felt glad, nevertheless, when she rode back into London. Here, she was nearer the heart of things. It would be to her London lodgings that the letter would come from Rob, telling her that he was to return. But no sooner had she opened the door than her mother-in-law came bustling out to greet her.

'Amy, dear, you've been away too long,' she said reprovingly. 'I trust you've written to Robin. I've been coming to the house whenever I could to see whether you had returned from Norfolk, and there is a pile of letters waiting, all in Robin's hand. But I must tell you, Robin will be home in three days! My dear, the King misses him. I declare I could have hugged the boy, for all he seems so cold-hearted. He's fond of Henry Sidney and young Barney, but it seems he really likes our Robin, too. He wants to appoint Robin a Gentleman of the Privy Chamber—a much more intimate post than Gentleman of the Ordinary. To be so near the King is a great honour, and I feel sure dear Robin will speedily find the favour he deserves.'

'Oh yes, indeed, how marvellous for Rob,' said Amy. 'But will it mean he'll spend less time than ever with me, Mother? I know I should be happy to see his advancement, but I love to be with him myself.'

'I understand,' agreed the Countess, to Amy's secret astonishment. 'When John and I were first married he had his way

74

to make, but Henry VIII's court was always graced by a Queen, so women flocked there.' She smiled reminiscently. 'We spent all our early years together,' she concluded.

'Yes, and you began your family early, and continued it right well,' said Amy wistfully. 'I feel that if only Rob could be with me more, we also might start a family.'

'Don't worry, child. You're young yet. Plenty of time for you to conceive many children. Your husband is making his way in the world, so that when you do have a family, life will be better for all of you. Soon he will be more established and in the joy of being together you will quicken with child.'

'Unless I'm too old for child-bearing,' muttered Amy, fortunately too low for the ears of the Countess, who continued merrily: 'But I must thank you for the letters you wrote whilst you journeyed. I'm sorry that I did not reply, but I'm not like you young things, full of clerkly arts.'

She bestowed a kiss light as a moth on her daughter-in-law's cheek, and left the house, waving vaguely at the window where she supposed Amy to be sitting. In fact, Amy was inelegantly sprawled on the couch, a velvet cushion choking back peals of laughter until the Countess was well out of hearing. She could never admit now that young Fane, her clerk, wrote all her letters except the ones to Rob, which she painfully penned herself!

In the flutter of preparation for Rob's arrival, Amy forgot her worries. She forgot even the miserable fear that sometimes assailed her that life would always be like this—elation at her husband's arrival, depression at his departure. It seemed to Amy that Rob followed his own bright, particular star, whilst she was forever earthbound, struggling with the petty problems of everyday living, without even the consolation of a child of Rob's to comfort her loneliness.

After the first ecstasies of reunion, Robert told Amy how excited he was, to hold such a position in the royal household.

'And Father has promised that I shall attend on Mary of Guise, the Queen Dowager of Scotland, on her visit to London in the autumn,' he told Amy triumphantly. 'Would you like to see her, my love? She'll be wearing the latest French fashions,

I'll be bound. I expect English eyes will start from their sockets—my gaze bulged a bit at Amboise.'

'Did Stukeley keep his promise to bed a different French-woman each night?' asked Amy, momentarily diverted by the recollection of Tom's boast.

'Lord, we didn't have time for *women*. Tell me, love, would you like to meet the Queen Dowager?'

'Oh yes, indeed, Rob, if the opportunity occurs,' said Amy. 'You don't know how I long to share your life, to see you as a courtier as well as my husband.'

Robert pulled her down beside him and glanced around the room. The windows were wide, letting in the August sunshine, but the door was closed. He lowered his voice, nodding towards the open windows. 'I must speak privately to you.'

Amy glided across the floor and closed the windows quietly. Then she turned expectant eyes on her husband's young face, solemn now with importance.

'Amy, my darling, I believe that Father plans to rise even higher in Edward's favour than he now stands,' he said quietly, choosing his words with care. 'He looks for complete control over the King—he says Somerset is full of idealistic and foolish notions which have set the nobles against him. Also, he is taking Edward more under his own wing. That's one reason why I'm to be a Gentleman of the Privy Chamber, for I'm young, yet old enough to protect and amuse his Majesty.'

'Well, I'm very glad for your father,' said Amy doubtfully. 'But why so secret, Rob? It's freely said in the streets that the Earl of Warwick is the power behind the throne now.'

Robert gave an impatient exclamation. 'God above, woman, *what stands in the way of my father assuming the role of Lord Protector?*'

'Do you mean *who*?' asked Amy quietly after a long pause. 'If you mean who, then of course I understand you. But surely there will be no need to do more than he has done already?'

'He must do more. What good does it do the country if my father and Somerset sit glaring at each other over the King's head and waste time and money spying on each other instead of getting on with the work of ruling the kingdom? Surely even living away from court as you do, love, you've realised that neither my father nor Somerset trust each other?'

'I realised that, but men have lived together without trust before,' Amy pointed out. 'Surely the Earl cannot mean to bring disgrace to Somerset and have him altogether cast out? Why, he's a *good* man. I've heard him speak, Rob, and he feels so strongly for the common people in their distress over rising prices and land enclosures.'

'Feeling is a high-sounding word: action would be more to the point. Whilst he wrings his hands and wails over their plight, no one is quicker to seize the new taxes to build himself new palaces; and though he professes the new religion he insists that the Princess Mary be allowed to hear mass, and fights for Gardiner's liberty. There's no man more likely to rouse the Catholics than their beloved Gardiner. Oh, Amy, you've a shrewd mind and a quick brain. Surely you've seen through Somerset?'

Amy shrugged helplessly. How could she say that she was beginning to see through the Earl of Warwick as well, though he was not nearly as transparent as poor Edward Seymour?

Instead she said discreetly, 'Well, I hope your father—if he goes ahead with whatever scheme he has in mind—doesn't forget the lesson he himself taught Kett. Whenever one enters Norwich, Castle Blancheflower towers high and one can see for oneself Kett's tarred corpse. It's a reminder to everyone of what can happen to those who try to better their own lot.'

Robert eyed his wife, his gaze calculating. 'What do you mean by that? Are you trying to say that my father is not a better man than Somerset? Do you think he will reach too high, and so come to ruin?'

Amy saw in his suddenly widening eyes the revelation of what this perpetual hungering for power might mean. Abruptly, Rob was only a boy who loved his father and wanted to see him live and prosper. The fact that John Dudley was mortal, and might over-reach himself and suffer for it, struck Robert with dismay.

'Don't worry, Rob,' Amy said, catching his hand. 'I meant nothing against your father, except perhaps that as I said, it

77

might be unwise to discredit Somerset too much. You must realise that Somerset is loved, but as yet your father has turned all his energies to looking after Edward, and the people know very little of him. Now let's forget about politics. Tell me all about France.'

Robert, distracted, began to tell her the stories of his travels, remembering for Amy's benefit the many amusing incidents that had taken place, and soon they were themselves once more, interested only in each other, with the power of princes—and protectors—far from their thoughts.

At court, the secret negotiations ran on oiled wheels—or so it seemed—and Amy stayed in her London lodgings to be near Rob. Then, on the eleventh of October, the Earl of Warwick became the Duke of Northumberland and little Jane Grey's father, the Marquis of Dorset, became the Duke of Suffolk. Other followers of Dudley's were honoured: his eldest son John took the title of Earl of Warwick. But the lavish bestowal of titles boded ill for Edward Seymour, Duke of Somerset. Only three days later, Somerset was arrested and sent to the Tower, and the new Duke of Northumberland hastily stepped into his shoes; though to the consternation of many he called himself not 'Lord Protector', but 'Highness', as though *he* were the King, and not young Edward.

'I told you Father would do it,' Robert crowed as he and Amy lay in each other's arms that night. 'Somerset will be charged with treason, you see if I'm not right. That's one charge no man can escape.'

'Don't, Rob,' Amy pleaded. 'Forget it all when you're with me. Pretend we're a simple country squire and his wife, in our manor, with no thoughts of royal intrigue to bother us.'

'They don't bother *me*, I've faith in my father to pull us all through safely,' Robert told her confidently. He gripped her tightly, making her squeak. 'Now for *our* fun. Escorting the Dowager Queen will be fun, Amy, and you'll trip along happily with the other ladies who manage the escort, you'll see.'

And Amy did see. The bliss of being near Robert, seeing

78

him in his role of courtier and yet not having to bear the ceremonies alone, for her mother-in-law kept close, allayed her nervousness and Amy was very happy indeed.

The Queen Dowager was a handsome, stately woman, aware of her position as an honoured guest, but never seeming overbearing or proud. The fashions worn by the Queen herself down to her humblest maid of honour set the Englishwomen buzzing with excitement and a desire to imitate.

'It's been a real experience for me, being in the presence of such a great person,' Amy told Anne, her eyes shining. 'She has had a sad life really, yet her smile is sweet and she was so nice to Edward. And never has she made any of us feel inferior of shabby. Yes, I like her.'

'But remember, she's mother to the Queen of Scotland and a daughter of the house of Guise; she must be treated with the utmost respect,' Anne said.

Amy's eyes opened wider and her mouth formed an O of astonishment. Amy, very conscious of her lowly position, had never done more than smile and curtsey when the Queen Dowager looked in her direction. But Anne, laughing, enlightened her.

'Not *you*, silly child. Robin! He's a charming young man, I admit, but he's rather pushful. I sometimes think he needs reminding that my own dear John is now Earl of Warwick, and a person of importance. Your Robin is too quick to put himself forward with offers of advice and assistance.'

To her amazement, the girl she had thought of as a fluffy kitten immediately turned on her, showing too plainly that she might be just a kitten, but like all cats great and small, she had claws.

'Surely you realise that Robin only saves John from tasks he seems to find overpowering?' said Amy. 'The Queen Dowager turns for some small piece of information and John steps back. Only then does Rob come forward—or so it seems to me.'

Anne flushed. There was no doubt that of all the Duke's fine sons, John was the least prepossessing. Smaller and more slightly built than the other lads, he had also inherited his mother's fair colouring, and with his lively, vivid brothers present he tended to merge into the background. But Robert seemed to find competition stimulating and took his place naturally as near the important personages as he could contrive.

So Amy found the taste of court life sweet. She watched Mary of Guise leave London, escorted by the Duke of Northumberland. Behind them rode a troop of a hundred men, forty of them dressed like exotic magpies, in black and white velvet.

After the excitement of the royal visit, Amy's spirits received a sad blow. She had felt her fear and dislike of her father-in-law increasing since he had deposed Somerset; now she began to realise her feelings were shared by others—many others. For after he had prudently given King Edward the most delightful Christmas that could be devised, the Duke of Northumberland proceeded to rush through a trial at Westminster, charging Somerset with felony.

'They'll never convict him on that charge,' Amy said contemptuously, but she didn't realise how powerful the Duke of Northumberland had grown. The judges were all men who hated Somerset—they would have convicted the ex-Protector on any charge.

And they convicted Edward Seymour, as Robert had confidently told his wife they would. But Amy, going quietly about the streets of London, heard constant murmurs against her new family; how the Duke of Somerset had at least *tried* to help the poor, which was more than a Dudley would do. They hoped that the King (such a nice lad) would not allow his uncle to be killed. But no one could understand that to Edward, nothing was nicer than seeing the man who had once ruled his life, keeping his pocket empty and his nose stuck into his books, brought low by the sporting Duke.

So Edward signed the death warrant with never a qualm, as Robert told Amy a trifle ruefully, and on 22nd January, Somerset died.

He met his end nobly, folk said. As he had tried to live, so he died. His speech on the scaffold was very moving, and when his head was struck from his body the people surged forward to dip their kerchiefs in the blood of the man they considered to be a martyr.

As for Northumberland, the people looked to the future with fear, for call him Earl or Duke, they knew him for a Dudley; son of that dishonest rogue Edmund Dudley, who had oppressed their forefathers in the reign of Henry VII.

'What should we do now?' asked Amy fearfully. 'Will there be civil war? The mood of the people is frightening.'

'Don't you *see*? My father realised that with Somerset to lead them, there might well have been a civil war. But without Somerset he can have peace to work out his plans for the country.'

'Well, I'm sure I hope you're right,' Amy said doubtfully. 'But with Somerset dead, couldn't your father spare you, for a few weeks? We ought to look over our manors together and see that the land is in good heart.'

'Oh, I think we might get away,' Robert answered easily. 'For one thing, fond though Edward is of me, he has plenty of other friends around him. And for another, we've not visited Cockisford Priory since the improvements have been completed.'

'We can stay with Father—most convenient really, Rob— and he'll teach you all about sheep.'

'Good idea. After all, I'm Constable of the Castle, and Steward of the Manor of Rising. I ought to show my face in the county,' agreed Robert with a grin.

He picked Amy up and whirled her round. 'We'll have some fun, lass, riding around Norfolk,' he said exultantly. 'It's not the weather for trips to the country yet, mind, and I'll have to arrange everything with the King and my father; but when the fine weather comes we'll take up country living for a while. And who knows? Perhaps we'll start our family.'

The waiting time was hard for Amy. The Duke seemed to make no effort to gain the people's affection. He was too busy consolidating his position and making sure that he kept the King's regard.

But at last the day of their departure arrived, and the young couple set off on the long journey to Syderstone. On the way they visited property which Edward had granted to Robert, and found it good.

They worked hard in Norfolk. Robert was made Joint-Commissioner of Lieutenancy for the County during their stay but this did not prevent them from hearing the rumours of how the Duke of Northumberland was becoming the most hated dictator the country had ever known.

The facts could not be hidden from Amy, though Robert would have preferred that she remained in ignorance, for throughout the land, in his greed for money and power, Northumberland burned, tortured and then grabbed the possessions of his victims. Mainly he persecuted in the name of the Protestant religion, but occasionally the mask slipped when there was a fat Protestant church to be robbed, and Protestant clergy cheated out of their lands and tithes by the insatiable Duke.

'I hadn't realised that your father was so deeply religious,' Sir John Robsart said sarcastically to Rob when he had himself tried without success to intervene in saving a friend's property.

Robert, reddening uncomfortably, said, 'Nor I, sir,' which made his father-in-law laugh and think hopefully that though the father was a rogue, the son was a good enough lad. He had apparently got a conscience at any rate, which Northumberland patently lacked.

Amy hated knowing that people hearing the name of Dudley automatically associated Rob with the Duke of Northumberland's brutality and greed. But she consoled herself with the thought that when people got to know her husband, they liked him for himself, saying to each other, 'You wouldn't think he was a Dudley.'

Robert, Amy knew, was in a quandary. He could not pretend to like the way his father seemed to be behaving, yet he would not deny the Duke was doing right. It was a habit with him to admire and love his parents; such habits are hard to break.

'Father had a difficult childhood,' he told Amy loyally. 'He was adopted by Sir Edward Guildford of course, and his mother married Viscount Lisle—they were good to him as well, I believe. But being the son of an unpopular man must have soured his attitude towards the people.'

'I wish he'd think of his own sons, then. Does he think none of his present dealings will affect his children? He must know that you will be smeared by his deeds as he was by his father's. Or is he too busy gathering money and power to think of others?'

She paused, seeing in her mind's eye the fires, the torture chambers, the rack. 'He is the most hated man in the kingdom,' she said in a low voice. 'Will he pull us down with him, when he falls?'

Robert said blusteringly, 'Falls, love? Why should he fall when he has the love of the King? You're talking foolishly. I'm for London anyway, where I can see for myself what is going on. Come with me if you wish, or stay here. But if you come, hold your tongue in front of Father. He can't bear criticism, especially over affairs of state, and religion.'

'I'm your wife, and I love you,' Amy said truculently. 'I'll return to London with you and I'll keep a still tongue in my head when your father is present. But that won't stop me thinking.'

So they set out together to return to the capital, both outwardly cheerful but both shrinking inwardly from what they might find.

8

Find me a monarch!

'Lady Jane Grey is to marry your *brother*? But Rob, don't you remember? At our wedding it was said that the King had his eye upon her for a bride.'

Amy's remark annoyed Robert doubly because he remembered tactlessly telling her that piece of gossip when she had first seen the King.

'That was three years ago, and in marriages of state, three years is a long time. Edward was a child, he's a young man now. He certainly wouldn't consider marrying Jane—he will probably marry a foreign princess one of these days. If—if his health improves.'

'Edward really is still ill, then?'

'Amy, I've told you and you must have heard it talked over amongst the family. Ever since he had measles in the spring his health has been far from good. He doesn't consider himself dangerously ill, but a famous Italian doctor came from an interview with the King shaking his head. Maybe he'll recover—who can say?'

'But why Guildford for Jane?' said Amy, reverting to the original topic of conversation. 'She is betrothed to Hertford, the Seymour heir. And even that has been one of those betrothals that somehow one never expects to see end in a marriage bed. But Jane and *Guildford*? They hardly know each other, and they're so young! Jane thinks of nothing but her studies and the Protestant religion, and Guildford is sporting mad.'

'Guildford will probably find her a dead bore,' admitted Robert with the sudden frankness that Amy found so endearing. 'Oh hang it, Amy, you'd winkle the truth out of an oyster! It seems a will has been drawn up by—by the Council. Edward has signed it. He's left the crown to Jane. As you remembered, she's always been a favourite with Edward and she's the most devout Protestant. Edward realises that if the crown went to Mary, who is next in the succession, she would bring back the Pope into England.'

'But, Rob, how can Edward will the crown away as though it were simply an object, and not the circlet that can be worn only by the anointed head of the realm?' cried Amy. 'This is your father's work, I'll be bound.'

The quick colour flamed in Robert's cheeks but Amy's eyes, bright with conviction, forced him to nod sullenly.

'My father advises and undoubtedly Edward listens. But if Jane didn't marry Guildford—a staunch Protestant like herself—she might take a foreign prince, which would never do; particularly if he were a papist.'

'Hertford is a Protestant,' argued Amy. Then, struck by a sudden doubt, 'Rob, does Jane know she is willed to have the crown?'

'I believe not. She has been told that the marriage is in the interests of her parents and her religion. My father thinks it is enough for her to know at this point, for who knows? The King might recover and live to father a family himself.'

Amy, looking sadly at her husband, thought she could read him like a book. Edward must be mortally ill or the Duke would never have taken the drastic step of marrying Guildford to Jane, a child of no particular significance. And John Dudley was running short of sons to marry where it best suited him.

It must annoy him now, Amy thought with quiet satisfaction, when he saw the best and boldest of his sons, most suited to captivate a girl's heart, married to a lass who could be of no possible use in his intrigues.

However, Amy and Robert attended the wedding, which was very gay with three young couples being joined in matrimony at the same time. Jane married Guildford; Rob's sister Katherine Dudley married Henry, Lord Hastings, and Jane's younger sister, another Katherine, married Lord Herbert, eldest son of the Earl of Pembroke, though since she was only thirteen and a tiny skinny creature, the couple would not live together for some time to come.

Jane was escorted down the aisle by two pages, and before them walked sixteen virgins, clad in white. Her hair hung loose as was customary for a bride, but some of it had been plaited and interlaced with pearls, a style new to Amy. However, no pomp and ceremony could hide the bride's pale face and trembling lips.

'She's such a baby,' Amy told her sister-in-law in an indignant whisper. 'How can her parents allow her to be mixed up in this wicked affair?'

'Hush,' hissed Lady Anne. 'You should realise, Amy, that you were one of the lucky few. Many and many a maid goes to her marriage bed scarcely knowing the man who is to be her husband. Love can grow from unpromising beginnings, especially when the man is handsome and the girl is young and can be easily swayed, like Jane.'

But Amy, looking at her new sister-in-law, was unconvinced. She was shy, certainly. After the ceremony she looked as though she might faint. But Amy detected in the line of her small mouth a certain firmness—inflexibility, even.

She heard with uneasiness that though Jane had at last been told that Edward had willed the crown to her, the information had been given only in the course of a quarrel between Jane and the Duchess, and Jane had scarcely heeded the words.

For despite promises, Jane was not allowed to return with her sisters Katherine and Mary to their parents' home. She was told that she must live with her husband at Durham House and that the couple would bed together as was customary.

'Is the King so near to death?' Amy asked Robert. 'Does Jane realise this? Was she told only the worst possible health could have kept him from the wedding?'

'Damn it, Amy, she must know the King is ill. Everyone knows.'

'Well, for all her cleverness, I don't believe Jane has fully realised what the death of the King will mean to her. Oh, Rob, she's scarcely more fitted to be Queen than I am! She's so immature and unworldly, how can her parents allow her to be forced into such a position?'

'She will have my father to advise her. And Guildford, of course.'

'Why, your family cheated her when they refused to let her go home with the marriage unconsummated,' Amy said bluntly. 'Anyway, should Edward die—which God forbid—what makes you think the people will accept her as his successor? The bread and ale your father handed out at the wedding? Three days' bread and ale don't buy allegiance, Rob.'

'I don't see why you should be so bitter against my father,' Robert said, stung. 'But for him I'd not have reached the position I hold today, and you would not be so well clothed and housed, with servants to run at your bidding.'

'We were speaking of Jane, Robert,' said Amy. She held his gaze and continued remorselessly, 'She has been forced into a distasteful marriage with your brother. She is being pushed into a false position by your father and her own parents, who are greedy upstarts hungering for the throne. I *cannot* stand by and not tell you that to me, these things seem shameful and wrong. I pray to heaven that Edward has a long and merry life, then we shall see how mortified your father will be when he finds himself with a daughter-in-law who hates him, and a surly son.'

And when Rob would have answered hotly, she turned and ran from the room, slamming the door in his indignant face.

Supper that night was eaten by the young Dudleys in constrained silence. Amy was determined to make no attempt at reconciliation and Robert was still hurt and furious over her words. But in bed, Robert could no longer stand his wife's silent condemnation. Cuddling close to her in the darkness of the June night, he told her that they must not quarrel over affairs of state.

'Because for me, Amy love, my father has always been right,' he reminded her. 'Our marriage could have been held up indefinitely had he not given me my wish. Now I'll wish

Edward a long and merry life as you do. Come, kiss and be friends.'

So the quarrel was forgotten in love-making, but it had taught Amy an unforgettable lesson.

The Dudleys might be unpleasant, but they were a closely united family. They hung together—and that's what I'm afraid of, she thought, with morbid humour. I'm afraid that the innocent sons may share the scaffold with their father, who richly deserves such a fate!

Amy would have liked to get to know Jane, but though she visited her several times during her stay at Durham House, she found the girl reserved and wary, and decided it was useless tying to be friends whilst Jane was virtually a captive. When Jane had won the right to return to the manor of Chelsea, Amy thought she would visit her there, but she had not allowed for the effect marriage would have on a sensitive girl like Jane, who was physically and emotionally immature. Jane arrived home and simply collapsed. She was sure someone was trying to poison her, she jumped whenever a door creaked in the breeze and nearly became demented when it was suggested she might like to extend her acquaintance with Amy Dudley.

So Amy regretfully gave up the attempt at friendship and concentrated instead on keeping on good terms with the rest of her in-laws. No easy task at the moment, for Guildford sulked because his bride had gone home, the Duchess raged over the stupidity of a schoolroom chit who could fail to fall helplessly in love with her favourite son, and the male Dudleys were night and day at the bedside of the dying King.

'It's dreadful to see Edward now, poor boy,' Robert told Amy when he returned home for a short visit. 'He longs for death—and who can blame him? Better by far to die quickly in battle or by the axe than as he dies—by inches almost. Doctors keep saying he will die in a day or so, yet still he lives on somehow, against his own urgent prayers.'

Amy shuddered. 'But why do you have to be with him so much, Rob? Waking or sleeping, a Dudley is in his chamber. Is it because your father fears that Edward might be persuaded to change his will, and you'll find yourselves with

Guildford married to the most adamant young Protestant in the kingdom, and Mary on the throne, setting the Pope on "those damned Dudleys"?'

'Saucy baggage,' Robert said, pinching her cheek. 'But shrewd. I think Father is determined that no one shall have private talks with the King. Cranmer has tried: he even attempted to persuade Edward to dismiss Father, but without success. So it looks as though we'll have a King Guildford yet, which will prove to you, Mistress Disbelief, that we Dudleys are geniuses, each and every one!'

Amy laughed at his confidence, but the events which followed so swiftly gave no Dudley, either by birth or by marriage, much to laugh about.

One night in early July, Rob rode up to their lodgings and went indoors quietly and quickly to have a word with his wife.

'Edward's gone at last,' he said tersely. 'God, one had to be glad for his sake, Amy. The stench of the sickroom lingers in my nostrils still. I'll be glad of the ride to Hunsdon if only to clear my lungs with the fresh night air.'

'Why Hunsdon?' asked Amy, genuinely bewildered.

'Well, Edward's death will be kept from the people until we have secured Mary and Elizabeth. Can't have them loose to raise insurrection and rebellion, can we, my darling? I am to bring the Lady Mary to London. When he has them safe, Father will proclaim Edward's death and tell the people that the late King willed the crown to Jane. You'll see, everything will go ahead as smooth as silk, for Father's plans are well thought out. A messenger has already left to go to Mary, begging her to come to her brother as he lies dying. Elizabeth too, of course, though she's not so important. But I must leave you, my love. I shall meet Mary, in case she should learn the truth along the way, and find supporters. Then I have to proclaim Jane Queen at King's Lynn. It's quite near Syderstone, isn't it? Why don't you ride down to Norfolk and meet me, or do you want to stay here for Jane's coronation?'

'Couldn't I ride with you?' Amy pleaded, but Rob shook his head.

'I ride with troops, and we ride fast, without respite. No,

my pretty, you come at your own pace and send word when you arrive at Syderstone.'

The following day Amy set off for Syderstone. The news that the King was dead had been well kept and Amy thought it quite probable that she would be back in London in time for Jane's coronation anyway.

In the event, she was wrong, for though she sent word to Rob when she arrived at Syderstone she only had a brief verbal message from him to the effect that he had missed Mary and would be chasing after her so could not come to Amy after all.

Amy hesitated, unwilling to return to London without her husband, so she was still with her father when news of the coronation of Queen Jane reached her. Almost simultaneously they heard that Mary Tudor had been at Kenninghall in Norfolk with a troop of loyal folk around her. Impatiently, Amy waited for news. Syderstone was remote but she was sure Rob would find some way of getting in touch with her.

Sure enough, news came, but not as Amy had secretly hoped, in the person of her husband. It was brought from London by special messenger. Amy heard the horse clattering into the cobbled stableyard and ran out. The weather was sultry and the horse, poor creature, was standing with its head hanging and sides heaving, in a welter of foam and sweat. The messenger was pale with heat and exhaustion; plainly his errand was an important one.

'Do you come from my husband, Robert Dudley?' Amy asked, in a torment of anxiety.

The man nodded, leaning against his horse and raising heavy eyelids. It was easy to see that he needed sleep, but he must be kept awake long enough to deliver his message. A groom came running over to take the horse and Amy beckoned to one of the stable lads, who stood eyeing the scene with openmouthed astonishment.

'Luke, help me get the man into the kitchen,' she said sharply, bringing the boy quickly to her side.

Between them they got the messenger into a chair and with the servants she had known since she was a child round her, Amy waited for his words.

'Mistress, all is lost. Queen Jane—that is, the Lady Jane—has been deposed and Queen Mary reigns. Your husband bade me bring you the news without fail, for he himself is—is ...'

'Come, man, I know nothing good can have happened to my husband if Mary is on the throne,' Amy told him, her voice taut with anguish. 'Tell me what you must, for I will only imagine the worst.'

Her words seemed to hearten the man, for he said hastily, 'Never fear, mistress, Lord Robert is fit and well. But he is confined to the Tower, awaiting trial. The charge will be treason.'

Amy heard a voice she scarcely recognised as her own thanking the man, and ordering the servants to see to his needs. Then she left the kitchen and went to her father, who was sitting with his big chair pulled close to an open window to catch the cooler breeze of evening.

Through her head were running the words Rob had spoken with such sleepy satisfaction. 'The charge of treason—that's one charge no man can escape.'

As Sir John turned enquiringly to face her, Amy told him the news in a few words, through lips still stiff with shock.

For the first time it occurred to her that her father was an old man. He turned pale, muttering, 'Treason? The Tower? Surely, the Duke only did as the King wished? Treason? The Tower?'

Amy soothed him with words she scarcely believed even as she uttered them. 'A mistake, the people's dislike of the father, religion, when Mary truly comes into her own ...' until Sir John sank back onto his cushions, half-comforted.

By now, Amy herself realised she had not heard the whole. She turned, and went back to the kitchen where the messenger was seeing off the mutton pie she and her father had started that day. By his elbow stood a half-empty tankard of beer which he nearly knocked over in his attempt to get to his feet when Amy entered the room.

'Sit and eat, but answer my questions as best you can,' Amy told him.

The man obediently sat down again and told Amy as much

of the story as he himself had managed to piece together.

'The Duke and his five sons are in the Tower; the Duchess also. Lady Jane was in the Tower already and is there still. Many others are being imprisoned. But not as many as there should be,' he added, warming to his tale. 'For many of the Council turned traitor. Why, though Lady Jane is a prisoner, her parents bought their freedom.'

'Wretches,' muttered Amy between her teeth. 'If *I* had a child . . .' She left the sentence unfinished. What were her chances of having a child now, with her husband shut up in the Tower, a charge of treason hanging over his head? She knew how unlikely it was that he would ever leave those walls except to go to his place of execution.

However, she managed to keep such thoughts to herself. She thanked the messenger and left him; then she told Sir John that she must go to London. She would leave the very next day, taking with her what moneys she could lay her hands on at such short notice. Then she went to bed—but not, alas, to sleep. She found pictures passing before her eyes, and none of them were pleasant. The Duke she could not feel sorry for however hard she tried. But those others, led into vicious folly by such a man, why should they suffer a traitor's death? The only crime the Duchess had committed had been to love and obey her husband. Amy kept her mind resolutely away from Rob. She would wait until she got to London and heard from someone in authority that Rob was in real and deadly danger before she allowed herself to think.

Tossing and turning, Amy slept at last, only to dream of blood and death. She awoke with the breath short in her throat and her heart hammering. After that, she dared not sleep. She lay watching the sky between a gap in the bed hangings until the soulless dawn light poured into the room, and she could swish back the covers and begin to dress for her journey.

9

To the dark tower came

'Anne! Oh, thank God you're back! I came straight to your lodgings for news, but you were out.' Amy jumped up from her chair and hugged her sister-in-law.

'Amy, dear, where did you appear from? Robin told us you were safe in Norfolk,' said Lady Warwick, sitting wearily down as a servant brought two cups of wine into the room. She waited until the door closed behind the man before continuing, 'I've been to see John, in the Tower. My husband, I mean, not Father-in-law. I don't believe they'll keep the Duchess a prisoner for long but in any case I wouldn't be allowed to see her. As for the Duke, I wouldn't *wish* to see him.'

'Visiting John? Why, shall I be able to visit Robert?' Amy asked, her eyes glowing.

'I don't see why not. You'll have to apply for permission and see members of the Council and so on, but they have permitted most wives to see their husbands. Things are all at sixes and sevens though. The Duke is ill abed and being looked after in the Garden Tower. Ambrose and Henry are in the cell known as the Nuns' Bower. Jack and Guildford share a room, so when I go to see my husband I see Guildford too. I think Robin is somewhere on the floor below them. They say the Tower has never held so many prisoners and even the guards are confused. However, it does tend to make one forget the deadly seriousness of their situation.'

'When do they stand trial? Will they stand together, or separately? Are we allowed to be present? Who will judge them?' Amy asked, the words tumbling from her tongue.

Anne laughed. 'Don't be in a hurry to get them to trial, love, for they are in no rush. But the day is arranged for the Duke and Jack—18th August. I don't think I shall be able to visit Jack again until after the trial, for today I was led in reluctantly. But provided all goes well, we should be able to resume our visits once sentence has been pronounced.'

'Why aren't they trying Rob at the same time?' Amy asked fearfully.

'Because he's not a peer of the realm, love. Oh Amy, I once dreamed of the day when the Duke would suffer for the wrongs he did my father, but I did not wish poor Jack to suffer also. I try to stay cheerful and confident for his sake, but I can't help fearing that after the 18th, there may be only a few more visits.'

Amy patted Anne's shoulder gently, not speaking until Anne had regained her composure.

'May I stay here with you?' she asked then. 'I had meant to go to my usual lodgings but it would be easier to live together until our husbands are—free.'

'Oh yes, please stay with me,' urged Anne. 'For one thing, if the worst *should* happen, all the Dudleys' goods will be forfeit to the crown. But between us, we have enough to keep body and soul together.'

'I've heard it said that Mary is determined on clemency,' Amy said comfortingly. 'Why, the very messenger who brought me posthaste to London said that she was pardoning many of the Council who had signed the document against her—Edward's will. We must be as cheerful as we can until there is further news.'

So the two young women waited.

On 18th August, Northumberland, Warwick and Northampton were tried and condemned by their peers on the charge of treason, despite many of those same peers having been as deeply mixed up in the conspiracy to crown Jane Queen as had the accused.

Then they heard that Northumberland had recanted and declared for the Roman Catholic religion; had heard mass. Shortly afterwards the Earl of Warwick followed his example.

'They have their reasons,' Amy told Anne. 'I suppose your

Jack is trying to save what he can out of his estate for you, love.'

She glanced curiously at her sister-in-law. Had Anne, too, lain in her bed at night, wakeful in the thick darkness, wondering, wondering, why no baby had been born to her? It gave Amy a sort of comfort to know that none of the Dudley boys had yet become fathers. Surely, the fault lay with them rather than with their wives? Then she gave herself a brisk mental shake. What was the point in thinking about children when her husband's life was in such danger?

She and Anne were at last told they might see Robert and Jack. By then, of course, the boys were fatherless, for Northumberland had been beheaded shortly after his trial, along with two minor conspirators, Gates and Palmer.

Amy entered Robert's room doubtfully, feeling even in the autumn sun the grimness implicit in the stone walls and barred window. She wondered whether Rob would sense her lack of sorrow over his father's death, and hold it against her. But Rob's shout of delight, his bear-hug, told her all she wanted to know. It was *her* he loved, above all others.

'But I do worry over Mother,' he admitted. 'She *lived* for Father, and us boys. If we all suffer a similar fate, what will become of her? She's a good woman, and she's been kind to you. Have you seen her?'

'Of course, darling. Anne and I went as soon as she was released. You didn't think I would be heartless enough to forget her?'

'No, no. But you've had worries of your own, poor darling, trying to get permission to see me.'

'Mary's been good, all things considered, Rob. I know it's difficult to believe, but she seems to bear no grudge and is quite eager to pardon as many of the offenders as possible.'

'She would have been in a poor state if she had carried out justice on all the conspirators,' Robert said drily. 'For there would be an empty Council chamber for her to fill and few noblemen left in England.'

'Nevertheless, we must be grateful to her. She means to be known as "merciful Mary", so they say. So don't despair, Rob.'

'Have you seen Mary herself?' asked Robert, surprised that his shy little wife had found the courage to fight for the right to visit him.

'No, not personally. But I saw the members of the Council and eventually got permission, so here I am.' She laughed at his wide-eyed stare. 'Like all women, Rob, I may seem meek but I can be a veritable tigress where my man is concerned.'

They laughed together, then Rob asked, 'Is my mother well?'

'As well as you could expect her to be, my darling.'

'She mourns Father.'

The remark was a statement more than a question, but Amy nodded. 'Don't think she isn't fighting for her sons though. There is no more earnest supplicant to the Queen and the sight of her, so gentle and pleading, would soften a harder heart than Mary's. But I haven't told you—Anne and I are lodging together. It's better for us both, we keep each other cheerful.'

'Would you do something to please me, Amy?' asked Robert suddenly.

'With all my heart.'

'Go down to Norfolk for Christmas. My hands are under attainder but not yet forfeit. You are a better landowner than I, your father constantly tells me! Will you make sure that all is in good order, see that those beasts that are ready for sale go to the Christmas markets and so on? I need money badly.'

'Surely you don't *pay* for being in prison?' Amy asked incredulously.

'Not exactly, no. But any extras, debts contracted before, even your own slender upkeep—all these things cost money. And my allowance here buys but a sparse and monotonous diet.'

Amy, knowing his weakness for good food, laughed and kissed him, promising that she would do as he asked.

'I did bring money with me when I left Syderstone,' she told him gladly. 'So on my next visit I'll bring you a fat purse of gold! Then you won't starve between now and my return from Norfolk, you poor creature!'

She left the Tower with a lighter heart than she had known for weeks. Robert was imprisoned, yes. But he was healthy, remarkably cheerful, and hungry! Of course, it's dreadful to be glad that he's hungry, she scolded herself as she returned to their lodgings. But somehow when you know it's really greediness, it brings everything down to earth and makes Rob seem like any normal young man, and not a prisoner in fear for his life.

Feeling almost light-headed with relief at finding Robert optimistic and physically fit, Amy greeted Anne more cheerfully than she had dreamed would be possible.

'Isn't it wonderful to see them? Aren't they well?' she demanded.

Anne looked dubious. 'I don't think Jack could be described as *well*. He's already been condemned, remember; Robin has not been sentenced.'

'Oh, yes, poor Jack. But he must not worry; I'm sure Mary will never carry out the sentence. Why, she has told the people round her again and again that she intends to be merciful,' Amy said a little impatiently. It seemed unfair that she should have to keep her own spirits high for Robert's sake, only to find Anne an easy prey to despair.

'Mary may want to show tolerance, but what if she marries Philip?' Anne asked, her voice hollow with foreboding.

'What difference will a marriage—even a Spanish one— make?' Amy said. 'After all, Mary would still be our Queen and surely her husband would not change her attitude towards her subjects?'

Anne shook her head. 'Mary will alter for her husband,' she declared. 'The Spaniards will bring the Inquisition into England and then to recant won't be enough.'

'Anne, don't meet trouble halfway! We've got plenty of real worries without you imagining fresh ones. Just live for today. The boys are alive and well. Robin wants me to go to Norfolk to see to our estates and collect any money that's owing. I'll go down a couple of weeks before Christmas, so you've time to arrange to move in with Mother-in-law until I return if you wish, or would you rather stay with your own mother?'

'I'll stay here. Mother-in-law is too painfully interested in the fate of our men, and my mother not at all. I'll miss you, Amy, don't be gone long.'

'I'll be back before you know it. I hate the thought of leaving Rob,' Amy reassured her.

So just before Christmas, Amy and her retinue set off towards Norfolk. Despite the chilly weather Amy rode her favourite mare, and they managed to visit all Rob's estates new and old before arriving at Syderstone for the festivities.

As she went about her work, prodding hoggets, bargaining over sturdy cattle, examining account books and discussing yield per acre, Amy had hope to buoy her up. For whilst she was still in London the Queen had told the Duchess of Northumberland that she did not wish the innocent to suffer for the guilty, and the Duchess was sure her sons would be safe.

Many a surly old countryman, glad enough in his heart to have the old religion back, asked the young mistress how Lord Robert was, in the Tower. They had succumbed to his charm as easily as Amy herself had done, four years earlier. She accepted with gratitude the small presents they pressed upon her, to give her husband when she returned to London. A fine wax candle, a handful of walnuts, some candied flowers, and a woollen blanket woven by a fond wife for her husband : 'But I'd like th'master to hev that, seeing as how that git mortal cowld shut up i' that narsty old Tower.'

Amy thanked them earnestly for their gifts, which she accepted because she knew they were open acknowledgement of their donors' fondness for Robert Dudley. She told them she hoped for Robert's release, adding—for who knew what ear was listening for the Queen—that Mary was a merciful and just lady, and wanted no cruel persecution in her realm. She managed to reach Syderstone for Christmas.

'Well, Father, I can see you have been busy at Cockisford. Our manors all have capable bailiffs, but none so conscientious as Mr Flowerdew.'

Father and daughter smiled at one another.

'I keep my eyes open,' Sir John admitted sheepishly. 'But how is the boy, Amy? Captivity for such an active one must prove irksome.'

'Rob is fine, really, Father. He's been granted the freedom of the leads, which means he gets some exercise. I left him money for extra food, and I've had little comforts—easy chairs, footstools, bedding and so on—taken to his chamber. It's a commodious enough room. Rob strides round it like a caged beast at times of course, but I tell him at least it's exercise!'

'I imagined he must be healthy enough, for you to leave him even to visit the estates,' admitted Sir John with a twinkle. 'But it's good to see you, girl. It's been several Christmases since I had a visitor, though Arthur comes occasionally to borrow money, the idle fellow.' His laugh and softening glance belied his words.

'And John Appleyard? Does he come to see you now and then?'

'John hasn't ridden over since your wedding. Yet I'm all the father that boy ever knew, and I treated him like my own son. But there, I mustn't grumble. You are here now, and that's what matters.'

So Amy and her father enjoyed Christmas together, though Amy was vaguely disturbed by his solitude and by his increasing desire to watch rather than take part in the activities of the house and grounds.

When she left at last, Sir John threw her into the saddle and held the bridle of her horse as they exchanged a parting kiss.

'Take good care of yourself, Father,' Amy said, smiling into his eyes.

'I will. But don't worry about me, you take care of yourself—and Robert of course.'

So she rode away down the drive, glancing back continually to wave to Sir John. As she wheeled her mount round the bend in the road Amy saw her father turn and go into the house, looking suddenly old, and lonely beyond belief.

It was the last time that she would ever see him alive.

Amy arrived back in London at the end of January, to find the city in a turmoil and Anne in a state of nervous excitement bordering on illness.

'There is a rebellion, Amy, against the Queen,' she whispered, when the two were alone.

'What has the Queen done wrong now?' Amy asked, mildly amused. More of Anne's bogeys, she thought. But this time, she did her sister-in-law an injustice.

'It's not what Mary's done, it's what she's going to do, Amy. The people know that she has given her word to marry Philip as soon as the country is safe for him to come to her. I don't believe anyone wants the Spaniards in England; not the most devout Catholics. So they plan to rebel against Mary.'

'Who will they push onto the throne this time, to make an unwilling puppet ruler?' asked Amy scornfully. 'Surely not poor little Jane Grey?'

'No, for the people would not stand another Dudley. Don't call her Grey, Amy, she's a Dudley now, like you and me. They plan to marry Lady Elizabeth to Edward Courtenay.'

Amy remembered the pale girl at her wedding, with the watchful eyes and tight lips.

'Poor Courtenay, whoever he may be,' she said lightly.

'Poor Courtenay! Why, he's the last of the Plantagenets, fabulously handsome I believe, and young too. Allied to Elizabeth's Tudor blood they could make a popular and successful King and Queen. Better than making us vassals of Spain, anyway.'

'Well, I shouldn't think they'll get much encouragement from Elizabeth,' said Amy frankly. 'She's a careful one, she is.'

'It would be wonderful for us if it happened, though, Amy. Elizabeth is a strong Protestant and a friend. She'd have the Dudleys out of the Tower in two minutes if she came to power.'

Amy shook her head doubtfully. 'It won't ever work, so don't get your hopes too high, Anne. Mary is best with her back against the wall. Look how bravely she outfaced Northumberland. When she has right on her side, she can be as bold as any man and her very presence inspires loyalty. Who is leading the rebellion?'

'Sir Thomas Wyatt, son of the man folk said loved Anne Boleyn, Elizabeth's mother. Isn't that romantic?'

Amy grinned. 'And who is leading the troops against this Wyatt?'

'The Duke of Suffolk. But rumour has it that he has led his men straight over to the enemy. Come now, doesn't that give you hope?'

'Far from it, Anne. A man who will betray his own child will whimper like a whipped cur when it comes to the point. No, I expect it will fizzle out like a damp firework.'

A week later the two girls hid behind closed shutters whilst Wyatt and his rebels fought in the streets outside. It appeared that Amy had been wrong and the rising would win the crown from Mary. But as Amy had said, Mary was at her best when desperate. She rallied the Londoners to her, appealing for their loyalty, and the rebel leaders were imprisoned. Sir Thomas Wyatt was now added to the prisoners in the Tower, and the Lady Elizabeth was sent for, from her home in the country.

Amy visited Robert as soon as it was safe to walk through the streets once more, but what she saw disturbed her.

Mary was not only furiously angry that the people should dare, after all these barren years, to try to come between her and the man of her choice. She was also bitterly hurt that the same people who had cheered for her only six months earlier, now hissed and muttered at her, and persecuted her priests.

She began to understand what the Spanish Ambassador had told her so often: England must be made safe for Philip, otherwise her marriage would not take place. And she was thirty-eight and had been seven times betrothed without coming successfully to the marriage bed.

So she began to rid herself of anyone who might prove a deterrent to her marriage. She began with ordinary, common people, though, who could do no one any harm. This somehow, thought Amy, made her actions more unpardonable.

Hurrying towards the Tower, the smell of death was already thick in the air, to those with nostrils sensitive enough to catch it. A few common people now, thought Amy with a shudder; but where will it end?

She saw Robert, still looking extraordinarily well despite his conditions of imprisonment, and gave him the money and details of their affairs for which he had asked. But he too looked grim.

'Are you afraid, Rob, that now there has been a rebellion, Mary may decide to make an example of you and your brothers?' she asked, not mincing matters.

Robert grinned at her, but she saw beneath his assumed cockiness the deep underlying worry.

'I suppose you know the Duke of Suffolk turned traitor to Mary and was one of the rebels?' he said, answering one question with another.

Amy nodded, twisting her hands together.

'I'm afraid that even though Mary may want to spare Jane's life, the Council simply won't allow it. Whilst Jane lives, anyone can raise a rebellion in her name however unwilling she may be. And if Jane dies, Guildford will die too, little though he may have deserved such a fate.'

'Jane doesn't deserve death either! She's a child—and not one of your father's own, simply one he chose to manipulate against her will. She's only just sixteen,' exclaimed Amy hotly, her eyes flashing.

'Lord, no! Good God, did it sound as though I meant she deserved to die? I suppose it must have. I'm sorry. But though I feel sorry for Jane, Guildford *is* my brother. He's mother's favourite child too, and honestly, Amy, the gentlest boy. He's very persuadable, being only nineteen, and would recant, I'm sure, if Jane would. As it is . . .' He sighed, and putting his arms round Amy, held her gently.

Suddenly, as though his fear had passed physically through his arms to her, Amy began sobbing quietly. Rob tried to wipe her tears and comfort her, though he had to admit he could see no escape. His brother and Jane would surely die.

'The sins of the fathers are indeed visited on the children,' he said bitterly. 'Why, oh why, did Father have to drag those two children down with him? Why? Why?'

He beat with his clenched fists against the stone wall of his cell, his face flushed and his lips compressed. For the first time, Amy thought, it was obvious how his inability to act was playing on his nerves.

Amy stayed with him, trying to talk calmly and soothe the man who a few moments earlier had tried to convince her that all could be well. At last he dropped into a chair, thanking her for the money she had brought and telling her to give his love to his mother, the Duchess.

'Be near her when bad news comes,' he urged.

So Anne and Amy persuaded the Duchess to stay with them for a few days, until the inevitable decision was reached. And it was a decision which Mary reached quickly, whilst her anger and hurt were still hot. Jane would die directly after Guildford, and the date was to be 12th February.

'Tomorrow!' gasped Amy. 'Now, Mother, don't think about it. Try to remember he's going where his father awaits him; try to be brave.'

But the Duchess was not even listening. Her lips moving in soundless prayer, she got to her feet and walked slowly from the room looking, Anne said afterwards, like a lost soul.

The girls knew the Dudley brothers would have been told that Guildford and Jane would die on the morrow.

'The executions are in the morning. I shall go to see Rob in the afternoon. He'll need me,' Amy told Anne simply.

Anne, weeping, said she could not see Jack on that dreadful day. She would only cry and make him worse; so on the afternoon of the 12th February Amy set out alone to visit Robert.

She walked past the scaffold within the walls of the Tower where Jane's execution had taken place, for a woman was allowed at least this semi-private death and spared the ordeal of a public execution on Tower Hill. As she passed the grim platform Amy realised with horror that Robert had been able to see it from his window. She began to hurry, trying to avert her eyes from the scaffold, the block, the sand and straw. But a movement caught her eye and despite herself she glanced towards it.

There, still lying on the scaffold, with the dress half off so that the childish white body showed, lay Jane's small corpse. It was the fluttering of some part of the gown in the breeze which had caught Amy's eye.

It was a cold day. The rime was still on the grass though it was afternoon, and the green was deserted. Amy dragged herself over to a grassy bank and began retching miserably, her head swimming and a hot dazzle before her eyes though her stomach churned coldly, and the frosted grass beneath her hands crackled icily, whilst her panting breaths hung heavily misty on the air.

Why? she asked herself. Why leave the poor child there, a good four hours after the execution? Jane's severed head with its bright chestnut hair lay on one side of the block, the eyes open and gazing sightlessly at the sky, the kerchief which had covered them hanging loose, its white dappled with scarlet. Straw and sand, strewn for the purpose, had soaked up the young life-blood, but Amy saw through eyes blurred by tears, that the hair was matted and congealed with blood, Jane's gown was dark with it, and her small lifeless hands were lying in pools of it.

Amy dragged her eyes away from the terrible sight and shaking violently, ran towards the Beauchamp Tower. Once there, she recovered her composure enough to mount the stairs to Robert's room and walk in with an attempt at nonchalance. But when he turned his stricken face towards her, she could only fling herself, sobbing, into his arms.

Rob, pale and tight-lipped, was trying to tell her something but she couldn't listen. Her voice seemed like a runaway cart, talking, talking, high-pitched and hysterical. She could hear her words and knew she should stop speaking but she was beyond her own control.

'Her little body, stiffening in the cold, no one to care for her. Her mother, indifferent. Is Mary not human? And what of her sisters? Her ladies? Could they not have seen to her burial? Oh Rob, her hair soaked up her blood—blood—blood!'

Robert struck her face sharply, making her cry out, but the flood of words, the uncontrollable hysteria, left as suddenly as

104

it had come. For a long time they clung together like two frightened children. Then Rob turned a chair round with its back to the window and sat down, pulling Amy onto his knee.

'They killed Guildford this morning,' he said quietly. 'I saw him leave, Amy. Weeping. His shoulders shook and he trembled, but he turned round and waved to me before they led him to the block.' A shudder shook him. 'I could have killed them, Amy, killed them! When they brought his body back for burial they covered his trunk with a sheet, but the movement of the cart shook the covering from the—the severed head. Jane passed the cart as she went on her way to the scaffold. She saw the head, Amy. Bloodstained, rolling lifelessly in the cart. The head of the man she'd married. They took her into the Lieutenant of the Tower's house, to calm her, I suppose. She was in there an hour, but when she came out she was quite composed. I couldn't hear what she said, but it affected many people in the crowd. I saw men and women weeping openly.

'She stood there pale and straight, trying not to show any fear, but she looked so *young*, Amy. A little girl, she seemed. There was mismanagement, for her women broke down and could not help her tie the handkerchief and then when the time came, she lost the block. I watched her turning like a child in blindman's buff, her hands held out before her. Everyone was silent and her voice rose shrill. "I can't find it, where is it?" she cried. Frightened then, like a child who's lost a lesson book, or can't remember the next line of a verse.' He laughed bitterly. 'Well, that's not so far out. By all accounts, she spent a lot of time being chastised by her parents for small imperfections. Anyway, someone climbed into the enclosure and guided her to the block and it was a quick end, thank God. If I have to die in a like manner, I pray I may have the courage Jane showed.'

'Don't think of it, my love,' Amy said gently.

'I *must* think of it, Amy. Death is for all of us, but I didn't realise until today that I'd never faced it for myself. And Jane's life didn't have the sweetness mine has. She never knew true love, either of parent or husband.'

He was silent a moment, then he held Amy so tightly that she could feel the heart pound in his breast. 'Amy, *I don't want to die*!'

'You had very little part in crowning Jane, you never caught up with Mary, thank God. You were safe from any implication in Wyatt's rebellion, shut up here in the Tower,' Amy said. 'I know you fear you'll be sentenced to death, but I can't and won't believe Mary would have such a sentence carried out. Why, I swear if she kills you, I'll kill her!'

At last Robert was able to give a shaky laugh and tell Amy he couldn't imagine her killing a mouse, and they began a resolute conversation about their estates, their backs still turned to that dreadful window.

Soon, however, their talk turned to affairs of the moment.

'Mary has certainly surprised England,' Amy said. 'Everyone was prepared for trouble when Philip arrived, but no one thought Mary would turn into an ogress. London is shivering in its shoes over the way she's behaving.'

'Did Courtenay get himself captured?' Robert asked idly.

'Yes, he is somewhere in the Tower. The Lady Elizabeth—or Princess, call her what you will—is to come to London. It augurs ill for her. I feel sorry for her, since it is widely said she would have no part in the uprising. But I bet Mary won't believe that. You know what sisters are, especially half-sisters. Always ready to think the worst.'

'You should know,' joked Robert and Amy smiled, remembering the way she and her half-sisters had bickered and fought whenever they met as youngsters.

'So Elizabeth is coming to London, is she?' mused Robert at length. 'Hmm, she'll probably end up here!' His tone changed. 'I only hope the Queen doesn't find some excuse, religious or political, to send her down there.'

He nodded expressively towards the window where the scaffold still stood.

'Surely she could not,' protested Amy. 'Why, Elizabeth is next in succession to the throne, should Mary die childless.'

'Yes, but as I said, you know what sisters are. Mary is the absolute opposite of Elizabeth: always has been. She must fear her influence, if only in religion. Elizabeth may pretend what she pleases but the people think of the new religion and Elizabeth in the same breath. And though Mary plans her Spanish marriage, she's old. Suppose she doesn't bear a child? Do you think she has any intention of letting the country return to Protestantism again, under her sister, daughter of the woman she called "the concubine", who seduced her father from her ageing, righteous mother? She pretends to believe that Elizabeth is no Tudor but the daughter of Mark Smeaton, Anne Boleyn's musician, though even *Mary* can't think that. Elizabeth got her colouring and her temper from good King Hal; she's his daughter without doubt. But Mary knows that if Elizabeth were to die, she could will the crown to someone with Royal blood but strong Catholic convictions.'

Amy pulled a face. 'I don't believe Mary's *that* bad,' she protested. 'Though the gibbets being set up at every street corner have made folk fear her.'

'There will be worse to come, Amy. She's a fanatic—the Queen I mean—and such people are dangerous. But here in the Tower we live from day to day; never knowing whether we shall suddenly be commanded to start our walk to the scaffold.'

He saw Amy's cheeks whiten and added hastily, 'I'm being moved up to share Jack's room soon, so with the two of us it will be more companionable. Why, you and Anne will be able to visit us together.'

But Robert gave Anne credit for more courage than she possessed. Countrybred Amy walked alone through the dirty, foul-smelling streets in the weeks that followed, for Anne could not bring herself to accompany her.

'I know you think I'm cowardly,' she said tearfully, 'but I'm so afraid, Amy! And my stomach is delicate. I'm overcome with nausea at the stench of rotting flesh from the gibbets, so that even if I came by coach I'd be poor comfort to my dearest Jack.'

The streets Amy walked along had changed. They were quieter, with the people in the overcrowded houses which leaned crazily towards each other across the muddy roads afraid to shout and call. No longer did cheerful cockney urchins tug at Amy's gown or beg for a groat to buy bread and beer. Instead they went about their business without jokes or laughter, stealing furtively along the kennels to pick over the rubbish. For who dared joke, or voice an opinion, now? Men—and women too—were being put to death for a wrong word.

The Lady Elizabeth had come to London as Amy had told Robert she would. But due to ill-health the journey had been a slow one and for three weeks she had been lodged in Whitehall Palace. But on the eighteenth of March she was sent to the Tower. Amy, a regular visitor, had been prevented from seeing Rob that day because of the torrential rain. All day it rained as though it meant to begin another Noah's Flood, and Amy was forced to sit beside the window panes, watching the water swirling in the gutter outside.

'At least the streets will be cleaner and smell sweeter,' she told Anne, as a furious wind carried a stream of water laden with rubbish down towards the Thames.

'It's a sign that spring is here,' Anne said hopefully. 'You know, the rain to clean the land so that the flowers may peep through.'

However, the following day dawned dry enough and Amy went to the Tower in her coach, for the water lying in the streets was still ankle deep.

'The Princess Elizabeth is a prisoner!' Robert told her as soon as she walked into his room. 'She's in good company, isn't she? The Dudleys, Tom Wyatt who led the rebellion against Mary, Courtenay, and Heaven knows who besides. She was landed at Traitors' Gate,' he went on, 'drenched to the skin, poor wench. So were her ladies. But she's full of spirit. She sat herself down on the steps and refused to go any further, and then someone said something that apparently changed her mind, and she walked into the Tower through the downpour as though she were Queen of all the world instead of a girl in danger of her life.'

'She *was* afraid, though,' Jack said quietly. 'Queenly she might appear, but a discerning eye could see her fear.'

'Aye, like a filly that smells blood,' agreed Robert. 'She had the tense air of one who would like to pull back, though she walked into prison as proud and straight as ever she walked in her life. She's got tremendous courage.'

'Yes, she's the type to stand unflinching through an ordeal and then break down in private,' said Jack. 'But news in prison travels fast, and we've heard of nothing but her courage here, so obviously any breakdown isn't going to take place within these walls.'

'She probably realises she has a long way to go before this particular ordeal will end,' Amy said soberly. 'I wish her luck, poor girl. What a wretched time she's had, always suspected of something, always on her guard. Yes, I wish her luck.'

But in the days that followed, Amy sometimes felt a twinge of something very like jealousy towards the Royal prisoner. Robert and Jack talked of her constantly, and sometimes Amy suspected that Robert had found some way of communicating with his childhood playmate. Certainly when she told him that her father was seriously ill and that she must go down to Norfolk to see him he raised no objection. Quite the opposite in fact.

'I'll miss you, my love,' he told her hastily. 'But I'm damned short of money and I'd like you to sell some of our land on my behalf. You know a good bit about land prices and so on, so I know you'll get the best bargain you can for us. I'd like to help Elizabeth if I could. She's short of money too, you know, but she's not got a loving little Amy to help her, as I have.'

'Of course I'll do as you ask, but won't it bring Mary's wrath on your head if she finds you've been helping her sister?' Amy asked half-fearfully.

'I'm helping an old friend, and she'll never find out who that old friend is. Elizabeth learned young how to hold her tongue. And I have to admit I'm backing a hunch, Amy. Elizabeth remembers her friends. If she should ever come to the throne she'd not forget we had helped her in her hour of greatest need.'

So Amy kissed Robert goodbye, clinging passionately whilst Jack tactfully peered through their window at the early daffodils dancing on Tower Green.

The next day, she was on the road for Norfolk once more.

10

Spanish marriage

When Amy returned from Norfolk, it was without seeing her father alive. He had died even whilst she rode with desperate haste along the winding lanes leading to Syderstone. But she had done as Robert desired and was able to give him the money he needed. She did not ask whether he managed to get a sum to Elizabeth. She guessed that he had; and knew that the transaction would be safer both for Elizabeth and themselves if it remained a secret.

When the Princess was released to house arrest towards the end of May, Amy told Anne that she was disproportionately glad.

'I'm only human, Anne,' she admitted. 'It was hard to see Rob looking pleased and secretive, hugging to himself the fact that he'd managed to communicate with her. I knew better than to ask a direct question of course, but if I hinted he'd just put on a teasing face and say, "If you want to know anything, better get yourself cast into the Tower. We prisoners keep our secrets." Honestly, Anne, there were times when I'd rather have been with Rob in the Tower than out of it.'

The girls were silent, thinking about imprisonment. Amy, who shared Rob's love of the outdoor life, frequently wondered how her husband kept his spirits up, knowing how he must hate being confined to one room most of the time. Jack, she knew, was in a far worse state. He had taken comfort from Robert's presence at first, but now he found his brother's cheerfulness irksome, and muttered with annoyance when Robert strode round their room until he had 'loosened his muscles' as he put it.

Robert could think of Mary as an annoying old maid who would eventually come to her senses and release him. To poor Jack she was fast becoming a nightmare figure, capable of endless cruelty. Anne had recommenced her visits with the coming of summer, for the Queen had the gibbets pulled down and the bodies removed so that her betrothed would be greeted by sweet-smelling streets and (she hoped) a crowd at least neutral and not actively hostile.

'She hopes in vain, though. The people are frightened by tales of the Spanish Inquisition. They fear Philip may bring it to England, I don't believe the Spaniards will get any welcome from the ordinary folk in the streets,' Amy told Rob when she visited him. 'I'm going to the wedding, though. I love a display of finery! Besides, I must go so that I can tell you what the Spanish Prince of half the world looks like in his wedding garments.'

So she and Anne, inconspicuously dressed, watched the great processions and saw small, elderly Mary clad in rich garments and small, blond Philip wearing even more magnificent finery. They were astonished to see how Philip smiled and waved to the crowds, how kind he was to his wife, and how handsome were many of the Spanish entourage.

'There wasn't a man to match you though, my love,' Amy told Robert loyally.

'You couldn't be the smallest bit prejudiced, I suppose?' teased Rob, whilst Jack fretted with impatience because the carving he was doing on the wall was not finished, and his knife was broken.

When the girls left, Amy found herself worrying about Jack. His physical strength seemed to have been sapped by lack of exercise and a poor diet. He took little interest in his food and would never join Robert in a sustaining meal. She thought his preoccupation with carving on the stone wall a bad sign, as though he was determined to leave something of himself to a world which would not know him long. He never spoke of the possibility of release and drew more and more into himself, so that any attempt to make him share in general talk made him hunch his shoulders and turn to stare broodingly at Tower

Green, where the scaffold had stood. Amy knew Anne shared her fears, but as the autumn advanced, their mother-in-law became increasingly cheerful.

'There isn't a Spaniard at court who hasn't listened to my pleadings for the liberty of my boys,' she told them. 'It's a blessing for us that the English haven't been friendly towards the Spaniards, for it makes them more willing to listen to me. They talk to Philip, and he talks to Mary and before you know it, the Tower gates will open and my sons will be free!'

She smiled delightedly at the girls, and Amy thought how very pretty Jane Dudley must have been once. She had lovely bone structure, and even now, after seeing her husband and many of her children die, her eyes, huge and sunken, looked out onto the world full of undiminished vigour.

At last the day came when she could tell Anne and Amy with simple triumph, 'It's all right. No more need for our worries. You'll get the pretty colour back in your cheeks, Amy dear, and Anne will lose that worried frown. Yes, the release order has come through. The boys will be out of prison in about three days.'

Amy grabbed Anne and they danced round the room, laughing and crying at once, whilst the Duchess looked on with an indulgent smile.

The next day the two girls went to see their men. Robert was jubilant, bright-eyed, as if he could personally have pushed down the walls of the Tower had he chosen to do so. Jack was peevish and weary, complaining only that the carving on the wall would lack its finishing touches.

Amy surveyed the carved stone with amazement. It really was a work of art, no wonder he had grown fond of it. But surely freedom must mean more to him than riddles, however significant.

'What does it mean, Jack?' she asked at length.

Jack had carved the family crest of the bear and ragged staff, and with it a lion. This was surrounded by a wreath of roses, acorns, geraniums and honeysuckle. Underneath this perfectly carved, was the rhyme:

113

'You that these beasts do wel behold and see
May deem with ease wherefore here made they be
With borders eke wherein there may be found
Four brothers names who list to serche the ground.'

'Isn't it obvious?' asked Robert impatiently. He had only found carving interesting to the extent of chipping out a fair copy of his device, a sprig of oak, and his initials.

'Not to me,' said Amy. 'You married a simple girl, my darling. What *does* it mean, Jack?'

But Jack would only say wearily, 'Work it out, pretty wench. It's my contribution to this rich life of ours. Work it out.'

But before she could puzzle out the meaning, the real business of their meeting had to be discussed. It was decided that Jack and Robert would go to stay at Penshurst with Sir Henry Sidney. Sir Henry had married the beautiful Mary Dudley and she was passionately fond of her brothers and eager to see them again. Amy agreed willingly to go to Mary's home and stay for a while, until Jack was healthier.

As they rode into the fresh air of the country Robert kept taking deep breaths, savouring the clean country smells after his long imprisonment in the unhealthy dampness of the Tower. Amy rode beside him on her favourite mare, Bronze Belle, a sweet-tempered chestnut her father had given her before his death.

But Anne and Jack rode behind them in a coach. Even freedom had been unable to restore Jack's belief in life, and his health would not allow him to ride on horseback, for he was still too weak. He sat silently by his wife, occasionally smiling at some passing scene, but otherwise withdrawn and quiet.

They had a wonderful reception at Penshurst, the Sidneys going out of their way to honour their guests. But whilst Amy and Robert hunted stag with their host, played at cards, danced the Galliard or the stately Pavane, and then sank into the depths of love-making in their big bed, Anne stayed close and quiet with poor Jack. Gradually, despite all her loving care and all the good things that Mary plied him with, he weakened.

Amy could pretend no surprise when, three days after his release, she and Robert looked their last on John Dudley, Earl of Warwick. He died as quietly as he had lived, moving almost imperceptibly from a doze to a coma, and from that coma to death.

Robert was full of sorrow, but he told Amy that Jack had grown more and more strange during their imprisonment.

'He was convinced that he at any rate would die,' Rob told her. 'He saw Guildford walk out of the Beauchamp Tower to meet his death, and Guildford was so much the younger. After that I think he almost wanted to die. And you know, Amy, there was less of the devil in Jack than in the rest of us. He followed Father, but I think knowing Father's devious ways broke Jack's spirit.'

Soon after her husband's death, Anne decided to go back to her mother's house for a while, though she did not think much of her new stepfather, Mr Newdigate, who had been a member of her father's household. However, she could appreciate her mother's desire to marry a man she could rule without fear that he, like her first husband, might one day lead her family into ruin.

'We're riding to Syderstone,' Amy told Mary Sidney as they bade their hostess an affectionate farewell. 'Everything is rather worrying, with attainders and one thing and another. I don't know what we'll do for money if the Crown impounds the wool and the sheep, but at least we'll have a roof over our heads and food we grow ourselves whilst the law takes its course.'

'Poor Robin, kicking his heels in darkest Norfolk, when he'd so much rather be flaunting his handsome person at court,' said Anne. 'But he wouldn't want to risk the flare-up of Mary's anger, when she wants none with the taint of heresy near her.'

Amy didn't answer. She felt sorry for Anne and for once thought that her childless state was probably for the best. Now Anne could, if she chose, marry again, and continue her life without any reminder of the years she had spent with Jack Dudley.

The journey to Syderstone was a long one, taking the young

115

couple the best part of a week, but to Robert it was sheer unalloyed happiness just to be a free man again, with the woman he loved beside him. He would urge his horse to a gallop for the pleasure of feeling the powerful muscles surge between his knees and the wind snatch at his hair. Then he and Amy would idle by a lake, watching a fish rise in the clear brown depths to snatch an unwary fly which swooped low over the surface.

They had a delightful homecoming at Syderstone and after a few days John Appleyard rode over from Wymondham with an invitation to spend Christmas at Stanfield Hall with him and his wife. But he brought one piece of unwelcome news.

'The Queen is with child,' John said. 'A Spanish brat in her womb, damn her! But of course she's pleased as can be, caressing her Philip until it's a wonder he doesn't flee back to Spain, for she's no tender young beauty!'

By the time the Dudleys joined the Appleyards at Stanfield Hall, the news was being discussed all over the kingdom. Some people thought that a baby might soften Mary's attitude, making her less keen to force her religious and political opinions on her people. Others took the more practical attitude that the Spanish child would put the Princess Elizabeth out of the succession and turn England into a minor Spanish state.

'What do you think, Eliza?' Amy asked her sister-in-law. 'You favour the old religion in your heart, I know. Will you be glad of a Popish princeling who can rule England after Mary's death?'

John's wife blushed, ill-at-ease with her pretty sister-in-law and her handsome brother-in-law. She was a short, dumpy woman with a florid complexion, but she had brought John a good dowry and was a competent housewife. And in addition she suffered in silence the knowledge that her husband kept a mistress both younger and prettier than she. Amy felt sorry for Eliza, but otherwise the two women had little in common. Not even mutual affection for John existed, Eliza merely regarding her husband as a good provider, Amy considering that his neglect of her father had hastened Sir John's death.

'Well, Eliza?' Amy asked, as the other woman twisted her

116

hands together diffidently.

'I'm glad the Queen is to have a child sure enough,' Eliza said slowly. 'But like most of the English, I'd as lief be ruled by one of my own kind. I've no fancy for a foreigner on the throne.'

'Well said, Eliza,' Robert cried, patting her plump shoulder. He was rewarded by a look of glowing admiration and a blush which increased the already deep colour in Eliza's cheeks.

But John had no time for such fancies. 'Those of us who have to earn a living can't be too fussy about religion,' he said. 'Maybe I favour the Protestants and Eliza here has a liking for the Pope, but it's of little consequence. We must ride with whichever mare rules—or as your father said, Robert, "Run dog, run devil, I must let it go forward".'

Amy winced at what she thought to be a tactless reference to the late Duke, but Robert did not appear to mind.

'I'm with you there,' he agreed. 'Whatever we may think, if one has lands to look after and business to attend to, then it's best to keep thoughts to yourself. After all, a man's *mind* is his own. Then you can outwardly at least follow the religion practised by the monarch. Your conscience shouldn't trouble you just because others speak out unwisely and become martyrs for your faith.'

'Your conscience wouldn't, would it, Rob?' asked Amy teasingly, but Robert, though he laughed, shook his head.

'No. I believe man should have freedom. We should be free to worship when and where we wish, to work our fields, to love a woman, to fight a battle.'

'We'll be as free as that under no monarch until we get to Paradise,' said Amy practically.

After their time with the Appleyards they returned to Syderstone. Robert was settling down well to life in the country. With their agent, Flowerdew, he rode over their lands learning all he could about sheep and pasturage, wood and water. But then in February his mother died.

'She said in her will that she wanted to be buried quietly, but she is to have a full funeral service in the Catholic manner,' Robert told Amy, gritting his teeth. 'I must go to the funeral, sweeting, whatever may occur in London. My mother loved us well. I must pay my last respects.'

'I'll come with you,' Amy said firmly. She didn't know how Robert would react to the full pomp of the funeral service. She feared he might be foolishly outspoken because his mother's dying wish—a simple burial with money given to the poor—would be set aside.

So they undertook the arduous journey to the capital and received the small legacies the Duchess had left to her children. She had little to give, but great and careful thought had gone into the bestowal of each bequest. To Ambrose she gave the only manor remaining to her—Hales Owen. She left fifty marks to Robert, and to Amy a gown of wrought velvet, elegant and rich, because she must have remembered how Amy had admired it.

Queen Mary attended the funeral, pregnant though she might be. And many others also beside the large Dudley clan, for the Duchess had been well liked.

But soon after the funeral Robert and Amy returned to Norfolk, for Mary, in a fury of religious zeal, was burning those Protestants who refused to recant. They could not, of course, ignore what happened around them, but living quietly in remote Syderstone they felt it less likely that Mary's wild eye would light upon them. Their life was full and pleasant, with frequent trips to Wells and Lynn, to Norwich and then on to Wymondham to visit the Appleyards; though the latter calls were difficult now, because John had installed his mistress, Bess Forster, at Stanfield Hall, and she and Eliza had to live under the same roof.

The Dudleys had news regularly from the court, so that on 30th April when bells were rung in the principal cities for the birth of a prince, a messenger reached Syderstone almost as Amy and Robert were exclaiming with dismay, to say that the news was false. The Queen was not yet in labour.

'Nor will she be,' said Robert joyfully as soon as they were alone. 'A silly old woman who wants to have a baby to hold her husband and keep her throne. She can't have a child at her age, her health's never been good; so she simply imagines herself pregnant. Foolish old creature, puffed up with wind and telling everyone she's with child.'

'Don't, Rob,' said Amy quickly. 'If you're right she must be terribly unhappy to have to *imagine* herself a mother. I'd love a child but I don't pine, because I have you. Mary has a polite, long-suffering foreign husband. They have to converse in *Latin*, it's their only common tongue—imagine that, my darling, and try to feel a little sorry for the poor woman.'

Robert put his arms round his wife's slender waist and rubbed his chin on her soft hair.

'I'd feel sorrier for England had her hopes been realised,' he whispered. 'But I'm sure she can't have children—look at her father! He tried hard enough, goodness knows, and had enough women. And all he got was a sickly illegitimate son or two, two legitimate daughters, and his heir, who died at sixteen. But why should we worry about her, my love? We have each other and as yet she hasn't shorn all our land from us. We have freedom. Let's use it.'

'Perhaps now that Mary's been told there isn't going to be a baby she'll stop the persecutions and burnings,' Amy said hopefully later in the year, when Mary had been made to accept the fact that the babe in her womb was mere wishful thinking. But if anything, Mary increased her ferocity. She seemed to think that God was punishing her by making her barren, so in order to win grace she must punish in her turn.

Messages came to Syderstone that Philip had left England at last, promising, however, a speedy return. Mary, said the messengers, was in despair and terribly lonely for her Spanish lord.

But it seemed to Amy that Robert was less interested in affairs at court than usual. He was learning the real pleasures of living in the country. They rode over their lands, spoke to yokels who clutched their forelocks and purpled with pleasure, and Robert ate tremendously and chuckled over Amy's anxiously worked accounts. Once again they swam in the sea, though Robert swore it was colder at Wells than Hemsby; they watched their own lambs grow up, they saw the shearers at

119

work, and they helped count their flocks.

In London, they knew, despair was plumbing the depths. The burnings of heretics grew worse: mainly poor men and women who stuck their chins out and refused to take back their words; a few insignificant Protestant clergy; a few more important ones. But on the whole it was the ignorant mass of the people who suffered.

Then to Amy's considerable astonishment, Robert came in one day to tell her to get their bags packed.

'A friend has sent a message to say that Mary wants someone to act as envoy between herself and Philip. My name was suggested as I speak fluent Spanish, and she is well disposed towards me. She has sent for us.'

Amy was infected by his pleasure. She packed quickly and deftly, with the help of her maid, Pirto. The two women were good friends, though Pirto was ten years the older. They had pleasure in similar things, both preferring the country to the town and both having unerring dress sense. Pirto nodded approvingly at the gowns Amy was choosing to take with her to London, whilst she got out the appropriate sleeves, kirtles and stockings to complete each outfit.

'But we wouldn't want to look old-fashioned and countrified, would we, my lady?' she said anxiously, looking doubtfully at the headdress in her hand. 'Who knows? The influx of Spaniards on the court may have led to a new fashion coming in so that the Spanish mode of dress is now generally worn.'

'Who knows, and who cares?' Amy answered joyfully, packing with neatness and despatch. 'Come, Pirto, that headdress will do very well. When we are near the Queen and have no fear of her displeasure—for why should she be displeased with us if she is going to allow my lord to act as go-between for herself and Philip—then we will see all the fashions.'

Their arrival at court, which was then at Greenwich, was inconspicuous. Robert had an audience with Mary and, defying custom, he dressed Spanish style. His charming impetuosity and good looks won the Queen's confidence. She gave him letters and verbal messages for Philip, and then he was kissing Amy goodbye.

120

'When I see you again I'll have gained Philip's favour,' he told her jubilantly. 'Then we shall dance at court once more.'

Amy forebore to point out that she herself had never danced at court, and what was more, there was not much dancing or enjoyment at the court of Mary Tudor.

She moved into lodgings with her servants once Robert had left, and found that she could enjoy her visit to London to a certain extent, provided she kept away from places like Smithfield.

'The burnings go on, though you do not see them,' Pirto reminded her a trifle severely. She knew her mistress was wise to appear outwardly complacent to the Catholic faith, but did not think she should be allowed to forget that her fellow creatures were suffering.

'I know, you don't have to remind me,' Amy said sadly. 'But Pirto, here we are near enough to Rob so that he can visit us when he comes to see the Queen. I'm not so selfish that I can forget the ordinary, decent people who are dying hideous deaths for the religion which I dare only hold in my heart.'

Nevertheless, when the summons came from the Palace of Hampton Court for Amy to have an audience with the Queen, she could not help feeling nervous. Why should she want to see me, she thought. What should I wear? Should I dress in my best to impress the Queen with my fine attire, or should I dress simply and demurely so that I appear inferior in every way? Then she remembered that Protestants dressed plainly, as a silent protest against the gauderies of the Catholic religion.

It was a very nervous girl, only twenty-four after all, who set off to meet her sovereign one warm afternoon in late summer.

II

The encounter

'Come this way, please. Her Majesty has been feeling ill, but this afternoon she seems a little better. I hope your visit will cheer her.'

The girl who spoke smiled amiably at her charge, trying to reassure this visitor to the court who was so plainly ill-at-ease.

'You're very kind,' Amy murmured. 'I'm afraid I didn't even ask your name. I'm rather nervous—it's the unexpected honour of meeting the Queen. I met the late King Edward at my wedding, but he was only a young boy then.'

The girl laughed as they walked slowly along the winding corridors of Hampton Court. 'I'm one of her Majesty's maids of honour. Magdalene Dacre is my name. I think you'll like Queen Mary, and she you. But you mustn't mind if she seems abrupt at first—maybe even harsh. It's just her manner, and as I said, she's not had the best of health. She already knows and likes your husband, Robert, and is eager to meet you.'

Amy blushed with gratification and said shyly, 'Why, if she likes my husband she'll surely wonder at his choice of wife. I'm no fine court lady I fear, though I've done my best to dress as her Grace would wish.'

Magdalene glanced approvingly at the other girl. Her gown of blue figured silk was cut in the conventional English fashion preferred by the Queen, who had not taken kindly to the exaggerated Spanish styles many other Englishwomen had seized upon with such fervour. Amy's gown was high-waisted with a flared hem, and the bell-shaped sleeves were criss-crossed with bands of darkest blue velvet ribbon. The high white collar which framed her face and the demure blue velvet coif partly hiding her shining golden hair made her seem a picture of propriety. But Magdalene noticed that the blue eyes sparkled with curiosity as they gazed round and she thought that Amy's soft lips, trembling slightly now with apprehension, could curve into a most enchanting smile when their owner was more at ease.

At the door of the Privy Chamber Amy was handed over to the care of another woman and led towards the Queen.

She saw a small, skinny figure in an over-elaborate gown of violet velvet. The red hair was heavily streaked with grey, the complexion marred by brownish blotches. The Queen's eyes, light blue and short-sighted, peered anxiously at the girl before her.

Amy thought wonderingly that this simply could not be the terrifying Queen Mary, who had people burned at the stake if they did not agree with her religion. This tired, anxious woman had none of the look of fury and zeal that Amy had expected to see engraved on her face. She reached the Queen, and sank into a deep curtsey, hoping her thoughts had not shown on her face.

Mary bade her rise and sat her down on a low stool, so that they could talk in comfort.

'I have a liking for your husband, for he brings me messages of hope and comfort from the King,' Mary said with that abruptness which Magdalene had warned Amy not to fear.

Amy answered steadily, 'I'm glad Robert pleases your Majesty. He is eager to please, I know, and enjoys being with Prince Philip.'

Her voice, to her surprise, sounded natural enough, though her heart was pounding in case she said the wrong thing, and annoyed the Queen.

'And you, Mistress Dudley, attend mass without reservations?'

The question was expected, yet it came so suddenly that Amy felt her heart leap. She glanced instinctively at her breast, almost expecting to see a tell-tale movement beneath the blue silk.

123

'I was brought up in the country, your Majesty, where mass was celebrated daily. To me, it is a part of my childhood,' Amy said, hoping the Queen would not guess how carefully she had learned this reply.

Mary smiled warmly and for a moment looked almost pretty. She did not seem to realise that Amy's answer was in fact no answer; an evasion.

'I'm glad. Many older people, of course, are more comfortable with the religion they have known for most of their lives. But younger people,' she sighed, unconsciously smoothing her thickened stomach. 'Younger people like change. They want to break from Rome, to probe new-fangled ideas, to consult astrologers and astronomers. Who wants to peer into the future? It's foolishness.'

She watched Amy closely to see how the girl received the remark. Amy felt that the worst hurdle had been crossed when they spoke of taking mass. Now she could smile frankly, dimples peeping.

'I'm interested in my future, your Majesty, but I would be afraid to try to discover what awaits me, for fear it might be horrid,' she said, and was relieved when Mary gave a bark of laughter and told her she was a minx like all girls, and faint-hearted into the bargain. Then she waved the women around them back to a distance and leaned her head nearer Amy's.

'Young Dudley—he's a good husband to you?' she asked abruptly.

Amy, startled, said impetuously, 'Oh, *so* good! He has ambitions which I can't share, being a woman, but he has much sweetness of temperament and a generous heart.'

Mary nodded absently, gazing at the elaborate embroidery she held on her lap. 'I've heard it said yours was a love match, though others say young Dudley married a Norfolk heiress,' she remarked.

Amy laughed outright. 'Well, I could scarcely be called an heiress, with my father owning three manors in Norfolk, and my half-brother married to a rich widow! I'm my father's only legitimate child of course, but at the time of marriage Father was very much alive and needed all the money he could

124

get to put back into his estates. Why he could only give me a portion of twenty pounds a year—I daresay I wear that much on my back at this very moment!'

A shadow crossed Mary's face at the mention of Amy's legitimacy, but lifted when Amy spoke of her marriage dowry of twenty pounds.

'Then Dudley chose you for his wife?' questioned Mary.

Amy might have felt affronted, but the Queen's tone held so much wistful longing that she could only pity the older woman.

'I believe so. We met whilst Robert was staying with the Greshams, near neighbours of ours at the time. After our first meetings he came down from London to see me, so I must believe that he was as fond of me as I was of him.'

'You say "was as fond". Do you mean he grows weary of you?'

Amy felt a slow tide of colour wash her face but she answered steadily enough, 'No, your Majesty. I believe our love has strengthened through trials such as his imprisonment in the Tower; his enforced absences in foreign lands. Would you wish me to leave you now?'

The Queen stared at her, surprised, then remarked, 'Have I offended you? My child, you must learn to hide your feelings. You see, we are both married and both childless. I have watched your husband and it's obvious that he's a strong, lusty young man who appeals to women. Yet he takes no interest in those of my maids of honour who seek to win his favours. Do you not wish for children? Are you unable to give birth to a baby? Could it be your husband who is at fault? You must not mind my questions, for I'm showing you my heart. I want children, and know my husband to be capable of being a father, for he already has a son. So I feel the fault must lie in me. How does the guilt lie in your partnership?'

Amy remembered this was more than an inquisitive elderly woman. This was her Queen. 'I want children, and believe myself to be capable of bearing them,' she said slowly, choosing her words with care. 'As for guilt, there is none, for we don't apportion blame. However, since as yet none of

Robert's brothers have fathered children, I generally suppose they need more time than many to start a family. To be sure, at times I fretted and worried, but it did no good. I have my husband, and I've learned to have patience. Maybe my patience will be rewarded and I will conceive.'

'Everyone preaches patience,' muttered Mary, more to herself than to Amy. 'I have no *time* for patience. I'm forty years old and my husband is across the sea. If he doesn't come back for years I'll be too old to bear him the sons we both desire.'

She glanced at Amy's wide, guileless blue eyes. 'Then I too must have patience,' she said kindly, as though she was unaware that she had spoken her thoughts out loud. Her thin, mottled hands worked on her lap, for *when* would Philip return? True, he had told her that he must obey the commands of his father to leave England for a few weeks. But already the weeks had stretched to months and though she had faith in Philip he had not returned. She could feel the tenseness of impotence and doubt building up in her mind, beading her forehead with sweat so that she longed to shout orders, to call for a pyre to be built big enough to cleanse this accursed land of every Protestant in it. Then her eyes caught a glimpse of the embroidery she was wrenching at, and she relaxed.

It was to be an altar cloth for her chapel at Greenwich and whenever she remembered the Church which it had been her duty and joy to bring back to English hearts, her cares fell from her.

Surely, she thought now, we are all in the hands of God? Surely he will look down on his handmaiden who has done so much for the true religion, and reward her patience and the years of barren waiting by giving her the child she longs for? If love is necessary for the creation of children then wouldn't her love for Philip suffice? She acknowledged with pain that she could not expect him to love her. She—ah, she had love and to spare.

Amy moved restlessly on her stool. The Queen's face had been so strange, her expression one of pain and her lips puckering and moving as though in silent conversation. Yet now she was gazing at her embroidery as though it were the child she longed for. Presently Mary looked up from her lap and continued talking as though there had been no break in the conversation.

'How does young Dudley enjoy country life? As you will know, I've had enough of it in my time, whilst he and his family enjoyed court favour. Now the boot's on the other foot, with the Dudley's rusticating whilst I am here, at the centre of things.'

'There are only three of the brothers left alive now,' Amy reminded her, greatly daring. 'We don't see much of the other two, but Robert and I are very happy down in Norfolk.'

She hesitated, wondering how much she dared say. But Mary was smiling at her with friendly ingenuousness.

'Of course, we miss our first home—the manor of Hemsby. We spent some happy months there when we were first married, with the sea so close that on stormy nights it was like being aboard a ship.'

Mary's smile broadened. Here was something she could do for Robert Dudley's pretty little wife. She had always liked giving presents. For a moment the wonderful feeling of being able to give, without stint, filled her.

'You shall have Hemsby back,' she said grandly. 'I'll see that the deeds are returned to you as soon as possible. Then when my husband and yours return to this country, you'll be able to enjoy a holiday with him at Hemsby, putting things to rights there.'

'Oh, thank you, your Grace,' gasped Amy, delighted at the ease with which Mary had restored their confiscated property. 'When Robert and I are back in Hemsby, we shall think of you with *such* gratitude.'

Mary, her cheeks mottling pink with pleasure, said gruffly, 'Aye, to be sure, but it's a small enough thing, after all. If you wish to show your thanks do as I do, and try to extend the spread of the true religion in the hearts of the people.'

She indicated the altar cloth on her knees and Amy leaned closer, admiring the lovely work, so painstakingly undertaken. The material was scarlet damask but so thickly and intricately was the silver thread stitched that Amy guessed when it was finished it would be difficult to tell from a distance whether it was red on silver or silver on red.

'I never learned to embroider, as you and your half-sister did,' Amy said regretfully. 'I can make a simple petticoat, but that's about all. I think Mother must have spoilt me, because even my samplers used to get finished for me so that I could run out and learn about the management of an estate with my father.'

'Your father taught you such things? But why is this? You have brothers.'

'Yes, half-brothers. But John Appleyard was sent away to a nobleman's home and when he came back for holidays he had no wish for further instruction. As for Arthur, he never was interested in estate management. I was lucky to have parents who were so wrapped up in my welfare. It has certainly come in useful, for when Robert is away I can act as his agent.'

'You mentioned my half-sister,' the Queen said abruptly. 'Do you know much of her? Is she, perhaps, a friend of yours?'

'She and Robert were friends as children, but I've only met her twice myself. Once at my wedding, when we exchanged a few words, once when I was with Robert at court and the Lady Elizabeth was present.'

Mary gave a grunt. 'You found her charming, no doubt.'

Amy said cautiously, 'I have no doubt she is a very delightful person, your Grace. But she is not much interested in country girls who have few talents.'

Mary chuckled. 'She's not much interested in women, child. But I expect she cast down her eyes and primmed up her mouth and made you think her a saint.'

'She need not worry over me, your Grace. What could it possibly matter to the Lady Elizabeth whether I think her saint or sinner?'

The words sounded sharper than she had intended and Mary laughed again.

'You didn't like her,' she said triumphantly. And when Amy would have hastily corrected her, said in a whisper, 'Well, I dont, either! Sly, she is, and over fond of the men, as her mother was before her.'

128

Then Amy saw on the face before her a glimpse of the woman she had feared to meet. Mary's mouth drew into a tight line and her eyes stared before her, their gaze cold and merciless.

'But for that woman, my mother would not have died as she did. But for the daughter, my reign would not be troubled as it has been. God, how I hate her!'

'Elizabeth's mother paid for her sins by an untimely death also,' said Amy boldly. She regretted the words as soon as they had been said, for why should she defend the Lady Elizabeth? But Mary did not hear her. Once more her hands fretted with the embroidery on her lap, her nails clawing and catching in the threads.

'Queen Catherine would have been pleased to know you are married to a son of Spain,' Amy ventured desperately.

To her inexpressible relief the eyes came back from times long past and the rigid frame relaxed.

'Yes, indeed. When I was making the decision over my marriage I prayed to be shown the right path. For I had nothing to guide me except his reputation and a portrait.' She smiled kindly at Amy. 'But I chose rightly. He is like your own husband; good and kind, devout and practical. It is the sad fate of those who wed ruling monarchs and are ruling monarchs themselves, that they may not see as much of their partners as they would wish.'

'My husband also spends a great deal of his time away from my side, and we are neither of us of royal descent,' Amy reminded her.

'Sometimes I wish I had been born a simple maid,' Mary told her, half-laughing, half-serious. 'I was a pretty young thing at fifteen or so; most men would have wed me for my long red-gold curls and blue eyes. But marriage for a princess is an important thing. I was a political asset whilst I remained single and heir to the throne, for whoever bedded me, wedded England. So I was promised to this one, promised to that one. But always something happened; my father quarrelled with my betrothed or thought another match more advantageous, so I wasted my prettiest years in waiting.'

129

She smiled at Amy and said briskly, 'But you are a lucky young woman. You married your handsome Dudley and you'll climb the ladder of life beside him. Whether you have children or not doesn't matter, because you love each other. You'll rejoice in his successes, but you won't be unduly perturbed if he doesn't have the brilliant future he craves.' She half-closed her eyes, looking at Amy as though she could see her future, more like a fortune-telling gipsy than Queen of England.

'He wants success and advancement, but it may be withheld from him,' she said in a droning voice. 'Stay by him, comfort his failures and make them seem small. He is a Dudley, remember.' She suddenly snapped her eyes open and looked with some surprise at Amy's concerned face.

'Did you have other young men before you married Robert?' she said, and Amy was almost sure the Queen was unaware of her moment of strangeness.

'Why yes, but to tell you the truth I had known most of them since I was nine or ten. They seemed more like well-loved brothers,' she confessed.

Mary laughed, remembering with delight the days when she had been nine or ten. She told Amy of those days, of her father's pride in her looks and achievements, her mother's deep love which surrounded and protected her. It seemed to Amy that in a way the ghost of that little girl gave the Queen her happiest moments. It was memories of her happy childhood that brought the gentle smile to Mary's face, and the same memories made her wish to be merciful towards all men and rule her kingdom through love. But as she grew more and more disillusioned with humanity, the child-ghost had less and less chance of influencing the woman she had become.

Today, however, in Amy's undemanding presence, Mary seemed to find comfort. The girl was simple and honest and she brought out the best in the Queen, making her remember her own youth with charming nostalgia because she called to mind only the pleasant incidents. After all, she was surrounded by people who knew the sort of life she had led. They knew how disturbed and unhappy she had been. She could not tell *them* of her youthful triumphs with young men. But Amy was new to city life. Together, that afternoon, the Queen and Amy saw the former's childhood through a roseate glow. Mary, when she became thoroughly involved, was a good storyteller. She wove a picture before Amy's fascinated eyes of the court of Henry VIII and Catherine of Aragon, when they were in love and all the world lay before their only child.

The Queen's ladies, clustered at the far end of the Privy Chamber, were glad to see their mistress so happy. To hear her loud laugh ring out, mixed with Amy Dudley's delighted giggles.

'She's good for the Queen,' murmured Jane Dormer to her companion. 'It's odd how sometimes the sight of youth and beauty makes her sharp and unkind, and yet at other times it seems to give her very real pleasure.'

'If you're comparing Amy Dudley with the Lady Elizabeth, remember Mary and Elizabeth are half-sisters,' answered Lady Margaret Douglas. 'Poor Mary would love to feel fond of her sister, but she is too aware that Elizabeth could so easily step into her shoes. Prejudice from the past blinds the Queen to any good in Elizabeth's character, but she can *afford* to see Amy Dudley in her true light for the girl is harmless. Indeed, they have something in common, both married to handsome men and both childless. I'm glad the Queen has taken kindly to the girl. From what one hears, it can't be all honey, being married to a Dudley.'

'He's faithful,' protested Jane Dormer. 'Goodness knows he has choice enough if he wished to stray from his wife; but he doesn't do it.'

'He's ambitious,' answered Lady Margaret grimly. 'And that can be worse in the long run than infidelity. Ambition can carry you far; it's already nearly carried Robert Dudley to the block. Who knows, his next ambition might lead his wife to share his fate. No, it's best to marry a man who is content with his lot.'

Jane Dormer was about to reply when they saw Amy giving a deep curtsey and the Queen beckoned to her cousin to lead Amy from her presence.

Lady Margaret obeyed with alacrity. She was curious to

meet the woman Robert Dudley had chosen to marry, and also eager to know what the Queen had talked about.

She led Amy out of the Privy Chamber saying kindly, 'Would you like to have a look round the Palace now that you're here? I believe this is your first visit, though your husband has been in and out of Hampton Court all his life.'

Amy, though wondering whether the last words were kindly meant, nevertheless said she would like to see the Palace.

Lady Margaret showed her the room in which Edward VI was born. She saw the very bed where Jane Seymour had given birth to her son and had later died. Amy noticed with awe that the silken coverlet of the bed was lined with ermine, and the hangings depicted a map of England, beautifully made, with little pictures of people doing their daily tasks woven into the work.

'See, here the Queen gives audience to foreign ambassadors, if any should visit us whilst we are here,' Lady Margaret said, showing her into a magnificent chamber where the very rushes on the floor seemed to sparkle pale gold in the sunlight.

'Aren't the hangings marvellous?' cried Amy, delighted with the strange pictures of foreign places and weird animals that decorated the walls.

'How did you enjoy speaking with the Queen?' Lady Margaret asked presently as they strolled through the beautiful gardens that surrounded the Palace.

'I was afraid I might say something to displease her, or perhaps make her unhappy. She becomes unhappy easily, does she not?'

'Yes, she hasn't had a happy life. But your fears were groundless?'

Amy looked thoughtful. 'Not altogether. She spoke strangely at times—it made me feel uncomfortable. I thought it best then to say nothing. I felt that when she is abstracted, thinking of the sad days that are gone, she would be quick to take offence.'

Lady Margaret nodded, realising uneasily that it was never wise to judge a girl a fool because she was young and pretty. Behind Amy's face, fresh as a wild rose, there dwelt a remarkably shrewd mind.

'But you managed to keep the Queen well amused, we could hear that from the other end of the room,' she remarked.

'Oh, once I had got over my first nervousness, it was quite simple,' Amy told her. 'We spoke of the time she had been happiest—when she was a little girl and the apple of her father's eye. She came to my marriage, you know, but I didn't mention it. Those days were unhappy ones for her, with the Duke of Northumberland growing ever more powerful and cruel.'

'You are a very sensible young woman, Mistress Dudley,' Lady Margaret was surprised into saying, and Amy laughing, said, 'Well, I have my share of *common* sense, I hope! One would have to be very feather-brained to remind the Queen of the Duke's rule. But as I was saying, I was married at Richmond, with the royal family present, but I saw very little of the Palace so this is the first royal residence I've really seen.'

'No, I can't imagine Robin taking you on a conducted tour of Richmond on your wedding day,' said Lady Margaret drily, and watched the younger woman blush rosily.

She really is charming, she thought as she waved Amy goodbye. A thoroughly sensible, well-brought-up girl. What a pity she could not be more at the court. But it would never do, Lady Margaret knew. The Robsarts were known to have brought up their only daughter in the Protestant faith, and though she now accepted the true religion with seeming docility, Lady Margaret thought that when the Queen was in one of her hysterical moods, railing against the Protestants and ordering the burning of yet more heretics, only a convinced Catholic could bear with her.

But Amy, riding home to her lodgings, was elated beyond measure. No thought of attending the court crossed her mind. How pleased Rob would be with her! She had seen Queen Mary and had not shown fear. She had amused the Queen, who, at her hint of how they missed their Hemsby home, had made a promise that it would be returned to them. With a feeling that she had made a friend of the Lady Margaret Douglas, and that even the Queen herself had rather liked her,

Amy rode gaily through the streets, humming a little tune under her breath, at peace with the world.

How pleased, how very pleased, Rob would be with his country wife!

12

At home and abroad

After her meeting with the Queen, Amy went back to the country, but news of Mary's frightful persecutions reached her even at Syderstone. In Norwich, as elsewhere in England, people were burned because they could not accept the Catholic faith. But Amy resolutely kept her mind on their estates and the management of them. She had heard from Rob that soon he hoped to be back in England, heralding Philip's return to Mary's fond arms. With that in mind, therefore, Amy did all the work she could so that whilst she was in London with Rob the estates could run smoothly without her.

At last the day came. It was one of those March days when the English countryside seems the best place in the world to be. A folicsome breeze played amongst the budding branches and overhead the sky was pale ice-blue, and the sunlight fell like clear gold water through the freshness of the morning, and lay in painted pools on the lawn.

Amy had finished an interview with Flowerdew on how many lambs should be kept, and how many sent to market. With the delightful feeling of having done her duty, she was giving herself the treat of wandering across the garden hunting for the first spears of the daffodils, exclaiming with delight when she found a patch of purple and gold crocuses in the long grass.

Mrs Allen, her housekeeper, came out into the garden. She bobbed a little curtsey to her young mistress, smiling at the pretty picture Amy made in her green and gold figured gown, out there in the green and gold world of spring.

'If you please, my lady, a messenger from London,' she

said, eyes twinkling.

Amy gave a squeak of excitement and, fleet-footed as one of her own lambs, ran across the lawn and jumped over a fat marmalade cat basking in the sunshine. In seconds she was in the cool, dark living-room, taking the message held out to her by one of Robert's servants.

'Thank you, Anstey. Off you go to the kitchen, Mrs Allen will give you some refreshment,' she told him, not wanting to open the precious letter in front of his curious eyes.

But as soon as he had disappeared her fingers were tearing at the seal and the sight of Rob's strong handwriting was almost as good as the sight of himself would have been.

'Dear one,' she read. 'Come to London as soon as may be, for I am here already and would like to have you with me. I do not know how long I may be in England, so don't delay. Your loving husband, R.D.'

Amy went and told the messenger that he could return to his master the following day. She and her servants would set out then also, but travelling more slowly, would probably reach London a day behind him. Then in a ferment of excitement she flew up the stairs, calling for Pirto in a voice high and breathless with elation.

'Put tablets of scented soap amongst my clothes, so they smell sweet,' she said distractedly. 'And let us take some perfume for Sir Robert. The nice, light scent we made last summer.'

'Sir Robert will have plenty of perfume from France,' said Pirto, smiling slightly. 'He won't have overlooked his toilet because he has been busy. Why, even in the Tower you said he was never untidy or ruffled.'

'Ah, but French perfume can't possibly compare with that from our own good Norfolk acres,' said Amy quickly. 'Put in a large flask, and be sure it's well stoppered. I've no desire to arrive in London with every garment reeking of roses and honeysuckle.'

Pirto chuckled, but by the time they reached London and Amy was in Robert's arms, he told her laughingly that what *she* smelled of was sweat and horseflesh.

136

'How rude you are!' exclaimed Amy. 'And if it were true—which it is *not*—it would be because I rode as fast as I could in order to be with you sooner.'

Laughing, he squeezed her tightly, then releasing her told her to go and bath whilst he ordered a good substantial dinner.

'The food at this inn is said to be excellent, and you've lost weight whilst I've been gone,' Robert said. 'I like my girl with curves, and pink cheeks. Your face is thinner. You need feeding up.'

'I need you home, that's all,' Amy assured him from the doorway.

The troubled look that crossed his face confirmed her suspicions. This was to be a fleeting visit, then. He had implied as much in his letter, but she had been unable to prevent herself from hoping that this time Philip would *have* to spend a few months with Mary. She knew Mary would have greeted the return of her lord with joy, not only because she wanted him by her side, but because this time he might give her the child she longed to bear. Could Philip really afford to antagonise Mary by leaving her before she had had a chance to conceive? Or would he think that after the false pregnancy which had already made him look a fool, it simply was not worthwhile to try to please his wife? Amy pondered the question as she changed her travel-stained riding-dress for the clean clothes Pirto was unpacking.

'Will you wear your Spanish farthingale, my lady?' asked Pirto, holding up the bell-shaped Verdigale, stiffened with circular wooden hoops and covered with dark blue silk.

'Of course,' said Amy, smiling at the other woman. 'Have you unpacked my best bodice and kirtle, Pirto? What should be more fitting than that the gown I wore to impress Queen Mary should now impress my husband?'

With Pirto's aid the beautiful blue silk bodice and the full kirtle were donned, and Amy's long hair brushed out and tucked into a small hood of finest lawn. Then Amy tripped happily downstairs to the parlour that Robert had pointed out to her. The meal was already steaming on the table, but Rob stood waiting for her, courteously refraining from beginning

137

on the food which looked so mouth-watering.

Amy noticed with an inward grin, though, that Rob had been unable to stand the temptation of a mug of English beer. He had a tankard in one hand, and was in the middle of the first long, satisfying pull when she entered. His eyes twinkled appreciatively at her over the rim as she approached, secure in the knowledge that her gown was new and fashionable, and that happiness alone was adding a glow to her cheeks.

As soon as the inn servant had finished serving them Amy said impulsively. 'Oh, Rob, it's good to have you home! Believe me, though our agents are worthy men, someone has to give them the yes-word before they take a step. I have had to think for us both, and brainwork has never been my strong point.'

'You're an excellent businesswoman, Amy, don't underrate yourself,' protested Rob, pushing a large hunk of beef into his mouth and speaking rather thickly. 'Your parents trained you better than most, for you can turn your hand to everything in the house and run an estate into the bargain.'

'Yes, but it worries me, Rob; then I get a little thin and that worries *you*. However, now that you're home again I'll get as fat as butter.'

Robert swallowed his meat too quickly and choked. 'I might as well tell you, love, I don't expect to be here for long. Philip has *plans*, and they concern me.'

'Men are cruel,' Amy said indignantly. 'The Queen has been sick with anxiety lest Philip never again honour these shores and now, if you please, Philip has *plans*. I believe Mary grows cruel because Philip is away, and not as the gossips like to say because he whispers "burn more heretics" every time he sees her. Anyway, what are these plans that will take you from my side and Philip from Mary's?'

'War with France!' blurted out Robert, his eyes shining with excitement. 'Imagine, Amy! If Spain and England join together to conquer the French, what spoils of war there will be! What honours will be heaped on anyone present! You must not think of our parting, just think of the glory I'll be winning on the fields of France.'

'Perhaps Mary won't let England be drawn into the war?' suggested Amy hopefully, making Robert shout with laughter.

'Perhaps pigs will fly! Philip can twist her round his little finger. If he wants English soldiers fighting in France then he'll get them. Why, if he asked her for the moon she would jump pretty high to try to snatch it out of the sky for him. Oh, don't you worry, the English will be fighting on French soil before many weeks are out.'

'Don't worry?' said Amy incredulously. 'What a fool you can be, Rob. I don't *want* the Queen to agree to join with Spain against France. Still less do I want my man involved in warfare. Why are you men such witless creatures when it comes to fighting? You might be killed in a dozen different ways, and I want you alive. I want us to live a normal married life together instead of all this bowing and scraping to a woman you despise and a man you detest. Don't go to France, Rob, I beg you.'

Robert frowned and his lips tightened into a determined line. 'It's the only way to get the attainder taken off our name. Why, if we do well, we might even be restored in blood! Anyway, I *want* to fight for my country. So should every honest Englishman.'

Amy checked the angry words that rose to her lips. What use was it to point out that he would not really be fighting for his country, but for Spain? What use to point out that an honourable name carved on a premature gravestone would not be much cause for rejoicing? She had known Robert long enough to realise that protests were useless. They would only lead to a fiery quarrel, with her probably flouncing off to bed in tears and Rob glowering by the fire half the night. Admittedly, making up their differences was delightful, but it never altered the outcome. Robert would do as he thought best—and she had to admit to herself that she would not have relished a man who bowed instantly to his wife's words.

So, changing the subject, she asked him how he was looking forward to seeing Hemsby again, once more their own property.

'Clever lass,' he said immediately, gladly leaving the subject of war, so fraught with discord. 'But if you looked half as beautiful when the Queen saw you as you look tonight I wouldn't have been surprised to find myself living at Windsor!'

Amy glanced fondly at her blue silk bodice, thickly sewn with pearls. There is something about blue, she thought, that makes people feel happy. Perhaps it's because sunny days are blue days.

As he thought he might be recalled to Philip's side at any time, Rob took lodgings for himself and Amy in London. They did a little sightseeing and watched a play, indulged in their mutual weakness for card games and visited friends. But at the end of the first week Rob put on his best clothes and told Amy to go to bed and wait for him there, as he might be late.

'I've an important meeting,' he said solemnly.

'I suppose it's with Philip, to learn what he's wheedled out of Mary,' said Amy scornfully. 'Don't try to tell me that you're visiting any other friend, all decked out in the Spanish fashion, with a jaunty hat, and a hip-length cloak, and those indelicate trunk hose.'

Robert did not know whether to laugh at her description of his tight-fitting nether garments, or to show his annoyance at the ease with which she had seen through his scheme.

He decided to laugh. 'They'll duck you for a witch, my lady, if you continue to forecast the future so accurately. Can you tell me what Philip will say, then, Madam Astrologer?'

'He'll say. "Too soon, my boy. Mustn't let her think I'm here just for soldiers," or some such thing,' Amy said promptly.

She bounced across their bedroom and began ripping off her gown in a way unlikely to prolong its future life.

'I've a good mind to stay at home after all,' Rob murmured provocatively as Amy flung the last of her garments to the floor and stalked with dignity towards their fourposter.

'Oh, go and play secret service spies with Philip, like two little boys,' Amy taunted him, pulling back the covers. 'You'll get no kisses from me tonight, Robert Dudley, I don't ... Oh!'

Dignity is hard to maintain when one has just had one's bottom pinched, but Robert dashed out of the room laughing, and Amy rolled into bed, muffling her giggles in the pillow and vowing she would have her revenge on her husband when he returned. But when he came back, tiptoeing into the bedroom, shielding the lighted candle so that he would not wake her if she slept, the expression of sulky disappointment on his face was enough to make her forget thoughts of revenge.

'Rob! What happened? Did you see Philip?' she demanded, sitting up in bed.

Robert put down the candle and began undressing with about as much ceremony as Amy had shown earlier.

'Yes, I did,' he said. 'And you *are* a witch, Amy. He told me that Mary was ill-at-ease over his coming; mad with joy one moment, suspicious the next. He said if I wanted to retire to my country estates I might do so, for there would be little news for a month or so.'

He climbed into bed, the picture of despondency, so that Amy had to bite back a laugh at the recollection on the cocksure figure who had left her a couple of hours earlier.

'Never mind, my darling. It will be nice to have some peace, and no doubt you can leave a man in London to bring you a message as soon as Philip needs you,' she comforted him, holding his curly dark head against her breast and smoothing the wrinkles from his brow.

'I don't think I'll bother to go to France,' grumbled Robert. 'He's a *man*, isn't he? Surely he can cook up some likely tale so that we can be off without further delay? It's so stupid, to be foiled at every turn by a little old woman who thinks she can become a mother in her state of health.'

'What is wrong with her health, then?' Amy enquired mildly.

Robert wriggled uncomfortably, not liking to be tied down.

'She *can't* be well. She's not yet forty-two but she looks sixty. And what about last year? Swelling up like a puffball, and then getting thinner almost overnight once they had persuaded her she carried no child. It's not natural. I don't think she'll live much longer.'

'Wishful thinking,' Amy murmured sleepily.

'Maybe. Nevertheless, we'll go back to Norfolk. I'm going to look about me for a property there. If the attainder is lifted or if I make a fortune in some way I'd like a manor near Syderstone. But something larger and more gracious, with a moat fed by a river in the grounds, and woods. Then we could raise cattle as well as sheep, and the hunting would be better.'

Soothingly, Amy talked softly of various manors she knew near Syderstone which might suit them, and presently his even breathing told her that he slept.

But when Robert woke her in the morning the old sparkle was back in his eyes and his enthusiasm for Norfolk seemed as strong as his desire to go to war with the French. In the tented privacy of the bed they made love, with passion and laughter, and Amy thought for the thousandth time how very lucky they were, that even in the most serious moments of their lives together laughter was never very far away.

They did not go straight to Syderstone as Robert wanted to see Thomas Gresham, so they agreed to spend a few days at Stanfield Hall with the Appleyards.

'Naturally, John will extend his hospitality to us willingly,' Rob said solemnly.

'Of course. John is a *fond* half-brother,' Amy retaliated, grinning. They both knew how uneasy John was in their company. He simply did not know how to treat them. Robert worked for the Prince of Spain and Amy was on visiting terms with the Queen of England. But their name was attained and their lands forfeit—they could be utterly discredited and homeless at Mary's whim. Yet Mary was ill, and he knew Robert had been friendly with Elizabeth when they were children. If she came next to the throne, it would be as well for the Appleyards to be the best of friends with the Dudleys.

But something seemed to have solved John's dilemma for him, because when they reached Stanfield they found themselves honoured guests. Amy thought he must have concluded that Dudleys always managed to land on their feet, so it would be as well to treat them with every courtesy.

He and his wife, Eliza, greeted Amy and Robert affably, therefore, and Bess Foster smiled with ingratiating friendliness every time Amy looked at her. This, however, Amy did as seldom as possible. The hard-faced young woman whose bold, light eyes flickered hungrily over Rob's broad shoulders and narrow hips was not to Amy's liking, and she saw with distaste that though Bess was John's acknowledged mistress, she did not hesitate to make a play for Robert whenever the opportunity occurred.

'That female gives me the creeps,' Robert told Amy in the seclusion of their bed. 'She's man-mad, that's her trouble. She would have me in her bed at the drop of a hat, the brazen bitch.'

'Quite a social occasion bedding her would be, Rob. I mean John sleeps with her, so it would be a threesome! Or do you think she'd encourage him to go back to poor Eliza for a night, while she seduced you? It's all right for us to laugh, but it must be dreadful for Eliza having her under the same roof.'

'Yes, and John is sometimes quite rude to his wife—and allows Bess to be rude as well.'

'If you ever take a mistress, Rob, I trust you'd never be fool enough to bring her within reach of my nails for half-an-hour, let alone a lifetime. If I were Eliza I'd have that hussy out of this house before you could say knife—and if she didn't leave I'd murder her.'

'God preserve me from women!' whispered Robert piously. 'In a way I admire your half-brother. I find one woman keeps me busy. Fancy keeping two satisfied and even having them both under the same roof! I wonder if they talk about his lovemaking, when he goes out and leaves them together?'

'He's insensitive, that's why he finds two women easy,' said Amy wisely. 'Probably one of them will stick a knife into John. Ho, serve him right! I've changed my mind, Rob. If you bring a mistress home, it's *you* I'd knife.'

'You never would, I'm too gorgeous to die young,' said Rob complacently. 'Besides, I'm not a big boiled pudding like John. I'd take some killing, unless you knew where to plant the blade

143

to the best advantage, and I'll wager you don't.'

'I don't believe I could murder you really,' admitted Amy. 'Don't let's talk about it. When do you go to Intwood? I'd like to come with you and talk to old Sir Richard.'

So the following day Robert and Amy rode together to Intwood Hall, glancing covertly at the remembered spots made special for them by their courting days.

As soon as they reached the Hall, Robert and Thomas went off together ostensibly to see a new peregrine falcon but probably, Amy thought, to talk treason. She and Sir Richard drew their chairs close, happy to speak of days gone by.

'Do you often hear from Mary and Harry?' Amy enquired presently. 'We move about so much, you see, and when Robert was in the Tower I was going between London and Norfolk on his errands. We lost touch, I'm ashamed to say, but I've never forgotten them.'

Sir Richard smiled, his mind on the days when Mary and Harry had run riot in his home. Happy days, that now seemed so much clearer than the uncertain present.

'Aye, you were good friends, you three.' He glanced slyly at Amy. 'And one would have been more than a friend, if your Robert had not come along.'

'Oh, Harry was like a brother,' protested Amy, blushing slightly. 'I expect he's married now?'

'Not he. When you suddenly fell in love with young Dudley he threw himself into other pursuits. He's a soldier; he fought in France and against the Scots. He has property, but he leaves the management to his bailiffs. He prefers a life of action and excitement, he says.'

Amy smiled, remembering Harry's preoccupation with the arts of war when they were children.

'And Mary?' she asked.

'Married, with a string of children. You'd not know Mary now. Do you remember how neat and fussy she was, looking down on you and Harry playing rough games? Well, now she mixes loathsome concoctions of boiled dockleaves and frog-spawn, thickened with starlings' eggs, to physic her husband who is suffering from boils.'

144

He laughed at Amy's astonished face and assured her the 'concoction' was to be placed on the boil and not swallowed, as she had at first supposed, adding that if she did not like the sound of Mary's physicking, it was as well she had not married Harry.

'For he would have expected you to follow him on his expeditions,' he reminded her. 'He always made you his second-in-command when you were youngsters: pushing you over garden walls to raid other people's cherry orchards; making you play the enemy when he wanted to fight the Scots or the French. Many's the time you were mired up to the waist, following out Harry's crazy schemes.'

'Well, it sounds as though we're all happy, in our different fashions,' Amy told Sir Richard. 'How does Thomas get on?'

'Thomas does well enough. But he'll do better when we get the Protestant religion back again and a more sensible woman than Mary on the throne,' said Sir Richard frankly, with a lack of caution which showed him very much the master in his own home. 'You won't see Master Thomas or his wife for dust when Mary dies and Elizabeth comes to the throne. He's got a head for figures, my son, and he'll end up riding high, see if he doesn't.'

'Mary may yet get herself with child, or will the crown to another,' Amy suggested, but Sir Richard snorted derisively.

'She's neither saint nor devil, that's her trouble,' he said. 'She isn't sufficiently wicked to get rid of her sister, as a worse woman would have done, and yet she won't will the crown elsewhere whilst a chance remains that she might have a child. It's my belief we'll see Elizabeth on the throne before many months are gone.'

When she and Robert were riding once more in the direction of Stanfield Amy could not help wondering aloud why Sir Richard too was so convinced that Mary Tudor had not long to live, and would soon be succeeded by her half-sister.

'No one who has seen her lately, Amy, and heard the hysteria rise in her voice over the least little put-off, could think her a healthy or a happy woman. She has waited too long for the chance to rule, and now that she's got the opportunity to use

145

her power, she's spoiling everything because of her fanatical feeling for the Catholic Church. She doesn't care about people's bodies, only about their souls. Well, men feel they are answerable to a higher Authority than Mary for the state of their souls, and they don't see why she should torment their bodies before sending them to the higher Authority. If you ask me, the most fervent prayer rising from the hearts of Englishmen today is that Mary's reign shall soon cease. It will free us from the Spaniard, too.'

'What of Elizabeth? Don't people fear she may also become a fanatic?' asked Amy.

Robert shook his head, leaning forward to untangle his black stallion's mane from the ornate red leather reins.

'No; she is their beautiful princess, who will free them from despair. Anyhow, those who know her realise that people mean more to her than churches. What is more, my love, if we play our cards right Elizabeth will serve us well. She's been my friend for years and I know she was grateful for our financial help when she was in the Tower.'

Amy sniffed. 'She doesn't like me much. We've only met twice but she gives me funny looks when she sees me. I wouldn't be surprised to learn that she'd got a weakness for you.'

'What woman has not?' questioned Robert, grinning and dodging a blow from his wife with quick grace. 'Anyway, you wouldn't mind a Queen being nutty about your husband, would you? It would be rather a compliment to your taste in marrying someone so—so . . .'

'So conceited,' Amy finished for him, smirking. 'Well, I would not be complimented, so if she does come to the throne she had better keep her claws off you.' She turned to face him, giving him her dimpling, teasing smile. 'Though I should imagine she'd be more likely to admire the beauty of the goods than try to sample them,' she added.

Robert gave a shout of laughter and his startled horse broke into a canter. Amy dug her heels into Bronze Belle's smooth side and soon they were racing joyfully towards Stanfield, their differences forgotten.

They did not stay long with the Appleyards after that, but were two months at Syderstone, sometimes seeing to their own affairs, and sometimes travelling about the nearby countryside on the look-out for a suitable estate. Then Robert's messenger came, with the expected summons from Philip.

'Will you come with me to London, love?' asked Robert, his eyes alight with excitement. 'Even though Philip has seen fit to summon me, it may not mean war. I may be in London for several months yet.'

So Amy decided to go with Robert, though London in the heat of the summer was not the healthiest place to be. They set off together on horseback, their mounts lethargic with the heat. But they were content to travel slowly, both secretly convinced that Philip would not have sent for Robert unless war was a certainty.

And so it proved. The Queen had agreed to an English force going to the continent, and amongst them would go the three remaining Dudley brothers: Ambrose, Robert and Henry. Robert would go as Master of the Ordinance, a post which required considerable organising ability.

'We Dudleys aren't the only soldiers you know going to France,' Robert said casually when he came home for a brief meal. 'A friend of yours from Norfolk is working under me. Excellent fellow.'

'Oh?' said Amy without much interest. She knew a great many ambitious young men would be eager to fight against France, and win what spoils of war they could.

Then one afternoon, when the rain was falling steadily from the lowering sky, the knocker was banged by an impatient hand. Amy, making a heavy martial cloak for Robert, sighed as she heard the manservant ushering someone into the room, but stood up nevertheless, letting her work slide into her chair.

The next moment she was squeaking, 'Harry, oh Harry!' for despite skin weatherbeaten by many campaigns and a neat brown beard he was still the irrepressible Harry Gresham she had known.

'Pleased to see me, Amy?' said Harry, grinning and shaking raindrops from his wide-brimmed hat.

'Yes, indeed. Come and sit by the fire, Harry. I've had one kindled because of the miserable weather.'

Amy spread his hat and cloak over a screen and then said expectantly, 'Well? Tell me of the battles you've fought and the maids who have fallen in love with you.'

'You'd be as bored with the hearing as I with the telling,' said Harry frankly. 'War is a messy business, not for women. Besides, the worst time to talk of war is just before the start of a military expedition. As for maids, I'll spare your blushes. How about you, Amy? How does married life suit you? Are you much at court? Does Robert share your love of the country, or are you a town-miss now?'

He spoke lightly, but his hungry eyes searched her face, half-hoping, half-fearing to find unhappiness there. But though he could see her youthful carefree attitude had left her, she seemed a contented woman.

'Married life suits me very well—you should try it. As for court, I have visited it only once.' She paused significantly, lowering her voice. 'You know how I was brought up, Harry. I have no love for the Pope, nor the Catholic faith. But that is something one does not speak about, except to close friends.' She smiled slightly, raising her voice to its normal pitch once more. 'As for Rob, he enjoys life equally, whether he is in London or on our country estates. I don't think either of us would like to be permanently exiled to the country, nor cooped up for ever in London.'

'If Elizabeth were to come to the throne, you probably wouldn't spend much time in Norfolk,' Harry said thoughtfully. 'I've worked with your husband these past few weeks and there's enough of his father in him to make me think he'll look for a higher office than he holds at present, should the opportunity occur. He would be a welcome addition to the court now, were it not for his religious beliefs being, at present, unfavourable.'

'Well, I daresay I'd enjoy living at court and wearing marvellous clothes,' said Amy lightly. 'Don't underestimate me, Harry. If you think I'd sicken and pine in Robert's shadow whilst he made a play for all the women, you've another think

148

coming. I'm still young enough to enjoy an agreeable flirtation and if Robert became unfaithful, I'd serve him the same trick! I would not sit back and be a wronged wife like Eliza Appleyard, I promise you.'

'If I'm around when you feel like throwing discretion to the four winds, I'll remind you of our old friendship,' said Harry, grinning. 'If you think to take another man I'd give better service than most.'

'You and Rob have one thing in common, you're both conceited,' Amy told him, flushing slightly.

'Ah, but I would have all the novelty of being your lover instead of your husband,' Harry said. 'It's not often I make an offer like that to a married woman, so think yourself fortunate.'

They laughed and Amy made to box Harry's ears, then paused. What would the servants think if they entered the room and saw her behaving in a familiar fashion with one of Robert's captains? Besides, she was sufficiently worldly to recognise behind the twinkle in Harry's eyes an unmistakable ardour. She might find herself in a most compromising situation, and she did not want that for her sake or for Harry's.

'Sometimes I wonder what my life would have been like if I had married you,' she said pensively.

'First must come a proposal, and that I never made,' Harry replied instantly, making Amy rock with laughter.

'Well, if marriage wasn't your intention, allow me to tell you I was sadly misled,' she said, wiping tears of mirth from her eyes.

'Ah, I was young and foolish then, Amy. But I've seen how a wife holds a man back. I wouldn't have been able to set up a Yorkshire mistress whilst I was fighting in the North, nor would I have been able to look twice at the pretty Mam'zelles.' He rolled his eyes and made and expressive shape in the air with his hands. 'I can't wait to get back to France and sample a willing French minx, who tells me "No, no", with her lips and "Yes, please" with her eyes.'

Amy pouted. 'I hope Rob doesn't get any ideas, that's all,' she said.

'That's the whole *point*,' Harry said triumphantly. 'Robert is a married man. He has his way to make in the world—yours too. He'll concentrate on his job, secure in the knowledge that he has a beautiful wife to go home to. I'm a footloose soldier. I do my work with a will and then take my pleasure where I may with a clear conscience.'

He rose, and Amy did not try to prevent him. It had done her heart good to see Harry, hear his ridiculous banter with the underlying note of seriousness. In the doorway he swept her into his arms and gave her a hearty kiss.

'There's something for you to remember me by,' he called as he strode down the narrow street, waving to the girl who smiled and waved back.

She thought of Harry with affection for the rest of the day, but when Rob came home late at night, her pleasure in seeing him completely overwhelmed her, so that Harry's visit paled into insignificance. She did wonder briefly whether she should mention that her old friend had called, then the knowledge that Rob was taking ship for France the very next day made her resolve to say nothing.

In bed, Rob roused her deepest depths of passion with his love-making, both of them knowing, though they did not speak of it, that this might be the last time their bodies ever met in the perfect fusion of love. Rob, caressing her silken skin, was aware of his hands as though they suddenly had a life of their own. He knew the sensitive fingers which now gave and received pleasure might be maimed in action. He imagined with sharp horror the many ways in which it was possible to die slowly from battle wounds.

I may never lie with her again, he thought. So despite his resolve to be fresh for the morrow, he and Amy spent the night love-making, trying to crowd into a few brief hours everything they felt for each other.

Yet when Robert returned from France, uninjured, he had to tell her that his brother Henry had been killed at St Quentin.

'But Ambrose and I did well. Philip will press for the restoration of our property,' Robert said coolly.

150

Amy, knowing how fond Robert had been of Henry, thought that he was hiding deep grief under a mantle of indifference so she did not reproach him. Instead she said brightly, 'We won't speak of it, darling. Tell me, how did Harry Gresham fare? You remember, you stayed with him at Intwood Hall when we first met.' But she did not really worry for Harry. He was a professional soldier and could take care of himself.

'Gresham? Oh yes, I know who you mean. A capable chap —brave too. Killed at St Quentin,' Robert answered briefly.

Amy did not speak. For a moment her whitened face was like carved ivory, then she forced herself to say steadily, 'I'm sorry. We were very good friends as children.'

It was the first and last time that the name of Harry Gresham was ever spoken between them.

13

Long live Elizabeth

With the war in Europe slowly coming to an end the Dudleys were restored in blood and Amy became Lady Amy officially once more, though her servants had never called her anything else. Most of their land was restored to them and Robert, as he had planned, began making efforts to buy the manor of Fitcham. It was only eight miles from Syderstone and with the property they already owned such as Cockisford Priory, they would have a considerable holding of land in North Norfolk.

Then the Queen thought herself pregnant once more, and Robert felt it incumbent upon him to suspend negotiations and go hurrying off to London to see if it were true. When he came home after a month spent away he was agog with the latest news.

'It's another mare's nest,' he said with a scornful crack of laughter as soon as they were alone. 'She's ailing again and determined to believe it's pregnancy. I don't think she'll live through the summer. Her face and arms are thin, yet her body is swollen up like a well-fed spider. She gave me an audience principally to see whether I thought Philip would come to her.'

'What did you say?' asked Amy anxiously. It seemed to her that during the whole of Mary's reign people had been giving her six months to live and yet there she was, full of sick fancies perhaps, but very much alive, and quite capable of revenging herself on anyone who displeased her.

'Don't worry, I'm not fool enough to offend Mary, even though I believe her to be dying,' said Robert cheerfully. 'In fact, I was tact itself. Told her to write to Philip and tell him she was expecting his child. Said I was sure that if he could come, he would come.'

'And will he?' asked Amy, although she thought she knew the answer.

'Not he! What, come over to this cold, unfriendly island to visit a withered old woman who thinks she's pregnant? He's been kind enough to her in the past but his ambassadors have told him she's dying. He is looking to the future already, Amy, in his slow, careful way. I wouldn't be surprised if he proposed to Elizabeth as soon as Mary's safe underground.'

'Don't, Rob. It sounds so heartless. I know she's done terrible things, but terrible things were done to her for years, remember.'

'What, should I think kindly of her, then? She who lit the fires of martyrdom in this kingdom?'

Amy shrugged and turned away. What good could it do to remind him of the fires his father had lit? And Northumberland's killings had been purely for gain of an earthly nature, with no thought, however misguidedly, of doing God's work. Amy believed the Queen did these evil things because she subconsciously wanted to be revenged on a world that had mistreated her. It went against her nature, Amy was sure, to behave as a tyrant; and yet her religion was sufficient excuse to justify her actions.

So throughout the summer people waited for Mary's death. Her ladies, even the most loyal, admitted sadly that she was very ill. She was subject to fainting fits and even when she was in moderately good health would sit for hours, her hands idle in her lap, just staring in front of her. Her eyes seemed to sink more deeply into her head. Gradually the flesh on her face shrank away, leaving great hollows beneath her cheekbones. Then she would become unnaturally animated, her skinny hands fidgeting nervously as she talked, falling suddenly still again when she passed into a state that was near to coma.

Towards the end of the summer, Robert was told definitely that the sale of Fitcham would not be within their means. He was restless and uneasy already, and decided to take the opportunity of returning to London.

'I want to be at the centre of things, when the old mare dies,' he told Amy.

'Why? There may be rioting or trouble of some sort. Why not wait here until you know who will rule?' asked Amy.

'Because those who are first to show their faith in Elizabeth and promise their allegiance will gain substantially, Amy. Believe me, I know the Princess. She is the sort that is loyal to the death to her friends, and she expects like treatment from them. I want to be one of the privileged circle round the throne this time. If I offer help and sympathy before her sister dies, I prove that I don't fear taking a risk, and if I'm one of the first at her side when the news comes I'll stay at her side throughout her reign. Elizabeth is like that.'

'Shall I come with you then, Rob? I might be of some help to you—to Elizabeth, even. She might be glad of a woman's company.'

'She'll have her own women, my love. Besides, my bet is that Elizabeth will want men round her when she first tastes freedom. Only to begin with, I mean,' he added hastily.

'Oh, go then. But if you think I'm going to moulder in the country away from you for long you're mistaken,' Amy said crossly. 'I happen to love you, God help me.'

Robert hugged her exuberantly, and telling her that they would both live to be grateful for his action, he left her alone with her servants at Syderstone, to wait for news.

Slowly the days dragged by. The heat was sullen, every day Amy awoke with the slight headache and listlessness in her body which usually presaged a storm, but the weather did not break. Every now and then she received messages from Robert, telling her little but hinting he was having an exciting time.

Autumn came, and the leaves whirled, brown and light, from the giant beech tree by Amy's bedroom window. The autumn colours which she loved surrounded her but she did not stray far from the house. It seemed to Amy that the whole world held its breath; waiting, waiting, for something that was not going to happen.

Amy saw the thickening of the lambs' coats and knew that

winter was at hand. November was half over, she thought.

'I don't believe Queen Mary is going to die,' she told Pirto plaintively. 'Of course, I shouldn't want her to die. But for the country's sake I feel she must. And this eternal waiting, whilst everything hangs in suspense, is unbearable. Why, even winter seems reluctant to arrive. A light hoar frost in the morning, turning the lawns grey, making the wool on the sheep steam when the sun comes up; but no real sharp biting cold; no snow. Everything in nature is waiting, as we must.'

Pirto scolded her for her fancies but suddenly, winter arrived, and a few days later, the long-awaited news.

'The Queen is dead—she died three days ago. The Princess Elizabeth is now to be our Queen,' Amy told her household. 'For the moment at least there have been no violent changes in the religious ceremonies, but of course persecution of the Protestants ceased as soon as Mary drew her last breath.'

'Will we join Sir Robert in London, my lady?' asked Pirto hopefully. She liked life in the country, but the quiet of Syderstone with so much going on in the capital was beginning to get on her nerves. She felt that a change would be good for both herself and her mistress.

'Yes, I think we should,' agreed Amy. 'However, we won't go straight to London. We'll stop for a few days in Norwich to hear the latest news.'

In Norwich they lodged in a pleasant tavern overlooking the wide market-place. Amy glanced instinctively up at the Castle as they entered the city gates, and hastily looked away again. After all this time the tarred body of Robert Kett hanging in his chains was still clearly visible.

She and Pirto enjoyed their time in the city. They went to the cathedral, where the clergy were holding mass as before, but with less obvious enjoyment and sincerity. They had anxious faces, Amy observed gleefully. She had heard how fat they had waxed during Mary's reign, whilst all about they were condemning people to the fire. Now they were having some anxiety in their turn, and serve them right, she thought. The rejoicings in the city were wildly exciting; bonfires blazed, lighting up the sweaty, happy faces of the citizens;

rich men threw money to the poor, and the ballad singers attracted big crowds when they sang of their new young Queen.

It was in Norwich that Amy heard her husband had been among the first to greet Elizabeth as Queen. Robert had brought the news that her sister was dead and that William Cecil was making all haste to her with the ring Mary had left as her token for the new ruler. Elizabeth had glanced, laughing, at his steed.

'Your horse has been hard-pressed, yet you have outridden the rest of 'em,' she said. 'So you shall be my new Master of Horse.'

Amy told herself she was glad, of course she was, that her husband had been singled out for such an honour. One after his own heart, too, for he would be responsible for all the Royal horses, their upkeep and general health. He was fond of all animals, but horses had always been his especial love.

'It will mean Robert will be very near the Queen, for he will have to be on hand all the time to see that she has sufficient horses in good health for formal and informal occasions,' she told John Appleyard when she visited him at Stanfield Hall. 'I only hope she will welcome me to court with equal enthusiasm.'

For rather to Amy's disappointment, there had been no summons from London, telling her that Robert wanted her by his side. Nevertheless, on towards London she and her retinue rode, little realising what disillusionment awaited them there.

Amy took lodgings near St Martin-in-the-Fields and sent a messenger to the Palace to tell Robert where he might find her. He was longer in coming than she expected, and when he did arrive his visit was strange and brief.

'You can't come to court, love,' he told her ruefully. 'It's full as it can be with all manner of people. Besides, you'd feel lost there, for Elizabeth is gathering round her all her old friends from former years.'

Amy was disappointed but understanding. Certainly she would not want to push in, especially if it might do harm to the Queen's regard for Robert. She would stay, she said, in her lodgings, and would see the coronation as one of the crowd if no other place could be found for her.

'Well, the coronation won't take place for a number of weeks,' Robert said doubtfully. 'Wouldn't you do better to return to Norfolk? You could visit friends if you feel Syderstone is too cut off.'

'I don't *want* to visit friends, I want to be with you,' Amy said indignantly. 'What's the matter with me, Robert Dudley? Have I developed six arms, or a squint? I won't interfere between you and the Queen, you may be sure of that.'

'I'm sorry, love,' Robert said remorsefully. 'I suppose it's because Elizabeth still feels unsure of herself. She likes men round her, but she leans on me. I'm young, as she is—most of her councillors are elderly and reliable. But she'll settle down once she has her affairs sorted out, and then what a time we'll have.'

Soon after he left, Amy realised that Pirto too was feeling the first faint stirrings of discomfort.

'It seems odd, my lady, that you aren't to go to court, since Sir Robert is holding such an important position there,' remarked Pirto. 'There are a mass of ladies at the court and I don't believe they're *all* Elizabeth's old friends. Nor do I believe a slip of a thing like you would add to the overcrowding problem.'

'Well, I never did think Elizabeth liked me,' Amy told her candidly. 'But of course she's never really known me. From what Sir Robert says I imagine I'm to wait for my presentation until all the fuss over the coronation is finished. Then I expect I'll take my place by his side.'

So it came about that when the coronation procession rode through the streets, Amy watched her husband in his place of honour as Master of the Horse riding immediately behind the litter in which the Queen sat. But Amy and Pirto were struggling to keep their places in the jostling, swaying crowd that lined the street.

Amy thought Robert looked wonderful astride a handsome black stallion and leading a beautiful snow white mare. He rode, straight-backed and handsome, controlling his horse with his knees so that his hands were free to hold the mare. But he did not see his little wife standing a-tiptoe to wave to him. His eyes were fixed on the glossy red-gold hair of the girl in the litter, and he never took his gaze from her.

'Sir Robert was dazzled by the splendour of her garments and equipage, my lady, that's why he didn't notice you,' Pirto said comfortingly to her mistress when they had fought their way through the rejoicing crowds back to their own quiet lodgings.

Amy nodded thoughtfully. 'Yes, I suppose so. She looked very splendid, I'm sure, but I was mainly watching Robert.'

Pirto chuckled. 'So were all the women. He *did* look a picture, didn't he? A sight to dazzle most wenches—and you the lucky woman he's wed to, Lady Amy.'

But as the new year turned from the cold of January to a fine, crisp spring, Amy was hard put to it not to show her discomfiture. Robert did not visit them as often as they expected in their pleasant lodgings, though Amy made sure there was always a light burning after dark so that he could not miss the house. He nearly always came at night and in haste, and though Amy did her best, she could not shut her ears to the rumours.

Sir Robert seemed to accompany the Queen everywhere. It was whispered that he was a married man but that the Queen wished he was single. It was he who had had the important task of riding to Dr Dee, the astrologer, who was asked to pick the day most suitable for the coronation. She would only send a *particular* friend on an errand like that, folk whispered in the streets; a man she could trust completely.

Then some weeks after the coronation Robert came to them one evening, and asked Amy politely if she and her household would move back into the country. At her startled exclamation he explained hastily that he did not expect her to bury herself at Syderstone.

'Why not stay with the Hydes, at Denchworth?' he suggested. 'You get on so well with Alice Hyde; she would be company for you. And we both love her children. It isn't too

158

far for me to visit you frequently, either. Come, Amy, what do you say?'

'Whose suggestion is this really, Rob? Do *you* want me out of the way or does Elizabeth? I'm not deaf or insensitive, you know. I've heard people talking.'

Robert looked relieved to be asked a straight question. 'Elizabeth won't have you at court,' he said baldly. 'She doesn't like women, especially when they're married to men she *does* like. She's told me she'd be better pleased if you were out of London.'

Amy could have cried with vexation. After all the years of waiting for Rob to regain the position he felt the world owed him, now she was not to be allowed to share it with him.

'All right, I'll go to Denchworth,' she said slowly. 'But I warn you, Rob, you had better visit me frequently or I'll make you sorry, see if I don't. And keep remembering you're a married man will you? I've no desire to be made a cuckold, even by the highest lady in the land. Elizabeth is in a position, I suppose, to play with fire and not get burned. You and I are not so invulnerable. Goodbye, Rob.'

'It won't be for long, Amy, I swear it. Just let Elizabeth feel her position more secure and she'll become accustomed to the fact that I'm a married man and want my wife beside me. Goodbye, sweeting.'

He kissed her and left, whilst Amy waved until he was out of sight. Then she turned back with a small sigh to tell Pirto that they would be leaving their lodgings as soon as they could pack all their gear. Pirto's startled look put into one glance what Amy was sure everyone else would soon be thinking. What was Robert Dudley up to, that he had no wish for his wife's eyes to be upon him?

Then she shrugged the thought impatiently away. Rob had always been ambitious: now he wanted a place at court, and he wanted the Queen's favour. If the only way to get these things was to keep his wife out of sight—and therefore out of mind, presumably—then he would have to do it. But he had told her it would not be for long. He had said he would visit her. She must be patient and wait until it was safe for him to show the Queen that he loved his wife and wanted her near him.

So Amy set off with what pride she could muster, to Denchworth and her friend Alice Hyde.

14

The sojourn at Denchworth

'Amy, little Amy! I thought you'd be too busy following that handsome husband of yours round the court to spare a thought for me, stuck out here in the country with a parcel of horrid brats. Do tell me all the latest gossip. Oh, how very glad I am to see you, my dear!'

'You did expect me, didn't you, Alice? I sent a messenger several days ahead of me.' Amy picked up a plump toddler and held him to her breast.

'Lord yes, love! But I half thought it must be a mistake, and how happy I am to discover myself wrong. Now don't let the children bother you, my dear, put Jackie down, he's playing with your necklace.'

'He doesn't bother me, he's adorable,' Amy told her friend. Over the child's curly head she looked frankly into Alice's honest brown eyes. 'I'm here because I love to visit you, of course. But I've left Rob's vicinity because I've been told by the Queen that I'm not wanted at court and she'd prefer that I left London. What do you make of *that*?'

'She can't *do* that to you, Amy! Robert is your husband, you've no children to prevent you spending your time at court. Can't you make a fuss?'

Amy shook her head. 'Robert agreed. Alice, from the rumours I've picked up I think Elizabeth is playing at being in love with Robert, and he's letting her believe he adores her because it's policy to stay in her good books. If I did try to bring him to heel I'd ruin his chance of a career at court. He'd never forgive me, you know. However, if I don't do anything but wait for events to take their course I shall still keep his love, and he promises that in time the Queen will accept me. What would *you* do?'

Alice considered, her head on one side, her sensible face puckered with thought. 'I'd have no choice, I suppose, but to do as you've done, though I'd expect my husband to visit me as frequently as possible to scotch any rumours. But you're not a prisoner here. You can come and go as you please, spend his money as extravagantly as you like. There's none—certainly not Robert, who was always generous—would deny you that right. So you have what fun you can, my pretty, and don't worry. Worrying won't help. You'll just have to wait and see.'

Shortly after she had settled in at Denchworth Robert came down to visit them as he had said he would. He seemed strangely ill-at-ease and rather offended Mrs Hyde by his arrogant, off-hand manner. But Amy had known him too long to put it down to his new position at court. It was his conscience, giving him a good hard prod.

When they were alone undressing for bed, Robert said resentfully, 'Why does Alice Hyde stare at me so? I thought your maid acted strangely, too. Rushing out of the room without a word when I came in—the merest bob for a curtsey.'

'Alice was not staring and Pirto did not slight you,' Amy said calmly. 'If you feel that perhaps they should treat you in such a way, that is your own opinion. I can assure you everyone here behaved perfectly normally.'

'You're annoyed with me too,' said Robert accusingly. 'You blame me because you're here in the country and not at court. But it's not my fault, it's Elizabeth's cursed jealousy. She wants to have me all to herself, she doesn't like to acknowledge the fact that I have a wife.' He waited for her to speak and when she did not reply went on morbidly, 'What a way to live, pulled in two by a couple of women! I must say I never thought you'd turn against me, Amy.'

'I haven't. Why wouldn't you stay downstairs to talk and play cards before coming to bed?' Amy asked, trying to change the subject.

'Because I was sick of their critical, staring faces,' Robert said sullenly. 'In God's name, woman, are you afraid of me seeing you naked now? Why do you turn away?'

'To blow out the candle,' Amy replied, surprised. 'What a strange mood you're in, Rob. Do you want me to relight the flame so that you can stare at me? There is still some light from the fire, I can see your face.'

Muttering under his breath Rob hunched an offended shoulder at her, and Amy got into bed. They lay side by side and Amy waited for Rob to make some move or remark. After all, he had not slept with her for several weeks. But all he did was give a great, stagey yawn and roll over. Amy guessed with a pang of most bitter anger that he was afraid for the first time in their married lives that if he made love to her she might become pregnant. But after about twenty minutes of trying to stem her tears, Amy gave a small, stifled gulp. At once, Rob turned towards her and she was in his arms, the passion that had been stifled in them both gladly breaking through the unnatural constraint.

Soothed and gladdened by his love-making, Amy slept well and deeply, only to be woken by Pirto's cry of surprise when she came to draw back the bedcurtains.

'Yes, Sir Robert has gone,' Amy said as coolly as she could. 'I suppose he had to be back at court. I only wish he had had the courtesy to wake me before he left.'

But when Pirto left the room her self-control broke and she burst into wild sobs, biting the pillow and muttering 'I hate her, I hate her', whilst the salt tears ran into her mouth.

Pirto must have noticed more than she had appeared to, for a few moments later there was a tap on the door and Alice Hyde rustled in, her florid face concerned.

'Don't cry, my love, don't cry,' she soothed. 'It's an awkward situation and one which will take some sorting out; but never fear. Everyone is saying that the Queen must marry, and since she certainly can't marry Robert then some foreign monarch, or perhaps even one of the unmarried nobles of the court, will come along and take her mind off her Master of the Horse.'

Amy struggled up in bed, saying distractedly, 'Oh Alice, what a nightmare! First, he was determined to share my bed but ignore me. Then we made love, and I thought everything was going to be all right, Queen or no Queen. But he felt so guilty that he slipped out of bed in the early hours, and was dressed and gone before I woke.' She gave a giggle which threatened to become hysterical. 'See, he pushed the bolster down his side of the bed in case I noticed he was missing and woke before he had got away! Why, if you had told me a few months ago such a thing could happen I'd have laughed you to scorn. There was nothing we desired more than a child, but now . . .' she broke off, her lips trembling.

'Why, you've plenty of time ahead of you to have children,' Alice said bracingly. 'Just don't worry about it, my pet. You'll have to let Robert dance attendance on the Queen in this absurd fashion until one or other gets tired of it. Remember, he does love you. When the Queen casts him off he'll come running back to your arms like a hurt child, and you'll comfort him and forgive his thoughtlessness.'

'You're probably right,' said Amy with a sigh. 'I'll get up now. Would you send Pirto to me? Though I'm not fat, praise the Lord, I still find stays difficult to get into unaided. I hope Elizabeth will see fit to alter the fashion regarding dress, though I'd rather she didn't bring about any marriage reforms.'

Smiling as brightly as she could, she indicated the leather corsets flung onto a chair where she had taken them off the night before.

As soon as Alice left, Amy jumped out of bed and ran to the looking-glass. She did not want Pirto to see her red-eyed and woebegone, so she wiped away the tell-tale tear stains and blew her nose vigorously. As she gazed at her more cheerful reflection, she noticed once again the lump on her breast. It had first appeared some months before and she had not worried at all, for it did not hurt, and was not noticeable—even Rob had not spotted it. But now she realised that it had grown larger. Her fingers felt it cautiously, but it was nothing, just an un-explained lump. She wiggled it experimentally with her fingers. No, there was no pain at all; no sensation of discomfort, even.

When Pirto entered Amy was already in her chemise and

together the two women kept up the pretence that all was well. Pirto helped her mistress into the despised stays, and together they spent an enjoyable hour choosing the gayest and prettiest clothes in Amy's wardrobe.

'Your peach kirtle and matching bodice, with the sleeves slashed with brown velvet?' suggested Pirto. She knew that few things took a woman's mind off her problems more effectively than clothes.

'Yes, I think so. I won't wear the partlet though, the weather is quite mild enough for my chest to be exposed. Then I can wear the amber and pearl beads to best advantage. The peach kirtle shows the petticoat, does it not? Shall I wear the white taffeta one, with the lace?'

Pirto wrinkled her nose. 'Wouldn't the straw go better with peach and brown than white? You have so many elegant foreparts which fix to a plain petticoat, yet you seldom wear them.'

'Yes, I know. And you don't have to tell me the forepart will be firmly affixed to the petticoat, and that many noble ladies wear them constantly, because you've said so dozens of times before. But I have this horrid fear that the wretched thing will fall off at the most embarrassing moment, leaving me in a plain linen petticoat under all my finery, like any milkmaid.'

'Very well, wear the white. After all, if harmony of colour doesn't matter to you...' began Pirto, with exaggerated politeness.

Amy laughed. 'The straw forepart with all its fine trimmings and embroidery let it be. After all, if it does fall off my shame will only be noticed by Alice's "parcel of horrid brats", and if it stays in place I shall have the courage to wear the things more often. Now how about shoes?'

And for several weeks life went on at the same pace, with nothing happening to disturb the calm at Denchworth. Amy played with the children, spent hours getting dressed each morning, and pretended desperately that she was not waiting for Robert to call on her. She found that despite her unhappiness she could still enjoy the changes of season, rejoicing as she always used to when the spring flowers began to show through the soil and the trees pushed forth their first buds.

She had a string of horses in the Hydes' stables for her pleasure, but quite often she would borrow a fat little pony called Pudding, that belonged to the Hyde children. Together she and Pudding explored the quiet lanes. His pace suited her present frame of mind and she was light enough to present no problems to the pony.

The month was April, and she was riding along the main road to London, half conscious of a desire to go right on riding until she could see Robert with her own eyes once more, when she saw another rider approaching. It was a man she knew slightly from her days in the city, but she doubted whether he would recognise her in the sad-coloured cloak which hid her garments, with the hood pulled well forward over her face.

'Good day,' she greeted him. 'You come from London? Any news of the court?'

He pulled off his cap politely. 'Aye, I've come from court, but there's not much that's new, milady. Only the same old stories with a different wrapper. The Queen pretends to look about her for a husband, but people are saying now that she'll have Robert Dudley or no one. She is closeted with him most of the day,' he put his finger alongside his nose and winked, 'and others say most of the night also. But for myself I'd say the Queen was playing a fool's game if it were true, for the gentleman is married. I'm riding to the house where his wife stays now, with a message for her. So I must be on my way.'

Replacing his cap carefully he set off, leaving Amy sitting on the back of the stolid little pony, stunned. So this was why Alice Hyde was so determinedly cheerful, always introducing her firmly to friends from London so that they would not commit any indiscretion without realising who she was. Tucked away in the big old manor house, with the children always around, folk watched their tongues. They did not want one of the youngsters to get hold of silly gossip and confide in their dear Auntie Amy!

Riding homewards was a slow business, because Amy stopped to pick a few pale primroses and sweetly-scented violets as an excuse for her late return. It would be her reason for avoid-

166

ing the messenger if he had lingered—that she had ridden far, and was tired.

But Pudding had other ideas. He enjoyed their quiet rides, but as soon as his head faced home he began thinking with pleasure of the warm stable that awaited him, and the meal of good hot mash. He had been spoilt since Amy began riding him, for she made sure he was fed at her expense with the best of everything, and her pocket always held an apple or some sweetmeats to reward Pudding at the end of the day.

So the pony fretted at the bit, pulling it forward so that he could chew it impatiently, even trying to break into a trot. Amy, smiling at his impatience, gave him his head at last and they ambled into the yard as dusk was falling.

The groom who ran to Pudding's head said breathlessly, 'Lady Amy, we were afraid something had happened. You're later than usual and a messenger has arrived from London. He's been drinking ale in the kitchen and waiting for you.'

'I'm tired, Jenkins. I'm going to my room. Would you tell the housekeeper to inform Mrs Hyde and send Pirto to me?'

She turned to walk into the house and was arrested by a surprisingly shrill whinny from Pudding. Laughing, she turned back and gave the pony titbits she had in her pocket, then she walked quickly indoors, and went straight to her room. When Pirto came up to her she found her mistress lighting the candles with one of the tapers that stood in a box beside the fire.

Pirto began to pull the curtains across the darkened windows, saying reprovingly, 'A messenger from Sir Robert, my lady. Come all the way from London. I was sure you'd want to see him yourself, and of course you'll want to send a message back with him. Are you sure you're too tired to come downstairs? Has something occurred to vex you?'

'Don't fuss, Pirto. To tell you the truth, I met the fellow on my ride. He said something which—which upset me a little, but he told me without knowing to whom he spoke and I've no desire to embarrass the poor man. Bring the message up here if it is written; if not, tell him you have my confidence. We have no secrets from each other. Or perhaps I should say, rather, I have no secrets from you.'

Pirto coloured hotly and Amy thought guiltily that she had been unnecessarily cruel. Pirto had kept silence, after all, only to save her mistress pain. But in the long run, the pain had been harder to bear when the gossip had been told her by a stranger, so that she knew everyone but herself must know of her husband's carryings-on.

Amy watched as Pirto lingered by the door, hoping her mistress would relent. 'He'd never recognise you, milady, and he's wearing the master's new livery beneath his cloak. You'd like to see it. Ever so nice it is—blue and silver.' Then as Amy did not answer she left the room. A few minutes elapsed before she was back again, carrying a roll of parchment sealed with the familiar bear and ragged staff of the Dudleys.

'The messenger was very put out, my lady,' she said diffidently. 'It seems Sir Robert wanted to have first-hand news of you. Now that sounds nice, doesn't it?'

Amy broke the seal and said absently, but with considerable sarcasm, 'Charming!'

As she read, the room settled into silence except for the snapping of twigs on the hearth and the creak of the logs as they settled deeper into their redhot bed of ash. Nothing else stirred. Pirto stood poised, ready to take a message verbally or to send for the clerk to write a reply. Amy sat like a statue, her head bent, reading. Only the flames moved, casting long wavering shadows into the corners of the big room, illuminating Amy's fair hair and brightening the creamy parchment so that it looked gold-edged.

Suddenly Amy broke the stillness. She stood up, and walking purposefully over to the fire she pushed the parchment into the flames. She and the other woman watched as it flared up and was consumed, then Amy ground the charred fragments to fine black ash with her shoe. As an afterthought, almost, she tossed into the heart of the fire the blue and silver ribbons which had been tied round the scroll.

Pirto stirred uneasily, and Amy turned round. 'I'm sorry, Pirto, I didn't mean to keep you standing. There's no reply. You'd better go and tell the messenger so that he can get on the road back to London.'

Pirto, used to being in her mistress's confidence, went unhappily down the stairs to tell the messenger there would be no letter to take back to Sir Robert, and that he should return to London at once. The man was annoyed, saying bluntly that this was not what his master had told him to expect.

'I was given to understand that Lady Dudley would lodge me somewhere for the night, and that I'd ride tomorrow with an answer for my lord,' he said sulkily.

'This isn't Lady Dudley's house, she is merely a guest here,' Pirto rebuked him swiftly. 'I'm sorry you could not have left earlier but my mistress was out visiting friends in the neighbourhood.'

She told the lie without compunction. She was not going to have the news that her lady was pining for her husband carried back to London by this young upstart. Sir Robert must be allowed to think Lady Amy was managing very well without him.

When she went back to Amy's chamber she found her mistress already beginning to get herself ready for bed. Her long hair was unpinned and she was combing it automatically whilst she stared unseeingly at her reflection in the mirror.

'I'll do that, my lady, if you're sure you won't dine with the Hydes tonight,' Pirto told her, taking the comb from Amy's unresisting hand.

As the soothing motion began, Amy turned her eyes up to Pirto's face, and the woman saw traces of tears on the girl's cheeks.

'Pirto, tomorrow we leave this place. I've a fancy to roam around the country. I'd like to visit my mother's family, the Scotts. They live in Camberwell. I'd like to go to London, too, and do some shopping.'

'Yes, my lady?' said Pirto delicately, not entirely giving up hope of finding out the contents of the mysterious letter.

Amy smiled for the first time since she had returned from her ride, a smile of genuine amusement and understanding.

'Dear Pirto. Of course I can trust you, though I wish you had been more frank with me. It is better that I should know what is going on in London, however much it may hurt me. The messenger told me Robert is living in Elizabeth's pocket by day and maybe by night also. In his letter Robert asks me if I would prove my love for him by agreeing to a divorce, should it prove necessary. He suggested that I burn the letter, which as you will remember, I did. I sent no reply—what should I have said? I imagine—though he did not say so—that he would want to divorce me on the grounds of our being childless, and I fancy such a divorce would lead to complications if it were ever granted. Also, I feel that when a man wants to say a thing like that to his wife the least he can do is say it to her face, and not try to escape a painful scene by sending a messenger.'

Pirto could think of no words adequate to express her sympathy. Instead she asked, 'But why leave Denchworth, my lady? The Hydes are very kind, they have made us feel welcome and at home. It seems madness to go wandering the country when we can be so comfortable here.'

'Here, Pirto, it is easy to hide the truth from me. Oh, I'm not doubting they do it with the best intentions, but I've no wish to be kept in the dark about Robert's doings. If I'd known sooner what sort of idiotic goings-on were afoot in London maybe I'd have been able to prevent things reaching this disastrous stage. Moving from place to place, people won't bother to guard their words, and I'll hear gossip which folk would hide under their tongues if they knew my name.' She gave a deep sigh. 'I'm weary, Pirto. I seem to ache all over. I feel as though I've lived through a hundred years since I first spoke to that messenger.'

She glanced up at the woman's face, impassive through her efforts to hold back tears.

'Do you think, Pirto, that bruised hearts mend? Is it ever possible to forget that one's husband is unfaithful every day in thought and word, even if not as yet in actual deed? I can't believe I shall ever trust love again, or rid myself of the belief that the first eight years of our marriage were a sham. He loved me merely because I was young and easily pleased, and because I was useful to him when he was in trouble. As soon as his good days came again he realised I would be in the way, and cast me off.'

Mistress and maid, they cried together now, Amy's body shaking with such great, racking sobs that Pirto was frightened.

'My lady, don't take on so,' she begged. 'Many and many a woman has discovered that her man was unfaithful. But they've got over it, taken it as one more burden a woman has to bear. Now dry your eyes, my pretty, and get into bed. I'll bring you a bowl of hot chicken broth. You'd like that, wouldn't you? And I'll get young master Andrew to show you the drawing he made of you and Pudding setting off today— it's enough to make a cat laugh!'

Amy managed a tremulous smile and nodded her head. She let Pirto brush out her hair and undress her, then got into bed as the maid removed the warming pan. Between the sheets, waiting for the hot broth, and her young visitor, she thought she had a lot to be thankful for. This infatuation of Robert's must surely be a fleeting thing? He had never before wavered for one moment in his faithfulness to her. Surely he was more in love with the crown than with she who wore it?

Pirto came in, carefully carrying the broth, and a roll of bread in the shape of a wheatsheaf. Andrew, following with his drawing, told Amy that her little loaf had been made for him.

'But I told cook to let you have it, because you're not well,' he said magnificently.

He settled himself comfortably on the edge of the bed and prattled of his lessons and the affairs of the house whilst Amy ate, a little amusement gradually creeping into her eyes as he talked on and on. The last of the broth finished, Amy's eyelids began to droop over her eyes. Her long golden lashes gradually sank onto her cheeks and her breathing grew deep and even.

'Why is she sleeping?' Andrew asked, awed that anyone could fall asleep whilst his shrill young voice was dinning in their ears.

'Hush! I put something in her broth. She's not well, poor dear. Now come out quietly and I'll douse the candles.'

'She doesn't look ill,' Andrew objected, eyeing the still form

171

in the bed curiously. 'She looks quite well—and very beauti-ful. She's like a princess with her hair loose, isn't she, Pirto?'

'Indeed she is,' said Pirto grimly. 'But she really isn't very well, Master Andrew. She'll be better tomorrow if we leave her in peace now. Come.' And she drew him quietly from the room, dousing the candles with a wetted finger and thumb to stop them smoking.

'The firelight is still playing on her face,' Andrew pointed out. 'Won't that wake her?'

'The fire will soon die down, Master Andrew. And before I make it up, I'll draw her bedcurtains. But by then she'll be well away, all her troubles forgotten. Now come away do, young man.'

Andrew went with Pirto obediently enough but his thoughts were in a turmoil. Why did they say Auntie Amy was ill when she looked so fresh and beautiful? When his mother was ill she was pale or red. He went in to have his meal with the rest of the family, but throughout the evening his mind dwelt on the mystery.

Though he did not know it, for the rest of his life whenever anyone spoke of a beautiful woman, Andrew Hyde would get a mind-picture of Amy Dudley, lying asleep in the fourposter bed with the blue hangings embroidered with silver lovers' knots. Her face in repose had the serenity of a child, yet the deeper beauty of her womanhood was the subtle charm which bedazzled his young mind. And never would he be able to believe that anyone so beautiful could be ill or unhappy.

In the course of the evening Pirto took Alice Hyde aside to explain that though her lady wanted to move on for a while, she did not think they had better leave until Amy had become accustomed to her present unhappiness.

'It's come upon her sudden like, ma'am,' she explained. 'Somehow, despite Sir Robert's strangeness when he first visited us here, she couldn't believe that he'd ever want to cast her off. I think she was right, he doesn't *want* to cast her off now. But he's ambitious, and he is being forced to choose between the Lady Amy and a place at the Queen's side. I think she's right, too, when she says we should move around. It will help her to forget her unhappiness. But I don't want her to leave you, ma'am, until she's straightened things out in her own mind.'

'*Can* she come to terms with a thing like this?' Alice Hyde asked incredulously.

Pirto nodded, calm determination on her face. 'She's got a stout heart, for all her slight frame, ma'am. She'll learn to live with what she knows, for she'll realise there is no other choice. But I've no doubt we'll be back to trespass on your hospitality again, ma'am, for we've been very happy here with you.'

'I'll welcome you with open arms,' Mrs Hyde said sadly. 'I can't help thinking that it's partly my fault that you must leave. If I'd been more frank, told her what was going on . . .'

'I have been to blame as well, but what's done is done. Now my lady and I must learn to live with what we know, and that is easiest done amongst strangers.'

A few days later, Amy and her retinue of servants and horses left Denchworth for Camberwell.

15

He travels fastest . . .

When she left the Hydes, Amy determined to make the most of her life. After all, she was young, she had her health and strength, and even though her husband was making a mockery of their marriage it had happened to other people, and they had survived it. Furthermore, moving continually about the countryside as she did there was little chance of Robert taking her by surprise, so that she cried out with pleasure at the sight of him, before she remembered their changed relationship.

She visited friends and relatives, and found both extremely pleased to see her, entertaining her lavishly and making much of her. Slightly puzzled, Amy asked a young cousin why this was.

The girl flushed, then replied frankly. 'Well, there are many who think they'll gain your husband's approval because they have given you hospitality so that you are kept happily away from court.'

Amy tried to keep her countenance and failed miserably. She felt the flood of scarlet rise to her forehead at the humiliation. So her friends were putting themselves in Elizabeth's good books by keeping her separated from Robert!

During her journeying she had discovered much that was unknown to her before. Folk had been thrown into prison for saying the Queen was with child by Robert Dudley, whilst it was an open secret that ambassadors who came to sue for Elizabeth's hand on behalf of their masters thought Robert a very formidable opponent.

The Queen showered him with gifts of land and money. He had been granted licences for imports, had honours given him.

Young though he was, he was a member of the Queen's council. She heard tales of how he was supposed to have said openly that his wife would be no bar against his marriage to the Queen, for he could put her away privily.

To do him justice, Amy did not believe he had ever said any such thing. Whatever his faults might be—and they were many—physical cruelty had never been one of them. He might hope to divorce her, but until he told her so to her face she would simply have to wait and see how the infatuation progressed.

But her cousin's frankness did one thing—it decided Amy to go to London herself, where she might be a charge on no one. She might even see Robert, she thought, and was shocked by the quick pleasure the idea could still give her.

The small lump in her breast was growing, and at times she was uncomfortably aware that it was no unimportant thing to be lightly forgotten. She had to admit it was a source of discomfort now; not particularly acute perhaps, but worrying. And sometimes her temper was short, making her have to bite back a sharp retort to many a friendly question. Perhaps she could visit a doctor whilst she was in London and learn how to treat the thing, whatever it was.

The question that worried her most, though, was how much longer could she carry on? Would the strained situation tell not only on her temper but eventually on her reason? Others had gone mad through love; she remembered the stories she had been told as a child of Juana of Spain. The infidelities of her husband, Philip of Burgundy, whom she had loved to distraction, had led to her raving madness. At his death she would not allow his corpse to be buried but ran away with the coffin, constantly having the lid removed so that she could gaze upon his features, for in death he was utterly hers. Yet she would not allow another woman in the room with his coffin because of his unfaithfulness.

Amy shuddered. Jealousy could be a terrible thing if you allowed it to control your mind. She vowed to herself that if she ever became aware of the fearful tinge of madness she would take her own life rather than live, witless and tormented, a laughing stock at court and a cause of humiliation and despair to Robert.

So really, going to London would be a test. She and Pirto arranged to stay in their old lodgings near St Martin-in-the-Fields. Pirto suggested that Amy might go to Robert's manor at Kew, but Amy told her firmly that she had no desire for the public disgrace of being asked to leave her husband's house.

They moved quietly into their lodgings and Amy began to wander around London, picking up bits of information, gossip, and plain scandal as she went. But the planned visit to the doctor received an unexpected set-back. Pirto, sent to make an appointment with an eminent man of Amy's acquaintance, returned with the message that he would prefer not to see Lady Amy, both for his sake and her own.

Put on her mettle, Amy ordered her carriage for late in the evening, and went round to his home. The doctor was charming to her, entertaining her in his small study so that they could talk undisturbed.

'You must have heard the rumours which have been circulating since Elizabeth came to the throne, Lady Amy. I'm sure Sir Robert has no intention of poisoning you, or causing your death by any means. But if some mishap *should* befall you, or if someone wishing to implicate Sir Robert should use foul means against you, any doctor you had consulted would be suspected. Believe me, my dear, you're safer away from *all* doctors. Act always as though you are in perfect health and you are likely to remain so.'

'I see,' said Amy in a shaky voice, after a lengthy pause. 'Then to admit to illness might hasten my end—not by Robert's hand, but by someone who would gladly see him convicted of murder?'

The doctor nodded reluctantly. 'Yes. It's better that you should be warned. I'm convinced that your husband would never harm you. But he is heartily hated by many, and some would not hesitate to use any means to bring about his downfall.'

'But since I am here, might I have your opinion in confidence of the lump in my breast?' asked Amy. She hated

176

herself for the question, but felt that it had to be said.

The doctor agreed, and examined her. He looked at her with some perplexity.

'Do you suffer much pain, Lady Amy?'

'A little discomfort, sometimes. Nothing acute.'

He nodded thoughtfully. 'I think it's an abscess. If it should form and burst, you should have this poultice made up and apply it night and morning.' He scribbled his prescription on a piece of paper and Amy, considerably relieved, thanked him and left.

Next day she told Pirto what the doctor had said and they cast about them for the best solution to the problem.

'I'll have to get in touch with Robert, though it goes against the grain for me to make the first move,' Amy decided. 'Will you take a letter to the court for me, Pirto? I'll write to my sister-in-law, Lady Mary Sidney, asking her to persuade Robert to come and see us.'

'But do you think Lady Mary will help us?'

'Yes, indeed,' Amy said decidedly. 'Mary is fond of Robert, I think he is her favourite brother, but she's been kind to me as well. Never will I forget the welcome they gave us when the Dudley brothers were released from the Tower. Don't worry, Pirto. If you can see Lady Mary and give her my letter, the news will reach Sir Robert unknown to the Queen.'

The next day Pirto set off on her errand. She found it unexpectedly easy to get into the royal palace simply by showing a message with Lady Mary Sidney's name on it; and when she saw the lady and gave her the letter, Mary Sidney showed surprising concern.

'Poor little Amy, we've felt deeply for her,' she said. 'Is she well? In good spirits? I wish I could assure you that my brother means only to further his career with the Queen, but I don't suppose you'd believe me.' She smiled ruefully. 'I'm not even sure I believe it myself,' she confessed.

The letter had the result Amy had foretold. That very evening, as soon as it was dusk, Robert slipped quietly into their lodgings. Amy felt the flood of happy colour come to her face and had to force herself to stand immobile by the fireplace, instead of rushing across the room and hurling herself into her husband's arms.

For his part, Robert could only gaze at her with troubled affection. Then, suddenly, the tense face and the eyes meeting his own so steadily brought words to his lips.

'Amy, my poor love, my darling! You've suffered, I can see that. But believe me, I wouldn't harm you. If I could undo our marriage and let you go your own way to a union with a happier, less selfish man than myself I would, but I cannot. If divorce was in question it would be because Elizabeth was promised to me in marriage, and then of course you would have to bear the brunt of blame for the divorce.'

'Never mind that,' Amy said firmly, though her lips trembled. 'I asked you to call because I felt we must talk. According to . . .' She hesitated. 'According to an old friend we are both in some danger. I, because someone might try to have me killed; you, because you would be blamed for my death. We must concoct a plan to keep us both safe.'

'Amy, I beg for your understanding. Elizabeth loves me. With her favour I can rise to great heights. But I don't love her—or not in the way you and I understand love. I admire her, for her brilliant mind and sparkling wit. But often I long for your gentle understanding. Yet I am tied to Elizabeth in a way it's difficult to explain. She holds my future advancement in the palm of her hand and also, strangely, my future happiness.'

'We did not come to talk of your relationship with Elizabeth. We came to talk of protecting our lives, Robert. Why should I die in order that you may lose your reputation? And even *you* cannot want to go through life with people thinking you a wife-murderer. How shall we avoid this horrid fate?'

She smiled slightly and beckoned him to take a seat opposite her, which he did slowly, reluctant to leave the question of his relationship with the Queen without attempting further explanation.

'I suggest that we become friends, and make sure that everyone thinks we are on the best of terms,' Amy said as Robert seemed tongue-tied. 'I know this may create difficulties with Elizabeth, but she's an intelligent woman, or so you keep telling me. She'll have to accept that it's the only way to save your reputation—and possibly hers as well. I think you should call on me regularly and spend some days with me. As it is, you pay for all my entertainments. If you stay with me it will be difficult for people to say that we are utterly estranged.'

'But where will you live? London is out of the question— too close—and it would be difficult, if not impossible, for me to visit you on one of our Norfolk estates. Elizabeth is unreasonably jealous and wants me within a few hours' ride of her.'

Amy nodded curtly. 'I understand. I thought that I'd live with Alice Hyde for a while. Then pehaps I could share a house with a widow or someone else in need of companionship, as I am.'

Robert's face brightened. 'I know the very thing! You remember Forster? He's my treasurer—a fine fellow. Well, he's buying a place in Berkshire for his wife to live with her friend Mrs Odingsells. Actually the place belongs to Dr Owen—his father was one of Edward's physicians. The doctor doesn't live there now, though his wife does.' He looked self-conscious. 'They're separated. Would you like to live there, Amy? Three women companions for you, and though the house is not spacious, I believe it to be comfortable and well appointed, with pleasant grounds.'

'It sounds ideal, especially for your purpose,' said Amy a trifle sarcastically. 'I'd be well chaperoned and no doubt you'd find a good reason for not sharing my bed. Didn't you say it wasn't a large dwelling? Then Pirto would probably have to have a truckle bed in my room. That would be cause enough.'

'You're right,' said Robert thoughtfully, unconscious of any sting in the remark. 'But that reminds me, Amy, I've heard rumours that you've a lump on your breast. My poor girl, your troubles certainly don't come singly, do they? Is it bad? Do you suffer much pain?'

'It isn't bad, and I'll thank you not to go talking about it,' said Amy sharply. 'I'm afraid, dear Robert, that it's unlikely to cause my death in the near future, if that's why you enquire so solicitously.'

Robert stood up, his brow darkening. "I'm sorry you think me so callous. I was genuinely concerned. But don't worry, I'll not talk of it. Goodnight.'

Amy saw him go, her impassive demeanour hiding wild inner grief. But she comforted herself with the thought that he had promised to visit her at the Hydes', and later at Forster's house, if she should decide to live there.

She spent a few more days in London, doing essential shopping, buying enough materials and trimmings to last her for years, Pirto told her laughingly. Then the carriages were loaded, her escort of a dozen mounted men in Robert's livery arrived, and she herself was tossed into the saddle.

'Won't you ride in the coach, my lady?' Pirto suggested. But Amy shook her head. She was heavy-eyed after a sleepless night, but she thought that she would rather have the clean air in her face than be cooped up in the coach, which managed to be both stuffy and cold, whilst the heavily rutted roads jarred the vehicle with every turn of the wheels.

Her arrival at Denchworth was in the nature of a Roman triumph. The children came shouting out of the house, Alice stood beaming on the front steps, and the servants all had a smile for Lady Amy, who had endeared herself to them by her few demands and by the largesse bestowed on them at her departure.

'Come into the sitting-room, my dear,' said Alice. 'Pirto, you can manage the bestowal of your mistress's luggage, can you not? There, now you may be easy.'

She pressed Amy gently into a softly-cushioned chair and eyed her keenly. The girl I first met has gone, were her first thoughts. She's so fine-drawn, and her eyes no longer shine with candour and merriment. They hide secrets, and look inward to sad thoughts.

Then Amy said gratefully, 'Oh, Alice, a comfortable chair, this pleasant room, and best of all, *you* to talk to! What more could I ask at the end of a journey? Tell me, how have you been whilst I've spent my time gadding about the country and buying up all the goods in the London shops? How are the children, my dear? And my best boy, Andrew?'

As she told Amy how the children were progressing at their games and lessons Mrs Hyde wondered whether she had been mistaken. Amy seemed as vivacious and happy as ever. Then she noticed her friend's eyes: even when brimming with laughter they had a look of watchfulness.

She's acting! she realised with sudden compassion. Poor little thing; yet how brave she is. Most girls who had been reared the spoilt only child of doting parents, as Amy had, would have bemoaned their fate, not caring how bad an impression they made on their hearers. But Amy had courage and self-respect, and Alice thought that whatever Robert might do, his wife would never find it in her heart to condemn him utterly.

So she did not mother her guest as she longed to, but asked her about the shopping in London, and how she had occupied her time whilst she was touring the countryside.

Amy answered freely and at last, blushing faintly, told Alice that she and Robert had come to an understanding.

'He will visit me and though we may no longer live as man and wife, we shall be good friends,' she said, with all the placidity she could muster. 'I've come to terms with it, Alice, as Robert has had to do. You see, I was wrong about him really, all along. I thought he had escaped the overmastering drive that led his father and grandfather to their ruin—ambition. It seems I was mistaken. I was everything to him until I got between him and advancement: for Elizabeth will only advance those who lie at her feet. I've had to choose whether I wanted to make life intolerable for Robert by trying to insist that we live together, or whether to accept this compromise. And really, it's no choice. He may not love the Queen, but he is fascinated by her. So we're going to be friends.'

'Well, it's your life,' Alice said, shrugging. 'But wouldn't it be best, Amy, if you divorced Robert and re-married? You're young and pretty, any man would be glad to take you for his wife.'

'I've had nearly eight years of Robert's love,' said Amy

181

simply. 'I don't believe I could ever live with a lesser man, and I certainly couldn't try to start a divorce before the Queen is ready for it. It's not as though I loved anyone else—I don't. There was a man I might have loved; but I think Robert spoils a woman for loving others.' She was silent for a moment, staring very hard at her hands lying in her lap, and Alice thought she was fighting back tears. 'I believe it has happened to Elizabeth, too,' she said at last. 'She's probably been fond of him for years, but now that she's had him with her constantly she has discovered that she loves him. Any woman would,' she finished, with complete conviction that Alice Hyde found very endearing.

'Well, no need to worry about it yet,' Alice said placidly, offering her friend a plate of little cakes. 'You may meet someone else you can love as you've never dreamed, and then it won't seem so impossible to upset Robert and the Queen, believe me.'

Amy, chuckling, helped herself to a cake and bit into it. 'If I loved another, what do you suppose Elizabeth would do to him if I tried to discredit her Robert in the eyes of the world? No, Robert made it plain he would free me when the Queen tells him she'll marry him. I wonder what the cause will be? Desertion, cruelty, adultery? It will be difficult to say I deserted him, and I rarely meet any men apart from my servants. And who would believe I could give Robert a beating? He's twice my size!'

'Don't, Amy,' said Alice involuntarily, but Amy told her that if she did not laugh about it she would probably cry and that would not help anyone.

So the young woman settled down in her room at Denchworth once more, sharing the lives of the happy, active Hydes, but with their instant understanding and sympathy when she felt that she would like to be alone.

Now that she and Robert had come to an understanding, Amy felt that life would become bearable once more; one day, perhaps, even enjoyable. She quickly fell into the ways of the household, helping Alice when she could, teaching the younger children their letters, wandering the quiet country lanes and visiting the beautiful old university town of Oxford.

Robert's first visit went off very well indeed. When in the company of the Hydes he behaved like an affectionate husband who wanted to see that all was well with his wife. He entered into their amusements, played with the children, talked freely to Amy. As she had foretold, when they were together riding in the countryside people they passed smiled and nodded, evidently taking it for granted that they were just another attractive young couple, enjoying each other's company.

For Robert, thought Amy, it was easy enough. He was fond of her, but she began to realise that he had a coolness in his nature that she lacked. For him, the snatches of time away from the court were a relaxation, a time when he could be himself. He did not have to court Amy, as he once told her he had to court Elizabeth. He did not have to be on his guard against others, in case someone else took an interest in Amy. He certainly never had to exert himself to make her jealous.

But for Amy, that first visit was a little foretaste of the mixture of heaven and hell that she would always know now in her husband's company. Like a child starved of affection, she cherished his every smile and kind word. But she was a woman; kind words were not enough. She longed desperately to be loved in return—to be desired even. She wore her prettiest gowns, though she had to keep her breasts covered, for the lump sometimes seemed about to burst, and she kept hopefully thinking that it would go. But it did not go, and Robert did not desire her. Ambition had a tighter hold on him than normal male feelings, evidently.

She endured two such visits, spending the days friendly and easy, the nights letting the tears soak unchecked into her pillow. Then she told Alice that she thought she would go into Norfolk for a short time.

'I long for my home,' she confessed. 'It would be impossible for me to live there, of course. It would be too far for Robert to visit, and there would be no suitable chaperon to quieten the Queen's fears that I might seduce her lover.' She laughed a trifle shrilly. 'I'll be gone some weeks, I may visit friends on my way back and shall certainly spend a week or so in London.'

'Have a good time, my dear, and forget your worries for a while,' Alice urged her friend.

'Why does everyone urge me to forget?' mused Amy aloud to Pirto as the coach wended its way towards Syderstone. 'They must know that though I would like to, I cannot. I hear my husband's conduct joked about in taverns and mocked in open market places. I hear people thanking God that I'm in good health, so that the Queen yearns for her horse-master in vain.' She pressed her hands to her hot cheeks. 'Oh God, what would I give for a liberal dose of forgetfulness,' she said warmly.

'You'll not forget whilst you let yourself remain fond,' Pirto said discouragingly. 'You should spend more time remembering how he neglects you than in recalling the days when he was your true lover.'

'Don't be a goose, Pirto,' Amy said sharply. 'The whole purpose of our reconciliation is to appear on the best of terms. If I was forever reminding myself of his sins it would be extremely difficult to appear civil, let alone affectionate.'

She saw Pirto colour and drop her gaze and was immediately ashamed of her brusque retort. 'I'm sorry, Pirto, I shouldn't have spoken like that. I'll admit to you, my dear friend, that I'm having a bad day with that wretched pain. That's why I consented to ride in the coach.'

Pirto was immediately concerned, and for the rest of the journey she talked of nothing but getting Amy to bed at a good tavern in Bletchley. 'I'll make up the poultice the good doctor advised us to use, and hot compresses to help the abscess to burst,' she said. 'And the landlord shall bring you a light meal that will tempt your appetite, and some mulled wine.'

Amy let her chatter on whilst her own thoughts strayed. She thought impatiently that the abscess was just a small annoyance to add to all the others. It could not possibly be responsible for the other pains. They did not come often, but when they came, she was on the rack. To move seemed impossible, yet she did it. She learned that on her bad days, she was wiser not to go downstairs with the Hydes. She seemed especially vulnerable then. The sight of a happy toddler stabbed her with the deep desperate hurt of a woman who knows she will never bear a child. Jogging along in the coach, she wondered when she had first allowed that thought to take root: never to bear a child; never to feel within her body the first faint flutterings of life that became bolder as the babe grew; never to know the triumphant, sweating, searing, bloody business of labour; never to hold close in her arms the tiny, palpitating, vulnerable creature which is a baby of one's own.

Yet though she now accepted the fact that she would be childless the knowledge was no easier to bear. On the contrary, it seemed to add an extra bitterness to her thoughts to know that she would cherish only the love of her parents and the transient sweetness of one man. Never would she know the maternal love she yearned to give, nor would she receive love from another man.

The second thought coming so naturally on the heels of the first gave her quite a shock. Never? Why should she assume that no man would ever love her again? Was she repulsive, then? Had the hurt within become visible on her face, like a hideous grimace? Yet even as she reasoned with herself, her logical brain was accepting and assimilating. She would know the warm affection of friends, the almost motherly love given by the faithful Pirto. But there would be nothing more.

The sides of the coach seemed to close about her, shutting her in with her painful, relentless thoughts. No brotherly love? she thought with panic. And, sighing, had to admit that Arthur, though he was carelessly fond of her, still harboured resentment against her because their father had loved his only daughter so much more than his profligate son. John had found her a nuisance as a child, and would now find her an embarrassment to a man who meant to get on in the world. Her half-sisters frequently said she was spoilt, and grudged her the 'good marriage' they believed her to have made. No love lost there.

But surely, somewhere, there must be a man who would love me, she thought. Even as she tried desperately to banish her fears of loneliness, a slow, dragging ache from her shoulder blades to the base of her spine brought out a light sheen of sweat on her face.

The pain? But surely—that was a thing to be endured? Something that came and went, leaving her free often. Surely it would not interfere with her life to any great extent? She tried to banish the knowledge that the pain, whatever it was, came more often now than it had a year ago. She remembered telling the doctor the pain was never really acute. Could she repeat that remark truthfully now?

She remembered a joke Robert had told her about Thomas Seymour, King Edward's Admiral uncle. He had given his nephew presents, money and affection. When he was telling Robert, he had joked, 'I cast my bread upon the waters, as the good Lord bids us, and what did I get back? Wet bread!'

She had laughed with Robert at the time, though she had felt guilty at doing so. For Tom Seymour's nephew had shown more than mere ingratitude. When he had signed his Uncle Tom's death warrant, the young King had proved how useless his uncle's generosity had been. With the executioner ready to carry out his task, 'wet bread' could be translated to mean 'no head'. Nothing for anyone to laugh about.

And her own bread, that she had cast so generously at Robert's feet? Ah, all that would be forgotten, now. She shook her head irritably, not wanting to think, and the pain clawed at her back like a tiger, making her gasp.

She felt the automatic resistance begin in her body: the tightening of muscles, clenching of fists and the breath held in her throat, as though by such puny efforts she could expel the pain. She began to consciously relax, uncurling her fingers one by one, breathing deeply and evenly, and the pain receded into the long throbbing surges that heralded the end of an attack.

'I need acceptance, Pirto,' she said unsteadily, opening her eyes and trying to smile at her maid's strained face. 'I must learn to accept things as they are, and not fight or rail against fate.'

'You don't, my lady. Oh, I know you may shed a few tears

186

in your own room, and sometimes you answer at random when your thoughts are with Sir Robert, but only those nearest you would know the hurt he gives you.'

Amy glanced at her mildly, seeming not to have heard. 'I must be thankful that I have been much beloved,' she said. 'I must accept with true joy the things that I have. I must not fret or worry over things I shall never possess.'

'Don't say such things, my lady. You sound as though you expect to die tomorrow! You're young, there may be another love for you yet—yes, *and* children, which it's my belief you would have borne in abundance had you married any other man than Sir Robert.'

'I'm afraid of death, or at any rate, afraid of dying. And I would have loved to bear children. But remember, Pirto, acceptance of one's lot is a virtue. If I am fortunate then I shall be happier because I've had small expectations of fortune.'

Pirto glanced at her mistress, distressed. It was not like Lady Amy to suddenly start talking in this morbid fashion. She wondered with a pang of superstitious fear whether her mistress had been given some warning of impending disaster. But the coach was entering Bletchley and Amy was leaning forward and smiling with pleasure as each remembered landmark was passed. In the bustle that ensued as the coach drew up at the tavern of their choice, Pirto forgot her fears. She hustled Amy up to the best bedchamber and helped her into bed with swift but gentle efficiency. Then she went downstairs to bully the landlord into allowing her to make up the doctor's poultice for her mistress whilst dinner was prepared.

They reached Syderstone after a long and tiring coach ride. But as soon as they came within sight of the mellow stone walls Amy thought that her journey had been worthwhile. Here, her only memories would be happy ones. Memories of days spent quietly with her father, learning how to run a sheep farm. Of their shared trips to Wells, and their guilty enjoyment of the salt marshes.

Here she had been happiest with Robert. The ordeal of the

187

Tower over, they had felt their love had been tested and not found wanting. In these pleasantly familiar pastures they had walked and talked together, and Robert had not been restless for court life, but content with his lot. He had even tried to buy Fitcham so that they might settle permanently in Norfolk.

But inside the house, having greeted the servants and her agent, Amy realised how much she missed her parents. Her mother had never been fond of Syderstone. Nevertheless she had lived here during the most formative years of Amy's young life. She had taught Amy the names of the flowers that she tended. Together they had made pot-pourri from the heavily scented roses; together picked the firm ripe peaches from the trees trained against the walls.

Her father's presence she felt strongest of all; indeed, when she sat down at his desk by the window of the little study she could almost feel him beside her. As she walked round the house she felt he went with her, a benign ghost, enjoying the air of bustle and activity that the dust-shrouded rooms had missed for so long.

And yet, contrary to her expectations, Amy did not make a lengthy visit. Syderstone proved too full of happy events gone by which could never come again. The very air seemed crowded with spirits—herself as a little girl, herself as a young woman, a wife; and that other Robert who had loved her once. They were all here, and she found her memories unbearable. She was conscientious, however, and did the work expected of her by Mr Flowerdew, her agent. Then she and her retinue set off once more towards Denchworth.

Her return coincided with one of Robert's visits, during the course of which he told her that if she would like it, she could move into Cumnor Place at any time.

'I'll visit you there as I have done here,' he promised. 'Come, Amy, look pleased! Alice Hyde is a good, kind woman, but taken up with her children and household. And she'll be more so in future, for I see she's pregnant again. At Cumnor, with three other fashionable ladies living in the house, you'll find much more to occupy you. Games, hunting, dressmaking—all are easier when there are no children to tie the wife down.'

'Yes, I'll probably be better without the children round me,' admitted Amy. 'I am beginning to find their presence rather a mixed blessing. I find myself wishing for the moon instead of being content with what I have.'

Robert looked embarrassed. 'Perhaps one day you'll be a mother, Amy,' he said with deceptive casualness. 'The Queen grows fond—mighty fond. Sometimes I wonder whether she might overcome her scruples if I told her she must wed me or I would leave the court for ever; then I could put divorce proceedings in hand.'

Amy was silent, a little smile hovering round her mouth. How completely devoid of tact this man was! And how blind! He had cast aside his love for her as soon as it became expedient to do so; it never occurred to him that despite herself, despite the way he treated her, she could still cherish him in her heart. He would not think that talk of divorce would fill her with despair, because then even the sight of him would be denied her.

Looking at him, admitting him to be cold, self-centred, calculating and unimaginative, she had to admit that she loved him still.

16

Cumnor Place

Amy was sitting in the pleasant garden at Cumnor, embroidering a little shirt for the latest addition to the Hyde family, a small boy only a week old. Around her, all occupied with tasks that would keep them out of the house and in the pleasant summer sunshine, were her companions. Amy eyed them covertly over her work. The three months she had spent in their company had told her a great deal about the lives and character of each.

Mrs Forster was a comfortable woman, both in mind and body. She was plump and placid, rarely saying a bad word about anyone. Yet Amy knew that before she reached her present haven of acceptance, Anne Forster had given birth to over a dozen still-born children. Sometimes she thought their shared sorrow was the reason Anthony and Anne Forster were such a loving couple. They had seen all their children born dead, gone through the agony of pregnancy after pregnancy, all of which had ended with dreadful suddenness, in miscarriage or still-birth. Amy did not think Anne could have been good-looking, even when she was young, but she had a sweet face, and her hair was still pretty; a bright brown, very shiny and slippery, so that it was continually escaping from the dozens of pins Anne used to keep it in place. So wisps of hair marred all attempts—spasmodic though they were—to achieve a neat and stylish appearance.

Mrs Owen was the complete opposite, both in looks and character, of her friend. She was thin and neat with beady inquisitive eyes. Her tongue was sharp, and her disposition acid, but she never pried into Amy's affairs; principally, Amy

190

guessed, because of her own separation from her husband. She looked barren, as indeed she was, Amy thought with a certain satisfaction. She could *not* like Doll Owen. The other woman's narrow shoulders and flat chest made Amy feel positively buxom.

For Mrs Odingsells Amy felt the most affection. She was a younger sister of Alice Hyde, but she bore little resemblance to that friendly, forthcoming creature. She was a widow, childless as they all were, a year or two older than Amy herself. But unlike Mrs Forster and Mrs Owen, Edith Odingsells talked very little about her past life. She was an attractive person, considerably more intelligent than either of the other women, and Amy had soon discovered that Edith shared her own sense of humour, so that they often looked over their companions' heads into each other's eyes, and shared a quiet joke. But more than that, even after so many weeks of each other's company, Amy had been unable to discover. Edith was not on the lookout for another husband, that was clear, both from her demeanour when Robert and his friends came calling, and from the place she had chosen to live. Amy sometimes amused herself by gazing curiously at Edith's profile and wondering whether her marriage had been so happy that she could not bear the thought of uniting herself with another; or so unhappy that she could not consider marriage with anything but distaste. At least, she thought ruefully, it kept her mind off her own troubles.

Robert was visiting her with a fair degree of constancy, helped of course by the fact that Anthony Forster also wanted to visit his wife regularly. Usually the two men brought other friends with them from the court, and they all made themselves agreeable, Robert exerting his considerable charm on his wife's companions, so that they thought her a most fortunate woman.

Of course, Amy knew they must speculate a little as to why she lived with them and not on one of Robert's estates. But her explanation of the convenience of living within easy reach of London, and with Mrs Forster too, so that Robert and Anthony could visit them together, satisfied the ladies' curiosity—or seemed to.

They knew, of course, that Robert's estates were mainly in Norfolk, and with Amy careful to visit London between Robert's trips to Cumnor Place, she hoped devoutly that a picture was being presented of a normal, loving couple.

Amy wondered idly what Edith *really* thought of her. She showed Amy the same cool friendliness that she used towards the other women. It was she who had marked the little shirt Amy was smocking with a complicated series of dots, so that Amy's unhandy needle might make a pretty pattern, but she had done it so much as a matter of course that Amy's thanks seemed unnecessary.

Now she sat reading a book, apparently completely enthralled by the words on the page before her. Amy wished she would read out loud: it would be a nice gesture and it would also put a stop to the continual chattering going on between Anne and Dorothy.

Mrs Owen was attacking her needlework as though it was a personal foe, so fiercely and quickly did her needle stab in and out of the taffeta, but it did not stop her tongue from wagging. Mrs Forster, painstakingly shelling peas, her hair falling across her unbecomingly flushed face, was glad to talk whilst she doggedly persisted with her boring task.

I need not listen, Amy told herself. I should concentrate on getting this shirt finished whilst I am feeling well enough to work. But it was impossible not to listen. They were talking about the various marriages the Queen might make. A *royal* match it must and would be, they declared. They were discussing with deepest interest what they would wear if such a wedding took place. Something eye-catching, they agreed.

'This kirtle, when it's finished, will catch most eyes!' cried Dorothy, proudly flourishing the taffeta on which she was working. Amy blinked and bit back a chuckle. The taffeta would indeed catch the eye, being the most vivid colour one could imagine—a really disastrous shade of green. However, Dorothy was unaware that anyone could find the colour gaudy. 'It's to be worn with a white under-dress, and that will be lifted to show a glimpse of scarlet petticoat. The partlet will

192

be white also—embroidered with pearl beads, I believe. A well-boned bodice of matching taffeta and sleeves slashed to show my best lawn chemise. Green and white, you see? The Tudor colours!' She looked round for their appreciation, but Mrs Odingsells was absorbed in her book and Amy was frowning over her smocking. She dared not look up, actually, for fear of catching Edith's eye. A white partlet and well-boned bodice, indeed! The partlet was normally worn to hide the breasts; the bodice was stiff so that the breasts would show round and full by contrast. But Dorothy had no breasts to speak of, thought Amy, so why bother with bones and partlets?

Then the very idea of that sallow, wrinkled neck and rather ferrety face rising out of a gown of white and brilliant green was rather awful. Poor Dorothy, it was about time someone gave her a lecture on colours and fashion. She should *never* wear white close to her face, it made her complexion look worse. And it would be a brave soul who wore that particular shade of green, too. Amy thought with another inward chuckle that Dorothy had put her finger on it when she said the dress would be eye-catching. So it would indeed—but not the wearer.

Anne Forster looked round and realised that no one had admired Dorothy's work. Always eager to please, she gasped with pretended admiration and raised her hands. 'My dear, it's . . .' she began. The corner of her elbow caught the edge of the bowl, and peas, pods and basin were scattered in the grass at her feet, whilst she scrambled ineffectually to pick them up, uttering small murmurs of distress.

Amy gladly threw down her work and knelt on the grass, teasing Anne for her clumsiness, her voice warm with affection. Edith put down her book and joined them and Dorothy felt herself obliged to lay down her half-made gown and help to repair the damage she had inadvertently caused. However, she snatched so crossly at the spilt vegetables that she knocked the bowl over again, spilling the peas the others had just picked up and bringing a cry of anguish from Anne Forster.

'Doll, how could you?' she said reproachfully. 'Oh, it's so difficult to see peas in the long grass, why didn't God make

193

them a nice bright red whilst he was about it?'

'Because you would give us roast beef and strawberries by mistake,' teased Amy, picking peas deftly from amongst the grass.

'Really, Anne, I *wish* you wouldn't call me by that common name! If Dorothy was good enough for my parents I should have thought you might have found it good enough for you,' said Mrs Owen tartly, a scarlet spot appearing in the centre of each thin cheek.

Poor Anne, doubly distressed, began to apologise, fumbling with the wisps of hair which kept getting in her eyes, trying to push them under her cap whilst Amy and Edith gathered the erring peas quickly and neatly and replaced them in the bowl.

It was there that Robert and Anthony found them, and all unknowing thought how happy they looked and what a pretty picture they made. Robert had grown used to Amy's slimness, and her pallor. He could admire her for the rich gold of her hair and the deep blue of her eyes, thinking that his wife was still the prettiest woman he knew, even when he came upon her unexpectedly like this, kneeling on the grass searching for something.

'My ladies?' Robert said. They turned towards him, the laughter dying from their faces to be replaced by admiration. He went and helped Amy to her feet, saying laughingly, 'How nice when a woman falls on her knees at the approach of her husband! And your friends do me the same courtesy. Tony, we are much to be envied.'

Anthony Forster kissed his plump wife on the cheek, saying heartily, 'Annie, what have you done now? You look hot and harassed, my dear. Why bother yourself with household matters when you have a large staff of servants to work for you?'

'I *like* keeping house,' his wife told him indignantly. 'You'd not be best pleased if you found me mending your shirts or making you hose, I know, but keep house I can and will.'

'If I catch you mending a shirt or meddling with any of my clothes, I'll beat you,' Tony threatened, laughing boisterously. 'For if there's one thing you cannot do, Annie, it's ply your needle to any good affect.'

He kissed her again, and Robert, remembering that Amy stood within the circle of his arm under the eyes of the other ladies, kissed the top of her head hastily, so that he should not appear remiss.

'It's a glorious day, Robert, I hope you're not too tired from the ride?' said Amy gently. Inside her head she was thanking God for making it one of her good days. Today she felt well and cheerful and would not have to fight a desire to quarrel with Robert, or indeed with anyone.

As the summer wore on, she had found prayer more and more essential to her. She usually knew of Robert's coming some days before his arrival and those days were spent in praying devoutly that the pain might come now—now, or when he left. Any time but when he was in the house and could not fail to see her anguish.

Sometimes her prayers were answered, sometimes not. But Amy discovered that with so much taken from her, she seemed to have found an inner strength that must be God-given. It enabled her to dissemble as she had never done in her life before, pretending health and comfort and good humour when inside the pain ripped and pulled, and her mind was dark. Then, it was the most difficult thing in the world not to show the bad temper and irritation, which seemed the only outlet for the pain. When Robert was not present and she had a bad day she tried to spend much of it in her own part of the house. But the house was small and privacy difficult to find. So even before the other women she sometimes had to act the part of an even-tempered and contented person.

It was becoming more difficult though, she admitted to herself. She put it down to the hot weather, which made the pain harder to fight. The result, she knew, was that the other women sometimes found her odd, and probably thought that reason enough for her to choose to live away from Robert for much of the time. Yet in Robert's presence her desire to please was so urgent that she could force the pain to the uttermost recesses of her mind, to be dealt with later, almost. She knew that it must seem strange to the other women that she was always at her best with her husband, yet chose to remain away

195

from him for long periods. But time, she thought bitterly, will probably tell them what they do not as yet understand. After all, she could not hope to keep her secret for ever, even though Anne and Dorothy visited London rarely, an Edith, never.

'Shall we leave the ladies, Tony?' asked Robert. 'We'll go into the house and freshen up after our ride, and then come out into the garden again. It's delightful out here; the scent of the flowers after the stink of hot horseflesh is very welcome.'

They were turning away when Anthony Forster saw the little shirt flung down on the grass, the needle still stuck in the coarse cotton material.

'Why, Annie, I know too well *that* is none of your work,' he said, pointing. 'So who should we congratulate, eh? Which of these lovely ladies hides a secret under her apron?'

It would have been hard to say which of the party was most embarrassed. Dorothy Owen froze into rigid disapproval. Edith Odingsells remained expressionless but suddenly arrested in mid-motion. The Forsters both went scarlet as they realised the hideous ineptitude of the remark. But Robert Dudley's face looked as though it had been turned to granite, and Amy's eyes filled with tears, though they did not spill down her pale cheeks.

Edith Odingsells was the first to regain her composure. She completed the movement of settling herself in her chair, picked up her book, and said evenly, 'Why, who but my sister, Alice Hyde? She has enough children, has she not? But nevertheless she gave birth to a fine boy a week ago. Hadn't you heard? We have been making her a few useful garments and Lady Amy is smocking a shirt. Won't you go in now, to freshen up?'

The men turned and made for the house, both of them looking remarkably like whipped dogs. Amy sat down, suddenly aware that her legs were trembling. What a terrible moment it must have been for Robert, she thought. No wonder he had stood like a statue—and no wonder he had fled so willingly!

The reason for his lack of composure was that the last time he had visited her, his natural desires had proved too much for his own iron will. He had gone into her room for a quiet talk

196

since Tony Forster had taken himself off early to bed with his good Anne.

Somewhat to his initial embarrassment Pirto had not been there. Amy had suffered patiently through a bad day and when in the evening the pain miraculously left her, she had bidden Pirto spend an evening with her friends in Oxford, as a reward for her constant hovering presence throughout the long, difficult hours. Pirto, who was indeed anxious to spend some time with her friends, had allowed herself to be persuaded. She brushed out her mistress's hair, helped her into the warmed bed with its lavender scented sheets, and left her with a book and a candle by the bedside, which Amy could snuff when she felt sleep overtaking her.

Amy had looked up from her book when the door opened, expecting slightly impatiently that Pirto had returned to remind her to pull the curtains round the bed so that she should not be woken by the early morning sunshine. Instead, Robert's dark eyes looked into her blue ones.

Startled, and embarrassed as much by his unease as her own, she had pulled up the sheet protectively so that even her creamy shoulders were hidden from view. She had no intention of letting him see her breast with the abscess, ugly and livid, marring the gentle curves of her body.

But the long months of siege on Elizabeth, the months of living the life of a monk whilst at court under the Queen's eye, and of not daring to touch his wife for fear she might quicken with child, burned in his mind and now his body like a red-hot brand. Then his ownership of the slight girl in the bed before him was questioned by her small action. She had dared—*dared*—to try to hide from him who owned it in the sight of God the beauty and desirability of her body.

His very masculinity cried out at the insult. What he wished to see, he would see. He might not possess her, but when he desired to look upon her beauty nothing on earth would stop him.

He took two strides across to the bed and jerked back the bedclothes savagely. Amy gave a startled squeak and instinctively tried to cover the abscess from his hot, searching eyes.

But Robert did not notice any imperfection. He saw only the delicious familiarity of her slim, naked body, and the wide blue eyes raised to his with a startled question in their depths. The next moment he was pulling off his clothes, and as his jerkin was hurled impatiently away it knocked over the candle, leaving them with the last small picture of the other. She could see his intention plain on his face, and in her eyes he saw the dawning of the desire which already consumed him.

So Robert coupled with no unwilling woman, there in the big bed in Cumnor Place. In the darkness restraint was forgotten. Two passionate people had been chaste against their natures and desires for too long.

'Might as well be hung for a sheep as for a lamb,' Robert said as they lay quiet at last, and he got up and bolted the door. The rest of the night was spent in love-making, all the more perfect because it was so completely unexpected—a gift from the gods. Amy had not even mourned when she felt him slip out of bed and fumble for his clothes in the grey light of dawn. It had to be like this, she thought. She had watched him dressing rather slowly, fumbling with his buttons and laces. Under heavy lids, her eyes smiled at him with an almost comradely understanding, and he had smiled back. Then, with his appetite sated, he had tiptoed in his stockinged feet across to the door, and slipped out, shutting it quietly behind him. It came to her then that they had scarcely exchanged a word, all through the night. The old familiarity of touch and response had come back to them so easily that they had needed no words. When Amy had got out of bed and summoned Pirto's nervous replacement from her usual morning task of clearing the rushes, the girl had suspected nothing. She had told Amy, quite chattily as she inexpertly brushed her mistress's hair, that Sir Robert and the other gentlemen had left.

'I expect they had important business at court, milady,' she said, trying anxiously to roll the long shiny hair into the sort of knot that Pirto had said was so simple.

'Yes, my husband likes to make an early start when he has a busy day ahead of him,' Amy said serenely.

And now here he was again, only three weeks since that last, memorable visit! Poor Robert, she thought. He really believes that one night of love could set me making baby-clothes! She was unable to stifle a smile and looking up, caught Mrs Odingsells smiling also.

'Their faces!' Amy said softly. The two older women were once more in animated conversation over court matters. They hoped to learn more now that they had visitors, they told each other archly.

'I thought I'd die of embarrassment,' admitted Mrs Odingsells, her voice low. 'But my dear, Mr Forster meant no harm—none in the world. He knows all our circumstances—goodness knows, his own wife has suffered so—and had he thought even a little before he spoke he never would have said what he did!'

'Does he know *your* circumstances?' said Amy quietly. 'He knows more than I do, then.'

Mrs Odingsells laughed. 'Well, let us say he knows me to be a virtuous widow! Scarcely the person to accuse of "hiding a secret under her apron". I suppose you were the only person not too badly embarrassed, though I realise you would like to have children, and may well do so. But I *would* like to speak to you. Perhaps I might come to your room one evening and we could talk privately.'

Amy was intrigued, though she realised that it would mean in return for Edith Odingsells' confidences, she would have to tell her own story. But perhaps it would be a relief to be able to confide in this intelligent, humorous woman.

When the men returned Amy managed to catch Robert's eye and give him a smile, accompanied by a tiny shake of the head. He caught her meaning and relaxed completely, making her very happy by the way he set himself out to entertain the company with tales of court life.

They went indoors to eat and afterwards they played cards and laughed together whilst the candles flickered and sent strange shadows across the walls, whose homely panels were covered by rich tapestries, all of them contributed by the ladies who shared the house.

'Shall we ride out tomorrow, my love?' Robert asked her

before they went to their rooms. Amy swept a curtsey, twinkling up at him. She knew he wanted to ask her the all-important question and hear the answer from her own lips, 'No, I'm not pregnant.'

As Pirto was putting her to bed Amy wondered whether to tell Robert the truth the next day—that she did not know her condition herself, it was far too soon. But she decided it was a needless cruelty. It would be ridiculous if she conceived now, when she had lost his love and he had taken her from sheer lust. Besides, she had always thought that there was some fault in John Dudley's sons that they could father no children, and she suspected Robert felt it too. For both their sakes she should not desire a child he would wish to repudiate.

So when they rode out next day through the lanes, with the white dust of summer rising around their horses' feet, she told him with composure that she was sure she would have no child. Relieved, Robert grew quite communicative about the Queen, and his life at court.

After a lengthy grumble about being made to feel like a pet lapdog on a short leash, he said suddenly, 'Mind you, though she will not definitely say she wants to marry me, she has said very definitely indeed that though she may not enjoy me, neither may I enjoy my wife. She would not object, I think, if I took myself a mistress to satisfy my carnal desires, but she wants all my love.'

Amy was silent, horrified at her own pain when she thought of him bedding with some fresh young maid of honour, when she needed him so badly. Then she suddenly felt that she hated Elizabeth, for making her wild, bold Rob into this vain courtier, who had not dared to let the Queen know he had slept once in nearly two years with his own wife.

The weather was hot, and somehow her quick retort had all the sharpness of a whiplash.

'What would the Queen say if I *did* have your child, Robert? Would it be so terrible if she found you still had a little willpower of your own left?'

Robert's face was already streaked with sweat but it reddened at the implied criticism.

'I follow my own road, my lady,' he said stiffly. 'If you should find yourself with child who would dream that it could be mine? Everyone thinks that Pirto always shares your room and I'll wager you haven't told her what occurred whilst she was in Oxford. If you think I'd not be believed, you forget the power of my purse. I'm sure there are ardent young fellows in your retinue who would like to bed you—and would swear they had done so to gain both your body and a handsome sum of money from me.'

The complete lack of compunction he showed struck cold into Amy's heart. She gazed up at him, speechless.

Misinterpreting her silence, Robert said cruelly, 'What is more, Amy, you showed such passionate ardour during the night we spent together, that it would be a kindness in me to find you a lover. You might pretend annoyance to find one of your menservants in your bed, but you'd soon be singing a different tune, my pretty.'

'But—but why should you so dishonour me?' Amy said, her voice small and thin. 'I told you I don't believe myself to be pregnant—I only said what if I did have your child? You mean you'd deny your own *baby*?'

Robert gave a crack of humourless laughter. 'By God, I would! There would be no place for me by Elizabeth's side if she found I'd slept with you and got you with child into the bargain.'

'But you; you know I'd not be unfaithful to you, though you are to me, Robert. If you should enter my room a second time then, am I to accept rape without complaint? For I'll never willingly lie with you again, Robert.' Her voice grew stronger as the indignities he had heaped upon her came to her mind. 'You *dare* to say it would be a kindness to find me a lover? You, who fawn at the feet of a cold-hearted, frigid, greedy woman? Who dare not let love into your heart in case it loses you your proud position as the Queen's lapdog? Well then, keep away from me in future, Robert. No more quiet rides together. My door shall be bolted every night, and during the day Pirto shan't leave my side. I know you now! You've shown me your true face after all these years. My God, how

201

can I have been so blind? You are indeed your father's son.'

She expected an outburst of hot rage, but his eyes as he turned them on her were cool and calculating.

'You're right. I've more of my father in me than anyone thought. But I've got my wits about me. I shan't lose my head as my father did; nor shall I lose the Queen's favour for your sake. As for your honour, I'll not enter your chamber again; but remember, we agreed on an outward show of friendship for both our sakes.'

She knew then that she had lost. The man who rode beside her was not her own Rob. If she had spoken as she had to Robert even a year ago, his outburst of rage would have been tremendous. But this man could weigh in the balance even a direct taunt at his pride. Amy felt her shoulders droop. The air suddenly seemed too thick for breathing and the pain, which had been blessedly absent, began to stir deep in the marrow of her bones.

'Why should I care if I'm poisoned and you get the blame?' she said listlessly, exhausted by the fierceness of her own anger, all wasted on this stranger. 'I might as well be dead as living with the knowledge that you hate me. And after the things you've said you can't suppose I should worry if you took the blame for my death? I've been a besotted fool, believing that you were fond of me beneath it all. Now I know better. Though I wouldn't deliberately harm you, neither will I defend myself from a death I'd welcome.'

'Don't wallow in melodrama,' said Robert contemptuously. 'So you'd welcome death, would you? Ha! A peculiar thing for a woman to say who spends a fortune of *my* money on her back, and squanders *my* money in keeping up appearances with her fine retinue and her horses and their upkeep.'

'Your doing, none of mine,' murmured Amy. She felt tired as she had not done for years, and the pain beating an insistent pulse through her body reminded her that she had ridden far enough. But the pain in her mind overrode all else.

'My doing, Amy? How is this then? Do I order your clothes? Do I command you to take trips into the country, visiting? Do I beg you to come to London?'

'You bade me keep the state of a great lady,' Amy reminded him patiently. 'You ordered my retinue and saw to the horses. I travel to London so that the people here think I'm living with you part of the time in your house there, but I lodge humbly enough, God knows. Now I'm telling you at last that I'm willing—nay, eager—to give all this up. The revenue from Syderstone is all I need. I can go back there and live. You won't have to visit me, and if someone is bold enough to travel into Norfolk to poison me he's welcome to try, but it would be a difficult task, for at Syderstone I know I am well-loved.'

The wistful longing in her voice, the tears which despite herself ran down her well-schooled features, were lost on him. He cursed himself for a fool. He, who had learned so carefully to control his temper, who never showed his feelings unless it was to his advantage to do so. Now, unless he worked carefully and quickly, he might well undo all the good he had done by visiting Amy with a fair degree of constancy.

'My poor girl, whatever led to this absurd quarrel,' he said. 'You're tired, and I was disagreeable. I'm sorry if I upset you, Amy. Let's turn for home now, and forget this foolishness. You must try to understand how it frets my temper for ever having to agree with the Queen, and you know that if you had my child she would cast me off and our fortunes would go whistling down the wind. But I shouldn't take it out on you, snarling at you as though you were responsible for Elizabeth's unbelievable jealousy and possessiveness. Will you forgive me?'

He turned his most charming smile on her, but he might as well have saved himself the trouble. Amy was occupied with her thoughts.

Syderstone! She could go there and be herself, for who would follow her into the heart of the country? And if they did follow her, and somehow succeed in killing her, was death such a dreadful fate compared to a life lived out in the shadow of Robert's hatred?

As the horses ambled slowly back the way they had come, Amy found herself thinking, how long have I to live, in any event? The pain whenever it came seemed to leave her

203

weaker; her strength was being sapped by it. Would not the pain itself kill her in time?

They left their mounts in the stable yard and went into the hall together. Amy, swaying with tiredness, told Robert she would go straight to bed.

'Pirto will stay with me. I don't expect I shall be up before you leave tomorrow morning, so I'll say goodbye now,' she said, whilst Anne Forster looked incredulously at her husband. He had not mentioned that their visit was to be such a short one.

Amy went slowly up the stairs, pulling herself up by the banister rail, so eager to be alone with her hurt that she did not care what people thought. When the pain consumed her, it was difficult to think of others; all her energy was concentrated on behaving normally until she was alone.

Watching her, as she moved upwards and out of sight, Robert found himself thinking for the first time that Amy did not look like a healthy woman. He had never realised before how radically she had changed during the past few months.

Frowning, he cast his mind back to a year ago. He remembered her light, dancing feet as she ran up and down stairs, the strength in her when she rode beside him, handling a nervous, moody horse as well as a man could.

I did not notice her changing, he thought. What has made her so different? She never runs upstairs now, or jumps up to reach a fruit above her head. He had grown used to Elizabeth's extreme slimness: now he realised with a little shock of surprise that Amy was thin, too. She was shapely to be sure, but her limbs no longer had the rounded healthy look he remembered, and her body had a frailty not entirely due to her loss of weight.

He remembered her remark—that she'd not care now if she were poisoned. He would never have believed that Amy, so full of spirit and vigour, could have said such a thing and meant it. But now, looking back, he was convinced she *had* meant it. It had not been said to aggravate him; it had been a statement of simple truth. In her present state—whatever that

204

might be—she no longer feared death.

It made him remember their difference of opinion—he thought it no more—and he cursed that she had so obviously dismissed him. He would have no chance to talk her round before he left the next day. He was none too sure, now, that she had dismissed his remarks as mere irritability as he felt she should have done. He cursed again when he realised the position she had placed him in. He would have to find a good explanation for their sudden departure to satisfy Anthony, and an even better one for their sudden arrival back at court for the Queen.

He could not be bothered to flatter the women by pleasant gossip over dinner but sat silent, playing with his food and trying to work out whether Amy had meant what she said. Surely she would not really go back to Syderstone, where he could never visit her, and allow him to bear the blame for neglecting his wife? He would have gone up to her room for a further interview, but he did not relish being turned out by Pirto—and he remembered Amy's vow to bolt her door. Short of knocking it down he would probably not get so much as a foot inside the room.

He did not give a thought to his wife as a woman; to the agonising blow that he had dealt her loving heart, or to her present state of mind.

Upstairs, Amy lay across her bed. For the first time in her twenty-eight years of life she actively and honestly wished herself dead. She had stood up to the pain of her body and the pain of his desertion with unbelievable fortitude. But this new pain, his contempt which was deep enough even to make him threaten to deny his own child, to accuse her of an adultery he knew she would never commit; this was the end. She felt as though she had been dragged through some unspeakable slime and was forever stained by its traces. Degraded and broken in body and spirit, she had not even feelings enough left to hate. Numbness gradually took over. She accepted a cup from Pirto and drank, sliding effortlessly into sleep, aware only as the drowsiness deepened that she never wanted to wake.

17

Freedom for ever more

It took Amy several days to recover, outwardly at least, from Robert's visit. She was very ill, with an illness that verged several times on something akin to madness. Pirto kept the other women from her bedside, but when she began to fear for her mistress's reason, she was so desperately worried and anxious that she confided in Edith Odingsells, who went at once to Amy.

Now she saw the pretty, neat Lady Amy Dudley in a very different state. Her poor, thin face was yellowed with illness, her great blue eyes fixed, her hair matted with sweat and neglect. Beside her stood a bowl of broth, untouched.

Bending down, Edith put her arm beneath Amy's shoulders and raised her. The broth was still warm and Amy was too weak to put up more than a token resistance. She tried feebly to move her mouth away from the spoon, but Edith lacked Pirto's knowledge of the frailty of the body in her arms. She was firm, not allowing the weak tears that ran down the hollow cheeks to stop her. When Amy let the broth trickle from the corners of her mouth she tilted her chin up ruthlessly, forcing the girl to swallow.

After that, she and Pirto nursed Amy between them. Soon, Mrs Odingsells saw the abscess, and a frown creased her brow. What was this thing that the girl never mentioned? Pirto was vague. Oh yes, she knew her lady suffered from terrible bouts of pain, but as to whether the abscess was the cause she could not rightly say. She did not think it could be, however, since the pains were all over her mistress's body and Lady Amy had never indicated that they came from one particular source.

Well, yes, they *had* seen a doctor—a good doctor too—in London, and he had said the abscess would burst. But that had been over a year ago and he had not been right yet, though they had applied the remedies the doctor had prescribed. No, they had not consulted a doctor in Oxford, or Abingdon. There were—well, certain difficulties.

Amy fought back to health surprisingly quickly once she had taken nourishment. And as soon as she had a chance to do so, Mrs Odingsells sat close to her patient and told her story. She thought it would quicken Amy's interest in living, and this, it seemed, was the important thing.

'I fell in love with a charming young man of rather doubtful origins,' she said, smiling slightly. 'My father did not approve —he thought Chris wild and unreliable and besides, I had been admired by an elderly widower who was a close friend of the family. However, in those days I was flighty and wilful, with no thought of respect for my elders. So I ran away with my charming Chris, and we lived together for several weeks before my father caught up with me.'

Amy looked with mild astonishment at the sensible, capable woman beside her bed. It seemed impossible to visualise Edith being young and thoughtless, let alone flighty and wilful. But she was languid, content to hear the story without interrupting with unnecessary questions.

'Of course, it was quite ridiculous, really. I had never worried about *how* we would live. Chris, much more practical, meant to blackmail the money out of my father. It was impossible. Father brought my elderly admirer with him when he came in search of us—we were staying with a young married friend who thought our escapade very romantic—and I had to hear a double lecture. Then my father's friend, Philip Odingsells, said he would marry me to save my name from dishonour, and I was wrenched from Chris's side and taken to my new husband's home, which seemed like a prison after my gay time with my lover.

'I'm afraid, Amy dear, that I bore a great grudge against my husband. He was rich, and tried to win my favour by letting me spend his money like water. He had several children already, most of whom I had known for years. His two eldest sons were both older than I, and resented my bad behaviour and the way I treated their father. I didn't care a fig for them—what *I* resented was my elderly husband's determination to beget more children. I found his embraces positively embarrassing, and was rather appalled by his energy—even Chris had not made love so perseveringly.'

Amy was surprised into giving a small chuckle.

'You may well snigger, my girl. You don't know how exhausting an old goat can be,' said Edith, and was rewarded by Amy's sudden spurt of laughter.

'Well, anyway, after some years, my husband brought me to London. I had never grown fond of him—by then I would have liked to bear children and blamed him because I had never conceived. He tricked me out in fine fashion to be presented at court—and there, who should I see but Chris! A soldier now, doing well for himself, with young girls always clustering round him to listen to his stories of foreign places.

'He recognised me at once, and to my joy, seemed eager for our relationship to begin where it had left off, some years earlier. So I took him for my lover, and in fact poor fat Philip found us in bed together when he returned unexpectedly to our town house from a trip into the country.

'There was a scuffle, and Philip was killed. I swore it was simply his heart, though I had seen Chris press the pillow over my husband's face. I kept silent because I thought I loved Chris. I certainly knew I had not loved Philip, never for one moment, despite his generosity.

'I was left a dower house and some money by Philip, and to my joy—but *not* to my surprise, because I was extremely vain—Chris immediately suggested that we should marry. I thought all my dreams had come true at last. After all, I was only twenty-five, and I had not known true love within a marriage before.

'Now, I can look back on being married to Chris and wonder how I can have been so blind. He married me for the money of course—and after a few months I found we weren't

208

even really married. One of the flock of pretty sixteen-year-olds had become his wife a few weeks before Philip was killed. But I didn't discover that until I found Chris lying with one of the dairymaids in the orchard. I would have killed them both if I'd had a knife to hand—I was a violent creature then. I upbraided Chris and in the course of the quarrel he threw it at my head that I had stood by and watched him murder my husband, because I wanted him for myself. He also told me he was already married, and would leave me that moment if I didn't promise to let him pursue his women in peace.

' "For, like you, Edie, I enjoy variety," he said with a grin. "I like many women, and many women like me. It may be you tonight, and your maid tomorrow." I had jumped out of the frying-pan into the fire. So I took the only path my pride would let me. I went back to my father and told him what had happened. I said nothing about Chris's part in my husband's death, of course. It was too late for that. Father had the marriage annulled and Chris disappeared with his wife—or wives, maybe. I'd had enough of marriage, you can imagine. So when my sister told me Mrs Forster was looking for a companion who would like to live with her, I was glad to volunteer. I gave up my inheritance from Philip to his sons; it seemed the right thing to do. Now I have a small sum which my mother left me when she died. I find it sufficient, especially living here. A silly story, is it not?'

'No, not silly; rather sad,' Amy said thoughtfully. 'But why won't you marry again now, Edith? You surely realise you were very unlucky, both with your husband and your lover?'

'Ah, but remember, Amy, I had indirectly been the cause of my husband's death. In a sense, I had murdered him, because if I had never been unfaithful with Chris, poor plain Philip would be alive today. No, I make trouble where men are concerned. Even Chris was unhappier for having known me. So I remain a widow and sometimes I think I have more contentment than I deserve.'

In her dreamy, convalescent state, Amy found it a relief to unburden herself in her turn. She took Edith's hand in her own, and related with the utmost economy of words just why

209

she herself was living at Cumnor Place.

'Poor Amy. I brought my fate down on my own head because I really loved no one but myself. And you have given love without fear or stinting. Yet your reward has been bitter.'

Somehow, the shared confidences made Amy's life happier than she had dared to believe possible. As her health returned, she found her most constant pleasure was her friendship with Edith Odingsells—not least because Edith was so different now from the restless, grasping girl she had been. A mature woman who had seen her own faults in time, and corrected them.

However, although she was no longer desperately ill, Amy knew very little relief, as time wore on, from the pain. But she had a secret that gave her a deep and private pleasure.

Despite her words to Robert, she now believed herself to be in the early stages of pregnancy. The thought that Robert would disown the child, that she would be called an adulteress by many people, did not worry her. She planned to give birth to the child at Syderstone, and she knew her friends there would willingly fall in with her story that she had adopted a child for companionship.

Sometimes when she was walking quietly in the gardens, where the richness of summer was beginning to fade, she found herself thinking, 'But I shan't be alive for long, after the birth of the child, so why should I not acknowledge it to be my own?' and wondered how she could be so certain of the imminence of her own death, whilst still planning for the future so serenely.

At other times, especially on her good days when the pain was only a blur within her, she could not believe that she was ill, and would plan happily how she would love her baby, manage its education out at Syderstone and sometimes, in a rosy glow, she would imagine Robert coming down to visit her and claiming the child delightedly as his own son.

But even in the midst of these happy daydreams, she was aware of a pulse like a clock, warning her that time was short and she should make the best use of the months that remained to her.

Towards the end of August Robert sent a messenger to her, telling her that he would be visiting Cumnor. She wondered at first how best to face him. But the inner voice that kept telling her the times she might see Robert were already numbered made her decide that they must meet as though their previous quarrel had never happened.

If he should ask again about the child, she ought to tell him the truth, but she thought gleefully she would make sure he did not ask. This small secret was her very own, not to be shared with a man that fate had thrown in her path ten years ago. She could not acknowledge that as father to her child he had any rights. After all, he had disowned any babies she might bear before she had any idea that there might *be* a baby.

Robert came and was charming to everyone; his attentiveness to Amy made all the ladies widen their eyes with envy—except Edith. *Her* eyes narrowed speculatively. What did he want from his wife now, then? Had he guessed that Amy would escape to Syderstone when she could do so, and live away from him, letting him explain to the whole world the cause and reason for his neglect? For though Amy had told no one of her hopes, she had confided in Edith that she might really go into Norfolk, for some months at any rate.

Amy herself watched Robert covertly. He was completely easy and friendly with her, but he did say casually to her in a teasing tone that he knew she would never willingly put him in an embarrassing position. Him! Who had treated her to every kind of indignity, who had threatened her unborn children with the slur of illegitimacy. Glossy with health, high-coloured and handsome, he never bothered to notice that his wife was an ill woman; never cared when he bruised her to her soul with his arrogant selfishness!

Yet something still stirs within me, Amy thought. Still my unbiddable heart beats more strongly because he is here, with his beauty and his charm and his graceful bearing. I can tell myself he is all the things my mind acknowledges him to be: I still cannot rule my heart to believe my head.

So before he left for the court once more, she found herself telling him for his own sake, that she sometimes thought she

211

would not live long.

'Don't pretend sorrow or anguish, it would be a pity to lose all that there is left between us, which is honest dealing,' she told him with a faint smile.

'Naturally, I'd be very distressed to hear of your death, Amy,' Robert said conciliatingly. 'Why, we are friends, aren't we? Good friends are always sorry to lose one another.'

'Ah, but we lost each other long ago, Robert. Remember? It was a crisp day in November, with flakes of snow in the air. A day to lighten the hearts of many. You rode to Hatfield and you declared your allegiance to the new Queen with your lips, but your eyes spoke of love. From that very second, my lord, we were lost to each other.'

Robert shrugged sulkily. 'I spoke of friendship. You speak of—of something different,' he mumbled.

'Nevertheless,' Amy said with finality, 'now that you know, when I take to my bed for the last time it won't come as a shock to you.' She hesitated, then added tartly, 'And you may *pretend* to your heart's content, sir; hover in the passage hour after hour, if you feel it does credit to your honour. But I tell you to your face you'll not be welcome at *my* deathbed. There, I'll have none but my true friends.'

He was silent, shaken by the vehemence in her that could deny him the right to see her in her last moments.

'You mean it?' he said at last, his voice low.

Amy nodded wordlessly, not trusting herself to speak. She knew that the hurt she inflicted on him by the denial was as nothing to the hurt she would be inflicting on herself when the time came. Against all reason, against her will even, she would want a last glimpse of him as a thirsty man longs for water. Knowing every word to be false, she would still want him to bend over her and whisper 'I love you,' so that at least she could die with the illusion of his love still intact. But the words had been said. She would not unsay them.

So Robert rode away from Cumnor Place and left Amy with her three lady companions, and the companion that was the most constant now of all—pain.

*

212

It was Sunday, September the eighth. Amy woke early, long before the first cock announced the new day. She lay quietly, savouring the fact that the pain was dulled, a growl at the base of her spine. As the room lightened, she became aware of noises coming faintly to her ears through the still early morning air, and parting the bedcurtains she slipped out of bed and went to the window.

Of course! The fair was coming to Abingdon today. What she could hear was the noise of preparation, being carried out as quietly as might be, so that when the good people of Abingdon awoke, the fair would be in their midst, ready for their enjoyment. Amy opened the window a crack. Yes, it was going to be a fine day. The air was cool on her face but over the stream mist was curled, and though the sun had not yet appeared the sky had a glow like pink pearls.

Amy glanced at the truckle bed and saw with satisfaction that Pirto still slept soundly. She closed the window softly, and feeling like a naughty child about to steal an outing she pulled on a thick, warm bedgown and went softly downstairs, anxious to disturb no one in the sleeping house.

Within half-an-hour she was climbing the winding stairs again, the stone striking cold through the thin soles of her slippers. The gladness with which she had greeted the morning was gone. The pain in her back was once more the familiar, gloating tearing of her weary body. She slid into bed, knowing a desolation so complete that the morning sky, now limpidly blue, seemed to her overcast, and full of foreboding.

The child she had believed she carried within her was just imagination, as Mary Tudor's babies had been. Ill-health had upset the balance of nature. But now Amy understood how Queen Mary had felt. Facts might have convinced her mind, but she could never convince her heart. Her heart said the baby had been there, and had been lost; not that it had never existed save in her longing imagination.

She was glad to see that Pirto was not stirring, and even more glad that she had confided in no one about her imagined pregnancy. Creeping further down the bed, alone with the disappointment heavy on her, she felt that she could bear no one

213

today. She felt like an empty shell, hollow so that every sound and movement was magnified into more pain. She wanted to be alone, to face the fact squarely that she had told Robert no more than the truth. She would bear no children.

But despite her unhappiness she dropped into a light doze as the sun came streaming into the room, and was awoken by an unsuspecting Pirto, pulling back the bedhangings.

'I've set out your best lavender gown for church, my lady; it's a hot day, so I've just put out the one petticoat and a light little bolster to give the skirt some fullness. But the farthingale might be cooler—would you prefer it?'

'I shan't go to church today, Pirto. I don't feel well enough,' Amy said firmly, disregarding Pirto's look of astonishment. 'What's more, I was up betimes and heard the noise of people and animals going towards Abingdon. It's the first day of the fair, and I want you and the other servants to go and enjoy yourselves: you can bring me a fairing.'

'I'll not go if you're feeling too ill for church, my lady,' Pirto said quickly.

Amy cast her eyes up to heaven. 'Pirto, as if I've not enough to bear,' she said crossly. 'You will go, if you please. And so will everyone else in the house, if I have my way. Believe me, I have a good reason. I want to be *alone* for once, and not surrounded by well-meaning busybodies.'

'If you're quite sure you'll be all right, Lady Amy,' the maid said unhappily. She knew that on days when the pain was particularly bad her mistress was quick to anger and found her tongue difficult to control. She must indeed be suffering if she could turn on her friend and servant in such a manner.

Over a breakfast of brawn, bread and ale which Amy hardly touched, she broached the subject of Abingdon Fair to Edith, Anne and Dorothy.

'It is a great event in the town,' she urged them. 'I wish you would go, truly I do. I've given my servants leave, and I'd be happier alone today. I feel such a need for solitude.'

'It's a day more fitting for the servants than for us, Amy,' Edith said, rather surprised. It was not often that Amy wanted to be alone: rather the opposite, in fact. It seemed that alone, she dwelt too much on her thoughts, and they could not be pleasant.

'What do you mean, today is not fitting for you?' said Amy sharply.

'Well, the countryfolk come into Abingdon on a Sunday. It gets rough and bawdy at the fair—or so I'm told. I'd rather go tomorrow when there are more gentlefolk patronising the amusements,' Edith said peaceably.

'Quite right, I wouldn't go on the Lord's Day,' approved Doll Owen, earning a look of deep dislike from both Amy and Edith.

Anne Forster, glancing timidly from one face to another, said undecidedly, 'Well, I don't know, I'm sure. I'd like a day at the fair, it's always a great treat. But I must admit I've never patronised it on a Sunday before. If you really think Monday would be more seemly . . .'

'We do,' Edith assured her. The look on Amy's face worried her. *Why* did she want them out of the house? The obvious solution that she wanted peace and quiet did not satisfy Edith Odingsells. She looked searchingly at Amy, but could read nothing in her countenance except the usual patient suffering.

'Of course, if you really feel Sunday is unsuitable I won't try to persuade you,' Amy said stiffly, but the colour which flooded her face showed her annoyance. 'However, I'll eat in my own apartment if you don't mind, and spend the day as quietly as I am able.'

She soon regretted her impromptu dismissal of Pirto. The pain was eating into her mind now, she thought, making it impossible even to enjoy the luxury of being alone because the thoughts that came to her were all dark. My future is dark, she admitted to herself. No glimmer of light beckons me on. All I want now that there will be no child, now that I've renounced Robert's love, is freedom. But what, after all *is* freedom? Even if I deny Robert and go to Syderstone is that freedom, when I can never escape from the pain? Of course not. The pain forbade even freedom, for she was chained by it, bound in its cruel embrace as it devoured her, body and soul.

Restlessly, her mind sought escape from her future, stretching ahead of her, a dark and lonely path. As the pain grows worse, she thought, I'll become more and more bitter and disillusioned. People will begin to dislike me, never realising that it's the pain that snaps and snarls at them, and not Amy Robsart. She smiled at her own use of her maiden name, then decided that she must make an effort to drag herself out of her slough of despond and be sociable with Anne, Dorothy and Edith.

She went through to the room where her companions were sitting employing themselves desultorily with the usual bits of embroidery, or mending.

'I'm sorry I was so abrupt earlier,' she said, trying to smile brightly. 'I had a headache—it's a very warm day, is it not? Now that I'm here we could play cards if you would like it. Or backgammon?'

So the four women settled down at a card table, and Amy found that in the interest of the game she became more cheerful. She was winning small amounts steadily, when Dorothy Owen said suddenly, 'Well, Lady Amy, lucky at cards, unlucky in love! That's what they say, you know.'

No one spoke. Amy sat with the cards halfway to the table. 'What do you mean?' she asked slowly after a moment.

'Silly girl, did you think we didn't know?' cried Dorothy archly. 'I must admit Sir Robert had me fooled—I thought he doted on you. Then one of my laundrywomen heard from a man in Sir Robert's retinue about the goings-on at court. Of how the Queen would like to marry Sir Robert: he has to keep you out of sight down here in the country in order that he can be free to entertain the Queen.' She eyed Amy with spiteful curiosity. 'I'd call that unlucky in love for you, my dear.'

'I would advise you not to listen to gossip,' said Amy coolly. She began to deal the cards and noticed with annoyance that her hands were shaking.

'I wonder how Pirto and the other servants are enjoying the fair?' put in Edith helpfully. But Mrs Owen had the bit firmly between her teeth.

'All the times we've thought you were at court, or at your husband's house in Kew, you've been in humble lodgings in

216

London!' she said triumphantly. 'I've been making some en-
quiries since I first heard how interested Queen Elizabeth is in
Sir Robert. You've always been mighty secretive towards us,
never discussing your affairs. *Now*, of course, I realise it is
because you have no affairs to discuss. You don't visit your
country estates because there you would be practically alone
with your husband. Here, in a smallish manor house, with
three other gentlewomen present, any intimacy between you
and Sir Robert would be difficult. And our dear young Queen
wouldn't like to know that the man she is wildly in love with
was having a relationship with another woman, even if she is
his wife.'

'I've never lied to you. Neither have I attempted to discover
why you yourself live separately from your husband,' said
Amy, keeping her voice level with an effort.

'Ah, but I've never attempted to pretend my husband had
not left me, I've never deceived anyone in my life,' began Mrs
Owen, her voice thick with spite and smugness.

'I do not pretend,' began Amy a trifle desperately. 'I am
only separated from Robert because of the life he leads at
court.' But she heard the unsteadiness in her voice and made
no attempt to override Mrs Owen when she interrupted.

'Come now, Amy, you might as well admit you've deliberately tried to mislead us. If you had been more open with us I
should never have had to discover your secrets for myself. I've
always disliked secretive people, I like a person to be frank
and open, and . . .'

'That's quite enough, I think, Mrs Owen. Come, Amy, deal
the rest of the cards.' Edith Odingsells' voice was quiet and
commanding but Amy knew when she was beaten. Her body
was shaken by huge shudders and her heart felt as if it was
trying to beat its fluttering way out of her breast. She fumbled
with the cards and they fell through her fingers onto the table.
Shaking more than ever, Amy pushed back her chair. It fell
over, clattering to the floor. Through lips that trembled un-
controllably, she said, 'I'm going to my own apartment,' and
avoiding the fallen chair, she turned and stumbled from the
room.

There was an embarrassed silence after the heavy oaken door had swung shut behind her. Then Mrs Owen spoke, her voice shriller than usual.

'Fancy her taking offence like that! Well, no doubt she'll soon be back to apologise for rushing out of the room without so much as a word of explanation. But then I've always thought her a queer-tempered girl. In fact, I've never really liked her. How dared she speak to me like that!'

'Oh Doll, how could you say those things,' wailed Anne Forster. 'I wouldn't have her hurt for the world. Poor child, how she must have suffered all these months! I suppose I've seemed quite heartless, but indeed my husband told me to act normally and not to repeat anything I heard about the Dudleys, for it was all wicked gossip. I've been as good as my word, too—you've had no gossip from *me*, Doll.'

'You've done a wicked thing to a sorely tried person,' Edith Odingsells said in a low voice. 'She never harmed you, never asked why your husband had left you. Why did you have to pry around in her poor little life to add to her pain? How would you like to carry her burden, unable even to confide in her friends? You're a vicious, spiteful woman, Doll Owen, I tell you to your face!'

Dorothy Owen's cheeks burned scarlet, but she sniffed disdainfully.

'Should we go after her?' asked Anne helplessly. 'Should we try to make everything all right again?'

'We can't make everything all right. Only Robert Dudley could do that. No, leave her alone for a while, until she's in control of herself once more,' advised Edith.

With no fourth person to complete their game, the women soon fell silent. They sat uneasily in the quiet of the hot afternoon whilst a late bluebottle buzzed round the room. Edith Odingsells picked up a book and began to turn the pages. Mrs Owen, her cheeks still unbecomingly flushed, began to work once more on the jabot of her new gown. Anne Forster gathered up a torn flounce on her petticoat with large, uneven stitches. Each woman tried to concentrate on her task and not allow her thoughts to stray to the girl who had run from the

218

room in such distress.

I've never liked her, Dorothy Owen thought defiantly. *It was time someone spoke out—I've always had the courage to say what everyone else was thinking.*

Anne ran the needle into her thumb and watched the blood well out into a fat scarlet cushion. *Poor child*, a voice said in her mind. *So heavy a burden, and I have done nothing to help her bear it. But in future I shall know better. When she has got over her distress, we must talk.*

Edith alone had her thoughts under control. Though she turned the pages of the book, she did not read a word. Her lips moved in silent prayer for her friend: that she might not feel herself forsaken and abandoned by everyone; that she would be able to conquer her feelings, and meet them at supper-time with her usual calm friendliness.

The bluebottle which had sounded alarmingly noisy in the stillness found the open window and flew down into the garden. Without its agitated buzz the silence seemed to hang like a physical presence in the air, making them long to speak. But no one said a word.

Amy shut the door of the cardroom behind her and walked as swiftly as she could along the upstairs corridor. Huge sobs were fighting for release, but she was deterined not to cry where the women could hear her. She would not complete Doll Owen's triumph by such an expression of weakness. She reached the head of the stairs and glanced down. How nice if it had been a well, into which she could plunge with certain death at the end. But the staircase was a series of gentle, beautiful curves and anyway, she thought defiantly, she would not let a spiteful, heartless creature like Dorothy Owen drive her to commit a mortal sin.

She went quickly down the steps, heedless of the pain, wanting now only to get away from the curious eyes and spiteful tongues in the room upstairs. She thought she would go into the garden for she wanted no one—no one—to find her. She could not remember that Anne Forster had been kind, and that Edith was very much her friend. They were suddenly a threat to the precarious little world she had built up, and already she felt its security tottering.

In her haste she stumbled on that last step, jolting herself as she miscalculated the number of stairs still to descend. It was such a little error, just an awkward movement really. Yet she heard a small, sharp *crack*, and felt a numbness spreading swiftly through her body.

She stood for a moment, swaying uncertainly. What was happening? She could no longer feel her own hands or feet, she had no control over a single muscle. As the paralysis spread, the pain could no longer be felt. She was conscious of the strangeness of being without pain almost as strongly as the strangeness of her inability to move her limbs. Then she began to fall.

A black tunnel seemed to open up before her. She was rushing into it, her mind which had been blank with surprise suddenly filled with thoughts. Something had happened to her as she stumbled; it had brought the numbness and the immobility. Now she would no longer have to worry about what had happened in the room upstairs, for she knew the black tunnel was her death approaching. What did it matter now if people scoffed because Amy Robsart could not hold her husband? Who would now despise her because she had borne no children? The pain had gone already, and would never claw mercilessly at her in death as it had in life. She would no longer be a burden to Robert's insatiable ambition, holding him back by simply existing. So *this*, she thought with wonder, is the complete freedom which all men strive after. And I was afraid—afraid of the ultimate freedom! She gave herself willingly now to death, diving head first into the dark tunnel, aware suddenly that at the end of it glowed a light as bright as sunlight shining from a blue sky through fresh green leaves.

It *was* sunlight, she thought exultantly, as the last sad stitch of life dropped from her spirit. And as her dazzled eyes grew used to the brilliance, she saw in a marvellous radiance the faces of her parents, smiling at her with unforgettable tenderness. Smiling at Amy Robsart, the beloved.

Closing address

My Lord, Members of the Jury. You have now heard the evidence of the life of this young woman from its bright beginning to its tragic end, with an inexplicable fall on a pair of stairs. The steps of these stairs were low, and the angle of descent gradual. A fall on such stairs might produce bruises, but not a neck broken so cleanly and sharply that no other injuries were sustained. In this circumstance, more than any other, lies the source of the mystery which has surrounded Amy's death.

Rumour would always have surrounded such a death perhaps, but the actions of others have lent fuel to the fire of rumour. Little evidence exists today of those events which at the time were of such importance that for a while England's fate hung in the balance. It is as if such evidence has been deliberately destroyed. Local records and archives are silent. Nothing. As you have heard, the Robsart family lived at Syderstone in Norfolk. Yet the twelfth-century church has records which begin only *after* Amy's death—what happened to earlier documents? Similarly in Wymondham she is not once mentioned in contemporary writings, though her father and half-brother are.

Now let us examine the part Robert Dudley played after his wife's death. The most striking fact is that he did not go to Cumnor Place on hearing the tragedy—indeed, he never went there again in his life! We must accept that in those days, for Amy's husband to have attended her costly funeral would have been against the custom, but why no stone to mark where she lay? Robert further confuses the issue by his calm acceptance of his wife's death, with no expression of surprise or grief. He did, however, write to the foreman of the jury at the inquest after Amy's death, and these letters show a frantic eagerness to be cleared of any suspicion, and no interest at all in his wife's early demise. In fact his letter make it plain that he would have liked to uncover a murderer, for this would have cleared his name better than anything else. Robert even sent a manservant to secretly sound out local opinion as to the cause of Amy's death.

Members of the Jury, you may well ask what sort of man is this, who acts in such a self-centred, callous manner at such a time. At this stage thoughts of murder may naturally enter your mind.

I would urge you to reject these thoughts, because of three facts, two ancient and one modern.

First is the character of Dudley himself. He was an attractive man who behaved generously to his wife and who was faithful until Elizabeth became Queen. He was also self-seeking, extremely ambitious and of high intelligence. Surely an intelligent and ambitious man, if he were guilty, would have pretended grief, gone rushing to the scene of the tragedy and certainly *not* have contacted the foreman of the jury by letter?

Secondly, no one seems to have realised Amy died the day after the Queen's birthday. Had Robert's worst enemy designed to injure him, he would scarcely have chosen the very weekend when Dudley would be sure to stay by the Queen's side—as indeed he did.

The third and modern fact is the most convincing of all. The late Professor Ian Aird studied Amy's death closely, and the results of his findings were published in the *English Historical Review* LXXI No. 278 in January 1956. Some seventeen months before her death, a strong rumour began to circulate that young Amy Dudley suffered from 'a malady in one of her breasts', and Professor Aird points out that should a similar situation arise today and a woman of twenty-eight be found dead of an unexplained broken neck, the doctor would first examine her breasts. If she showed signs of advanced cancer then a post-mortem examination would almost certainly reveal

cancerous deposits in the bones, causing them to be so brittle that a mis-step or jarring footfall could cause a spontaneous fracture of the spine—in other words, a broken neck.

Surely, now, Amy can be cleared of the accusation of suicide which has hung over her head for four hundred years? To be sure, she rose unusually early on the fatal day, and tried to persuade everyone to go to the fair at Abingdon, leaving her alone in the house. But pain affects the mind so that sometimes the sufferer simply has to be alone. And Amy was very unhappy. Also, we know that she did not succeed in getting rid of any but her own servants. We know she played cards, but the cautious ladies who were her companions would only say that they were playing a card-game when Amy left the room suddenly, without explanation. No mention of discord: but is it likely that three women would sit in their room until the servants returned from the fair, never being drawn by sympathy or curiosity to see where their companion had gone?

You may as well come to the conclusion that they *did* go in search of Amy Dudley—and that finding her dead at the foot of the stairs they believed she had killed herself whilst the balance of her mind was disturbed by something that had taken place in the cardroom. No good could then have come of revealing the quarrel.

Members of the Jury, you may now believe Queen Elizabeth and Robert Dudley innocent of the crime of murder, but the eradication of all the records I have referred to still has not been explained. On this score, there is one further fact to be examined here. In 1947 the pavement of St Mary the Virgin in Oxford, where Amy was buried, had to be relaid and the opportunity was taken of exploring the area where Amy's body was expected to be. But someone had been there first. It was found that the area had been dug over to a depth of six feet and the soil and bones hopelessly intermingled. Surely this is the action of someone who believed, however mistakenly, that it would be better to obliterate all traces of whoever had been there?

So it may be assumed that though guiltless, *someone* was sufficiently worried to meddle with evidence which, in the

event, could well have proved without any doubt how Amy Dudley met her death.

Finally, I would ask you to try to put yourselves in Amy's place. A young woman, very much in love with her husband, who finds herself smitten by a painful and deadly disease and realises her husband has deserted her. Try if you can to rationalise the actions which have puzzled people for centuries. Why didn't she see a physician? Why did she neither insist on living with Dudley at court, nor leave him completely, so the breach was obvious? Why did she send her servants to the fair at Abingdon?

Members of the Jury, I hope Amy Robstart no longer appears a foolish woman suffering from nothing worse than hypochondria. To visit as often as possible a husband under sentence of death for treason; to face a Catholic Queen who burns Protestants for heresy when you are a Protestant—these are *facts* and they are not the actions of a milksop. If modern medical evidence is right she was also remarkable for dissembling a mortal illness; not for her own sake, but for the sake of the man who most cruelly left her alone with her agony.

I ask you to find for Amy Robsart.